KIELI

As the Deep Ravine's Wind Howls

Yukako
Kabei

Illustrated by:
Shunsuke Taue

THE STORY OF A CERTAIN PRIEST
AND FALLEN ANGEL ON A WINTER MORNING 1

CHAPTER 1:
WHAT'S WITHIN YOUR GRASP,
WHAT SLIPS THROUGH YOUR FINGERS 9

CHAPTER 2:
AS THE TOY SOLDIER WEEPS 45

CHAPTER 3:
THE TRAVEL-LOVERS OF CAR NINE 79

INTERLUDE:
THE STORY OF A CERTAIN PRIEST AND ANOTHER
VERY EMINENT PRIEST LONG BEFORE SPRING 107

CHAPTER 4:
A DANGEROUS YOUNG LADY AND A KIND BEAST..........117

CHAPTER 5:
IN THE LYRICS OF AN OLD, OLD SONG... 183

CHAPTER 6:
AS THE DEEP RAVINE'S WIND HOWLS 221

THE STORY OF A CERTAIN UNDYING, GIRL, RADIO,
AND WINGED BEAST UNDER THE TWILIT SKY 297

KIELI

As the Deep Ravine's Wind Howls

Yen
Press

NEW YORK

KIELI: As the Deep Ravine's Wind Howls
YUKAKO KABEI

Translation: Sarah Alys Lindholm

Yen Press
Hachette Book Group
237 Park Avenue, New York, NY 10017
www.HachetteBookGroup.com
www.YenPress.com.

Yen Press is an imprint of Hachette Book Group, Inc. The Yen Press name and logo are trademarks of Hachette Book Group, Inc.

First Yen Press Edition: September 2012

Library of Congress Cataloging-in-Publication Data

Kabei, Yukako.
  [Yuukoku no Kaze wa Nakinagara. English]
  As the deep ravine's wind howls / [Yukako Kabei ; translation by Sarah Alys Lindholm]. — 1st Yen Press ed.
     p. cm. — (Kieli ; 7)
  Summary: Kieli is a reclusive girl isolated by her ability to see ghosts until she and her dorm "roommate," Becca, the spirit of a former student, meet the handsome but distant Harvey who can also see ghosts and is one of the legendary Undying, an immortal soldier bred for war now being hunted by the Church.
  ISBN 978-0-7595-2935-9 (pbk.)
  [1. Fantasy.] I. Lindholm, Sarah Alys. II. Title.
  PZ7.K1142As 2012
  [Fic]—dc23   2012015968

10 9 8 7 6 5 4 3 2 1

RRD-C

Printed in the United States of America

THE STORY OF A CERTAIN PRIEST AND
FALLEN ANGEL ON A WINTER MORNING

The priesthood is a profession for con men.

He'd known someone who used to always say that at the drop of a hat—the crotchety old man who lived on the first floor of the apartment building kitty-corner from theirs when he was a kid, he recalled. None of the adults in the neighborhood had ever paid any attention to the rant, but when he considered his current circumstances, he couldn't help thinking the old man might have been onto something. Yes, maybe he'd dozed off Saturday night while he was prepping his Sunday service, and now it was morning and he was madly jotting down an outline of the sermon while he crammed breakfast into his mouth after a hasty shave; but half an hour from now he'd have to stand calmly at the pulpit and deliver a long-winded oration that was eloquent enough to look as though he'd prepared it carefully in advance. For a moment, he toyed with that career option: if he ever lost this job, perhaps he could make a living as a con man.

The young priest gave his writing hand a break, sighing slightly and taking another bite of his bland bread. He gave his notes a quick read-through. Then he added a few more lines, his mouth gaping wide open with the bread still crammed inside. His topic was Voyage 7:4—the passage about the demon who appeared in a saint's dreams disguised as an angel and tried to lead him astray. The modern-day Church's canon consisted of the original holy book that had been passed down from the time of the mother planet, additions made during the era of the Eleven Saints and Five Families, and a set of psalms recounting the hardships of the voyage, all compiled together into one volume.

His personal copy of it, an old, well-worn one he'd been using since his school days, was currently serving as a writing surface. The dry scratch of his pen over the coarse paper he'd placed on the holy book bounced faintly off the walls and ceiling, disappearing almost immediately.

"Ugh, I'm so tired."

He really did have to finish his notes this time, and then he had to give the actual service, but he yawned as he stretched his arms out, feeling as if he'd already done a whole day's work. This wasn't a great posture to let anyone see him in—slumped heavily against the back of his chair with his crossed legs propped on the edge of his desk—but it wasn't as if anyone else was around.

It was an ordinary, peaceful (other than his last-minute rush to finish the preparations he should have done yesterday) Sunday morning. He was sitting in the little sacristy that adjoined the chapel. Thin beams of light dyed blue and orange and other colors filtered in through the half-open door. It was just a little country-town chapel, though, with only one very plain stained-glass window in the wall behind the altar. He felt a little depressed whenever he remembered the majestic sight of the entire *wall* of stained glass in the cathedral in the capital. When he'd managed to snag the last open slot in Father Sigri's special seminar, he'd thought things were finally starting to go his way...but maybe he used up all his luck on that, because afterward there was no path to career advancement for him in the capital.

It was five years ago now that he'd taken up his post at the Church outpost in this town in the North-hairo boonies that was too tiny to even have its own train station. He'd come after he'd graduated from seminary and finished his research. He was the only priest working here, in fact, but it was such a nothing little town that even a young priest with hardly any experience could cover the place just fine.

Forget "nothing"—there was *less* than nothing.

Well, the environment is good here. Yeah. The environment.

Lately he was trying to convince himself that it was nice to be in such a relaxed place, but it was still hard not to feel listless when everything was the same day after day. It was making him steadily lose the motivation to actually put effort into his job.

"Father!" a voice suddenly called through the door. He hastily tried to sit up straight, and instead almost fell right out of the chair. When he craned his neck around from the unnatural in-between position he ended up in, a familiar-looking local boy was just cracking open the door and sticking his head in.

"G-good morning. You're early today." He greeted the boy with a smile. A stiff smile, since he'd just crammed the rest of the bread into his mouth. It wasn't time for the congregation to assemble yet, and he'd been completely off his guard.

He gulped and then said, "What's up?"

"Listen, listen! I found a stray angel!"

After all that trouble to keep up appearances, he ruined everything by blurting a dumbfounded "Huh?!"

Now he could hear muffled young voices chattering excitedly outside the chapel, so presumably a whole group of children was gathering there. The priest stood up, leaving his book and notes on the desk, and followed his visitor outside. The boy was actually jogging, as if to silently urge him to hurry up.

Autumn was just turning into winter. Cold, dry air bit at his cheeks, with periodic bursts of the warmth and scent of the fossil-fuel smog from town. Ahead of him, he saw five or six local kids coming into the chapel yard, all clustered around what appeared to be a female figure wearing a large shawl.

They were pulling her along by the hands, and she meekly let them, walking with her head tilted down. *She's walking a bit unsteadily—* Almost the moment he registered that thought, she stumbled and pitched over headfirst to the ground.

"Miss Angel!" all the kids cried anxiously. The whole question of whether she was an angel or not aside, he was certainly worried enough to rush to her side. He sank to his knees next to her without a thought for the dirt he must be getting on his priest's robes.

"A-are you all right, miss?" he asked, peering into her face, and then immediately forgetting to even close his mouth. He just gaped.

Golden hair tumbling in gentle waves out of her shawl and down her shoulders, one lock catching on finely sculpted lips—she was a breathtakingly beautiful young woman. A beautiful young woman in a wretchedly scruffy state: half of that long hair was snarled into a bird's nest, and the skin he imagined was normally lily-white and smooth was now grimy with the wilderness's yellow sand, as were her clothes. What was more, she seemed to have scraped herself in the fall. Blood was beginning to seep out of a garish wound on her cheek.

"See? See? She's an angel, right?"

"We found her at the edge of town. She must've fallen down from the sky and gotten hurt!" For all they were genuinely worried about the woman, the kids were all cheering about it with sparkling eyes. Yes, he could see where they'd gotten the idea.

And now black blood like coal tar was oozing out of the cut and starting to crawl around above the wound like something sentient, almost like maggots. With grotesque movements, the maggots pushed all the gravel out of it, and it closed up before his eyes in fast-forward. A few seconds later, the skin was smooth again as if nothing had ever happened. Only a few traces of sand and blood remained.

Voyage 7:4, the passage about the demon who appeared in dreams pretending to be an angel, came back to his mind with a vengeance.

"Father, what's wrong?"

"Hey, is the angel all right? Did she hit her head or something?" the children he'd elbowed aside asked curiously, looking over his shoulder. With his eyes fixed on the woman, he managed to force his voice past the rock that seemed to have lodged itself in his throat. It came out stiff and halting.

"Listen to me, kids. You pretend you never saw this woman. Do you understand?"

After the words left his mouth, he felt thoroughly disappointed with himself. *So now I'm another one of those adults who says things like this to kids...*

He repented right then and there his immodest complaint that this less-than-nothing town was making him listless. "Nothing" was fine by him. Now he knew that those peaceful, boring days had been a blessing after all. As for what he had to do to protect those peaceful days and the townspeople— he didn't agonize about it for long. He couldn't see any real choice.

He dove back into the sacristy and picked up the communicator that transmitted to the capital.

But had she actually shown any signs of harming him or the children in any way?

Afterward, he would regret his actions in that moment time and time again.

Maybe the crotchety old man who'd lived on the first floor of the apartment building kitty-corner from theirs had it right, and the priesthood really was a profession for con men.

CHAPTER 1

WHAT'S WITHIN YOUR GRASP,
WHAT SLIPS THROUGH YOUR FINGERS

There was a slight nervous constriction in the back of his throat. He hesitated for just two or three seconds, but then at the sound of the girl's even-more-nervous voice saying "T-try opening it," he opened his closed eyelid. The conjunctiva hadn't been exposed to outside air in so long that it was painfully oversensitive; for a split second it felt as if someone had stabbed him. Harvey unthinkingly closed his eyes. Then he opened them again, slowly, and gave two little blinks.

At first, all he noticed was that a blurry, milky-white film seemed to be covering his left eye's field of vision. His right eye steadily adjusted, though, and although his vision was still so radically different from one eye to the other that everything was disjointed, eventually the images on his left and right retinas managed to overlap. There was the same familiar counter, the same old shelves lined with bottles and glasses. After these past few weeks, Harvey had thought he knew this bar like the back of his hand, and yet now everything seemed a little off. *Huh, so this is what it looks like with two eyes.*

He lifted his left hand to eye level and opened and closed his fist a few times, until—

"*Well?*" demanded an impatient male voice. When he shifted his gaze, the right eye was a little slower to respond, and his vision swam dizzily. The rest of the world caught up to him a beat after his head stopped turning. There: he could see the portable radio sitting on the counter, and the anxious-looking girl standing beside it clutching the bandage he'd peeled off of his eye.

Her face right there in front of him in three dimensions was too real, somehow. Harvey's mind reeled a little. So the first feeling he had about the whole thing wasn't relief or nostalgia or any of that stuff so much as the—awkwardness? discomfort?—of wondering, *Is this really Kieli?*

Her expression started looking even more anxious as she watched him, probably because he was just staring at her without saying anything or evincing any kind of reaction. Harvey realized he ought to say *something*, so for lack of a better idea he reported the facts.

"I can see. More or less."

After several stiff-faced seconds in which she seemed to be digesting exactly what his words meant, she got that familiar old expression: biting her lip and looking on the verge of tears, but not actually crying. Oddly enough, that was what belatedly brought home to him that, yes, she really was Kieli after all. And then he finally did feel relieved.

The bartender looked just the same as ever that day: a black vest over a shirt with a stand-up collar. The only sign that he was dressed up at all was the bow tie around his neck, and even that change was hardly what you would call dramatic. When he shyly asked her how he looked, Kieli told him what she honestly thought, which was that he looked "about the same as usual." His face fell. It turned out that he considered this his absolute Sunday best. "But I like that!" Kieli amended hastily. The truth was, she really did like the bartender's usual outfit, because it was the most like him.

Right now, he was out in the center of the room, accepting

his guests' blessings and teases with a shy smile—pressed shoulder to shoulder with the woman who'd become his life partner today.

"Kieli, I'll take another beer over here, too!"

"And another round for us!"

"Oh, and can we get some ice? Sorry to bug you."

"Oh! Yes, coming right up!"

Beer and ice…and didn't the bartender ask me to bring up some wine from downstairs? Kieli was spinning in circles and craning her head in all directions as she carried drinks and hors d'oeuvres back and forth from the bar, just to make sure she didn't miss anybody's order. She was literally dizzyingly busy. This number of customers would be routine at Buzz & Suzie's Café back in South-hairo, but frankly this bar just wasn't as successful a business, so it had been a long time since Kieli had worked a shift this hectic.

Still, this was a far cry from the deserted feeling the place used to have. The Adolph Sax had slowly but steadily started attracting regulars lately.

And among those customers was Yana.

"Sorry to make you work all alone like this, dear. Here, I'll help you," said a sunny voice from across the counter where Kieli was just setting down the big container she'd scooped ice into. She figured she might as well bring it all out now. When she looked up, a friendly looking woman in a simple yet stylish dress was standing there smiling at her.

"No, Yana, I'm okay. You go ahead and sit down," Kieli answered, flustered.

"Are you sure? I'll just take this, then." Yana reached out to pick up the bucket crammed full of ice cubes. Looking at it now, Kieli could see that she'd definitely put too much in, and she started to feel awkward. She wished she'd held back a little more.

The only adornment Yana wore to signal her position today was the wreath of artificial flowers perched on her head like a tiara and draped with a lace veil. Personally, Kieli thought it wouldn't hurt to deck herself out in a little more finery on a day like this, but on the other hand, this style suited Yana's personality so well that it looked pretty great on its own.

"Oh, this?" said Yana, glancing up toward her own head and smiling. "Isn't it nice? It's handmade, you know."

"It's beautiful."

"You like it? Well, then, when it's your turn I'll go even more all-out on one!"

"Huh?" Kieli squeaked, caught by surprise at the change of subject. Yana's smile turned into more of a grin, and she leaned her face in close to Kieli conspiratorially.

"So, Kieli, how's it going with you two?"

"'Going'? Nothing's 'going'! Sheesh, go back to the party. You're the woman of the hour!"

Kieli stuck out both hands and forcibly pushed Yana back, and the older woman relented with a joking cluck of her tongue. She picked up the ice and headed back out to the floor. The bartender, who'd been surrounded by a crowd of heckling regulars, immediately jogged up to her and took charge of the heavy ice bucket, which only inspired more teasing whistles from his guests. The contrast between how thrown off he was by the teasing and how Yana let it all roll off her back with a smile was really funny. Kieli stood back from the crowd for a while, watching them with a smile of her own, until she remembered: "Whoops, I have to go get that wine."

She'd almost forgotten that particular chore. She left the counter and headed through the door that led down to the cellar, taking care not to forget the radio. She'd seen a rat down there once, and it was just a little scary to be there by herself now.

"That has got to be a scam. I'm telling you, it's a messed-up world. A woman so young marrying that bartender? It's some kind of conspiracy for sure."

"Yeah, yeah. There you go again," she told the radio, which had started leaking complaints the moment they were out of sight. Kieli knew that he was only grumbling out of habit when he was actually really happy for them, so she responded on autopilot as she made her way down the stairs.

Yes—the bartender had gotten married today! It was a characteristically modest wedding: Yana wasn't a passionate believer, and obviously the bartender (who technically had a history as a rebel against the Church) wasn't either, so instead of having a Church ceremony, they just invited all the regulars to the bar and threw a do-it-yourself party. The romance had begun three months ago, during the Colonization Days in the fall. Yana had started visiting the bar while Kieli and Harvey were in Westerbury, and apparently during the course of some small talk, the two of them had discovered they had the same taste in music and hit it off. True, the master was a full twelve years older, but he didn't always quite have his act together, so Kieli thought cheerful, capable Yana might be the perfect bride for him.

She hoped with all her heart that they would be happy.

Kieli turned on the cellar light and piled bottles of wine and ale into a nearby case by the yellowish glow of its bare bulb. Figuring she might as well bring it all out now, she filled up the whole case. It held about fifteen bottles.

"Kieli...you're putting too much in," the radio around her neck said disgustedly.

"I can carry this much. Upsy-daisy..." She got a grip on the case and tried to stand up, but sure enough, it turned out to be pretty heavy, and it wasn't too easy to lift. Still, Kieli gave it another try, putting her spirit into it. She'd just managed to get it a few centimeters off the ground when someone else's hand reached out and took one side of it for her. She squeaked and lost her balance momentarily at the sudden change in weight. When she looked up, still reeling, a lanky redhead was looming over her with a "good grief" expression on his face.

"W-welcome back," Kieli said, a little flustered.

"I keep telling you to quit being so reckless...There's no way you can carry that by yourself."

"It's your fault for not helping, you jerk. You just up and left the second the party started," griped the radio.

"I was walking around outside, letting my vision adjust," Harvey answered coolly, averting his eyes and sort of squinting. Kieli figured that was probably true enough, but she was dead certain he'd really run away from the party because all the commotion seemed like too much of a pain.

"Did you congratulate the owner?"

"I'll do it later. You hold that side."

They took hold of the handles on either side of the case and lifted it together, making their way upstairs. Harvey held his side in one hand, but Kieli gripped hers with both hands and grunted with effort as they walked. She had to admit she probably would've thrown her back out trying to carry it by herself. She'd gotten overenthusiastic and filled it too full.

Kieli stole a glance at Harvey's left hand on the opposite handle out of the corner of her eye. It'd been about three months since he'd broken his hand in Westerbury, and the injury had healed, but all his joints had been visibly standing out before the injury. Now that hand seemed even bonier than ever…His right arm, which was currently stuck in his coat pocket, was no different than it had been three months ago. It still cut off around the elbow, with a fragment of metal frame sticking out of the stump.

Kieli looked away from Harvey's arms and up into his face in profile, deciding to ask about something else.

"How's your eye?"

"Vision's still swimming," he said shortly, looking straight ahead. He stumbled a little on the stairs.

It was only this morning that he'd taken the bandage off his right eye and started getting it used to seeing again. After a little over a year, the eyeball he said he'd lost last winter at least appeared to have regenerated. Since his sight in that eye was still poor and made for too much of a difference between the right and left halves of his vision, Harvey claimed it was actually more tiring not to wear the bandage, but personally, Kieli still thought she'd rather he left it off. She'd been afraid she might never see those two coppery eyes together again, and now here they both were. This morning, Harvey had looked at her with two eyes and smiled just a little.

Harvey's right eye, and the bartender's wedding. Two good things in one day.

There had been bad things too, recently. One time Harvey had disappeared and not come back for almost two weeks, and she'd been worried to death. Then when he finally wandered back into the bar he'd just said something about finding a lead about Beatrix that ended up not panning out. (When she and the Corporal royally raked him over the coals for it, he gave them a slightly peevish apology.)

Maybe it's time to give up . . . Harvey had always said he was sure Beatrix was fine, but that day, for the first time, he said something negative.

In the end, they were about to have spent a whole winter here on the parish border with no clues about her to show for it. Kieli had desperately hoped to see Beatrix again before the spring—after all, in a little over two weeks, on the day when winter crossed into spring, it would be her seventeenth birthday. *Beatrix, you said you'd celebrate my next birthday. You promised me . . .*

She could hear lively cheers coming from upstairs. She pulled herself out of the funk she'd been falling into and kept heading up. *We're celebrating the bartender today. I shouldn't let myself look depressed.*

When they got back up to the ground floor, they were greeted with a flash of white light accompanied by a satisfying snap. Blinking in surprise, Kieli looked toward the center of the floor and saw a large, extravagant camera set up on a tripod. Someone was taking wedding photos of the bride and groom. Come to think of it, she did remember hearing that a photographer friend of the owner was coming over at the end of the party.

The bride sat in a chair with the groom standing close enough to press up against her side. He smiled bashfully, she beamed brightly, and the flash went off, casting a white light over them both. Kieli left the case of drinks in a corner of the room and watched the proceedings until Yana's voice called out, "Okay, Kieli, you're next!" and, her photograph session over, got up from the chair and made room. Kieli stared at her in surprise.

"Me? But I don't need…"

"Nonsense, it's fine. Come on, get over here."

And then Yana was running up to Kieli, taking her hand and not giving her a chance to say no. Something about Yana's cheery forcefulness reminded her of Suzie, and Kieli liked that about her, but sometimes it made her shy away. Suzie had married rock music–loving Buzz, too. That was another thing they had in common.

Pulling Kieli along by the hand, Yana trained her smile on Harvey.

"Hey, why don't you get a picture together?"

"I don't want to," Harvey replied immediately. His voice was curt, and he was wearing the exact same expression he used to when he was shying away from Suzie's forcefulness, too. Even Yana looked daunted at that. No considerate "No, thank you," no polite "I'll pass, thanks"; just a straight-up "I don't want to." Privately, Kieli was a little disappointed with him, too. She shot a glance at him, checking, and he sighed. "No reason for you to have a run-down old radio in the picture with you. Get one of just yourself," he said, lifting the radio off her neck. It gave a grumpy burst of static that clearly meant *Who are you calling "run-down"?*

"Okay, then...I'll take the opportunity, thank you." Kieli nodded hesitantly, letting herself be placed in the chair in front of the stage. It would rude for *all* of them to refuse Yana's kindness, after all. To tell the truth, though, she would have liked it best if she could have gotten a picture of the three of them together: Kieli, Harvey, and the Corporal. She did understand how it would be bad in various ways if there were pictures of Harvey floating around, but she couldn't help thinking she'd like a photo similiar to the one at Tadai's house...one that would capture Harvey's smile permanently like that. Was that greedy of her?

"Here, put this on."

Before the cameraman took the picture, Yana took the wreath off her own head and put it on Kieli's. "What?!" Kieli's hands flew to her head in confusion. She'd thought they were only going to do a casual snapshot!

"Er, I can pose without this."

"No, you can't take it off. We're going to get a shot of you all dolled up."

"Hey, Kieli, lookin' good!" hooted the regulars watching them, which only made her more flustered. Now she was getting nervous. She reflexively raised her head when a voice called "Okay, look this way," and was blindsided by the instantaneous snap of the shutter. However, the photographer holding the cable didn't seem happy with the shot. He tilted his head, looking dissatisfied. "Hmm...relax your expression a little, okay? Let's get another shot." Which was easy for him to say, but the more she consciously tried to smile, the more her face just twitched.

She found herself looking for Harvey in search of help, and located the redheaded man sitting on the case of wine they'd carried upstairs and having a smoke. He was watching the whole thing with complete indifference. When he noticed Kieli looking, he abruptly averted his eyes, reaching for his pack of cigarettes—even though he was already smoking one—and for some reason grabbing a fresh one and trying to stick it in his mouth, too. He let the lit one slip out in the process, creating his own one-man commotion.

What is he doing?

It was so funny, the giggle just spilled out of her, and in that instant the shutter clicked for the second time.

And thus a picture of Kieli on a winter day at the end of her sixteenth year was captured on film.

Watching Kieli from a distance getting a wreath clapped on her head and being cheered at by the regulars, he felt a tiny bit sympathetic. He didn't think she was the type of girl to handle being the center of attention like that very well. Not that he felt any urge to go help her out—he was even worse at it than she was.

Photos, huh?

Saying she wanted to build something together in the

sandbox back at Shiman's camp, and then that promise (which he'd like to erase from memory and pretend never happened)…he didn't know whether Kieli realized it herself or not, but he could tell she probably wanted some kind of memory that would clearly last. Which only made him feel more weighted down, so he ended up acting defensive without meaning to.

"Kieli looks so pretty in that. You could almost mistake her for the bride," the radio sighed in a voice full of emotion, like a father who'd just walked his daughter down the aisle.

"What are you, a doting parent?" Harvey jibed exasperatedly. The Corporal was way too partial to her. Though now that he mentioned it, Harvey did have to agree that the understated little wreath of flowers with its simple white lace looked tailor-made for Kieli (…*Does that count as being partial?*). Still, the smile she was giving the camera was so awkward and stiff that he didn't think anyone could mistake her for the woman of the hour.

"She's grown up so fast…I can die happy now that I've had the chance to see Kieli all dressed up like this."

"You're already dead," Harvey snarked on autopilot. He was busy tipping his ash into the tray he'd brought with him from the counter when the radio's static suddenly cut off. There were a few seconds of silence. After an odd pause, he heard the usual white noise start up again, along with a slightly subdued voice.

"Say, Herbie…"

"Harvey."

"I want to ask you a favor."

"Huh? Don't just burst out with something like that. It's creepy."

"When I break down and stop working for real, take me to Easterbury. To that grave at the mine."

Harvey settled his cigarette back into place and let his eyes roam the hall as if this were nothing much, really. He didn't know how to respond for a moment. The cigarette's thin stream of smoke dissipated into the white strobe light and the bustle of the bar, nearby but at the same time sounding far away, nothing to do with him. He could hear the photographer saying, "Relax your expression a little."

Harvey turned to look at the radio, the movement of his neck sort of stiff and awkward for some reason, and frowned. "…What are you saying?"

"Hmm? Oh, I'm just talking about 'somedays.'" The radio's tone turned joking. *"I ain't kicking the bucket for a good while yet. I've got enough bones to pick with you to last another fifty years, easy."*

"Ugh, not another fifty years," he answered. The whole conversation was seriously souring his mood now, though. *Stupid Corporal, bringing up something like that.*

Over the regulars' heads, Kieli's eyes caught his in a silent plea for help. Something made him avoid her gaze. Habit sent him reaching for his pack of smokes, like he always did when he felt uncomfortable. When he bent to pull a fresh one out with his mouth, the half-smoked one already between his lips fell into his lap. "Ow!" *Jeez, what the hell am I doing?*

He heard a little giggle from the center of the room. When he managed to rescue his cigarette and look up again, a stupid little sound of surprise escaped his lips. Behind the faintly smiling Kieli, though he doubted either she or the other guests noticed it, the ghosts from the band were leaning out over the edge of the stage and striking poses for the camera with their instruments, eager to get into the picture.

Sheesh...

As Harvey sighed, the flash lit up Kieli's face for the second time.

Late at night, with the party over and the guests gone home, the bar seemed even more horribly quiet after how bustling it had been all day. He distinctly remembered the opposite phenomenon being the norm for this bar not too long ago... But the number of dead customers gathering for the late-night concerts had started to lessen little by little in inverse proportion to the growing number of regular customers during the day, and tonight they seemed to have finally reached the point where not a single one showed up. There was only the four-member ghost band, quietly performing a slow number on the dimly lit stage.

After Kieli and the new bride had gone upstairs to bed, Harvey somehow ended up sitting at a table with the bartender.

"The day's over now, but congrats."

"I really don't know how to feel about hearing that from you."

"Why?"

"Eh, never mind. Thanks."

They clinked their drinks together across the table, and Harvey brought his half-full glass of amber liquid to his lips.

"You gonna drink? I don't see that too often."

"Well, today's a special occasion." When he tilted the glass, ice shifted with a barely there sound and touched his lip. Harvey didn't know whether it was because he was an Undying or because of his specific constitution that alcohol didn't affect him, but either way, to him it might as well have been water. So he'd never particularly sought it out to drink. Though he did often think he'd *like* to get drunk once. Speaking of things you didn't see too often, he noticed that the bartender wasn't polishing any glasses today, either.

"We'll be clearing out soon. I'm thinking we'll start traveling again."

"Don't be shy. You're welcome to stay here. Yana and I both like having people around."

"Yeah, well, I don't want to be a freeloader in a newlyweds' home," Harvey answered, not bothering to hide his distaste. The bartender hunched his shoulders, looking displeased. It was true, though. And even if it weren't, they'd ended up staying here a long time; longer than he'd planned. He'd considered this wedding the perfect nudge to get them moving again.

Harvey put his glass down and straightened up just a little on his stool.

"Thank you for everything... Be happy together."

He bobbed his head in a tiny bow. The bartender knit his brow, clearly wanting to say something, but in the end he just sighed, apparently giving up on it.

"What about Kieli? You're taking her with you, right?"

"Well, yeah, that's the plan."

The conversation broke off for a time. The band's current number was just drawing to a close, too, and the quiet in the background made their own silence feel all the more uneasy. It was the bartender who eventually broke it, in a more serious, almost admonishing tone.

"Just so you know, Kieli's more than some stranger's kid to me, too. She's Setsuri's gift to this world, and I care about her. So take responsibility and make her happy, you got that?"

"……"

He couldn't nod. But when he just stared with downcast eyes at the ice cubes sinking to the bottom of the amber liquid in his glass as they melted, the bartender repeated, "Harvey." It sounded like this one question he wasn't going to back down on until Harvey answered.

So Harvey reluctantly opened his mouth, but the only words that came sighing out were "…I'm gonna be sick."

And with that, he let his head thunk down on the table in front of him. "Huh?!" came the bartender's surprised voice from somewhere above him. "What, don't tell me you're drunk?!"

"No," he tried to say, but somewhere along the way it turned into a groan, so instead he shook his head without lifting it. The hard table felt uneven against his forehead. He wanted nothing more than to be left alone, so he let himself lie flopped there in that position and tried to project a "go away" aura. After a few moments he heard the bartender give an exasperated sigh.

The performance ended and the band took a break. With a brief word to the other musicians, a man climbed down from the stage and walked toward them. It was the bandleader. He was also the saxophonist, a rare thing to see in a rock band—but in truth, the hands holding his instrument had decayed in his grave long ago.

When the bartender turned to look at him, he jerked his chin toward the stage with a bit of a sardonic smile. "Yo. You want to join us for a number?"

The younger man blinked. "Huh? Me…sir?" he responded, with a strange belated politeness toward his former leader. Then the bartender cast a questioning glance in Harvey's direction, so Harvey assumed an indifferent expression and left his face firmly planted on the table. (He didn't want the guy looking to him for help.) The bartender shot him a miffed look, but he rose from his chair nevertheless and gave a shy smile. "Well, okay then…"

Harvey'd never once seen him playing the old acoustic guitar he brought out from around the side of the stage, and yet it appeared well looked after. The leader gave a satisfied nod at the sight of it, and the other players welcomed the bartender, clearing a place for him at center stage. Before the leader returned to the stage, he addressed Harvey.

"Would you listen to us? You're our only audience."

"…Sure."

After some simple tuning, the ghost band with one lone physical guitar in its midst began its eerily real concert. They'd given the bartender the lead guitar part. Harvey was no music expert, but even to untrained ears his playing sounded clumsy in spots. Seeing him like this, it was easy to believe he'd been the lowest guy on the totem pole when they were all alive. Though it was thanks to that he'd gotten released from prison, of course.

For a while Harvey drank alone, at his own pace, letting the chords filling the room wash over him without thinking about them overmuch. Personally, he found tobacco more useful than alcohol for distracting himself out of a bad mood, but he'd screwed up and left his cigarettes in the pocket of the coat Kieli'd taken upstairs.

Ugh, I'm gonna be sick…

A chunk of ice fell into his mouth. He chewed it with a grimace.

Make her happy.

How? he felt like asking. He had the feeling he'd get yelled at (by the Corporal) for asking someone else that, though, so he kept quiet.

But however you looked at it, no matter how much he might want to, there was no way he could make her happy *forever*, was there? Things might be fine as they were for now, but Harvey strongly felt that one day Kieli would have to find her own path toward a future all her own. At the same time, though, he also sometimes wondered whether feeling that way was only his way of shirking responsibility, and the longer he thought in circles like that, the more it seemed to trigger some kind of immunological response within him, until he felt like throwing up. But at least he didn't try to just walk away from the whole thing, which meant he'd grown a little…right?

At some point while he was spinning his empty glass on the table to distract himself, he realized he'd missed the last chorus, and the band was already getting near the end of the song. They'd asked him to listen, but halfway through he'd started thinking about other things, and his attention had wandered. He focused back on the stage. Sure enough, when he shifted his gaze too suddenly, his right eye lagged behind, making him dizzy.

Finally the images overlapped and he could focus on the stage—

Huh?

The empty glass slipped from his hand. He half-stood up from his chair without thinking and sent the table rocking, the glass falling over with a clunk.

In the center of the stage, the bartender's hands had stopped on the strings.

"…Well, take care of yourself."

"Hang in there."

"Be nice to your wife. Don't drive her to run out on you, got it?"

As the band members abandoned their performance to give their congratulations to the bartender, who was now standing stock-still, their outlines began to blur and the stage lights started to pass right through them. The vocals and guitar…the bass…the drums…one by one, the sound of each instrument faded away without waiting for the number to be quite over.

By the time all the music had cut off, leaving the song on a strange, unfinished note, only the bartender, the saxophonist, and the tired old sound equipment were left on stage. Now that it was almost vacant, the tiny stage seemed suddenly bigger.

"Heh, you just never seem to get better at that, do you?" the bandleader laughed jokingly. The bartender didn't laugh or make a retort. He bit his lip and hung his head, guitar still hanging limply from his shoulder.

"You're going...?"

"Yeah. Looks like it's about that time. Business is picking up, and it wouldn't do for us to haunt the place forever, would it? You're fine now, right...?"

The leader gave his answer with a smile, and then his form began to fade and melt into the light, as if to follow the other members. The bartender didn't nod or speak; he just stared at the floor in silence. But then all of a sudden he lifted his head as if he just couldn't stand it anymore.

"Wait—please wait! I still..."

"Don't look at me like that, you dolt. Otherwise we'll miss our chance to pass on again."

The bartender's hand reached out pleadingly, but it only slid through him, scrabbling at the air. The bandleader gave his old friend a gentle smile. Both the smile and the low, chiding voice sank into the quiet that filled the bar, steadily vanishing.

"You've started to live your own life, to walk your own path to the future. You can't stay chained to the past with us forever."

"Be happy, okay?...I won't tell you to be happy enough for all of us. Find your own happiness..."

* * *

The brass sax lingered until the bitter end, suspended wistfully in midair even after its player was gone. Eventually it too dissolved into silver static and melted into the air around them, and the stage was empty of all sound and light.

There was only the bartender in his black vest, standing still in the middle of the newly fallen dimness, his guitar dangling forgotten at his side.

"Now that's just mean..." the man said hoarsely, and let out a tiny laugh.

"Right up to the end, I was the worst player—I was the one who stuck out like a sore thumb—and I got left behind *again*...It's just mean, isn't it?" he grumbled, half to himself. Then he turned to Harvey with a smile that looked at once exhausted and somehow cheered. "Hey, Undying. This was the right thing, right? I guess this is the natural thing. I know it wouldn't do for me to make them stay here forever because they were worried about me..."

The tipped-over glass had rolled to the edge of the table unnoticed. It looked as if it was about to fall off. Harvey reached out and caught it with his left hand, and set it back down with a clink before he answered.

"...Yeah. I think it was the right thing."

It was the same answer he always would've given, but before, he would've been able to give it instantly. And yet somehow here he was, unable to get the words out now without a pause.

The bartender began cleaning up and didn't speak again. Harvey was left with nothing to do with himself. That and the fact that he didn't think he could go much longer without a smoke prompted him upstairs to go rescue his cigarettes. When he made his way up the creaking staircase to the second floor, Kieli was leaning on the hallway wall right at the top of the steps. A bit startled, he asked, "You're still awake?"

"Uh-huh…"

Kieli nodded without looking up or moving from the wall. *Oh, so you were watching that…* Harvey searched his mind for something to say, but before he could find anything she lifted her face to him with an unexpectedly bright smile.

"We'll have to work with Yana and do our best to keep this place lively."

It stabbed him in the heart how transparent her fake cheer was, and in the end he couldn't come up with any smart, sensitive words for her; he could only give her an unreadable look. "Oh, no! We didn't let the Corporal hear their last concert. I bet he'll be angry, huh? Sorry, Corporal!" she chirped in an unnaturally hyper-cheerful voice, and jogged back to her bedroom. Harvey watched her retreating back in silence. Then he let out a sigh of something like self-loathing.

"Be happy"… He found himself wondering how many times those particular words had been passed back and forth in this bar today. Him to the bartender, the bartender back to him, the band members to the bartender, and probably lots of other times in other conversations he hadn't heard.

Rather than a blessing, he kind of thought that "Be happy" might be a phrase you used to distance yourself, in a sense. A way of saying "I can't do anything else for you, so make the best of it on your own."

Suddenly he began to hate those words with a passion. *Why did he say that?*

"Harvey!"

He was making a displeased face at his own thoughts when Kieli popped right back into the hallway. The mask of false cheer she'd worn a moment ago had slipped off, and her smile was gone. Still, she didn't seem depressed, either—if anything, she looked pale and stunned.

"The Corporal's acting weird. He won't answer," she said, running up to him and holding out the radio.

"Weird...?"

"I can't hear his voice."

Harvey took the radio from her and squatted down there in the hallway. Kieli squatted across from him. The first thing he checked was the power, but it was on. "Corporal?" he called. But just like Kieli said, he didn't answer. When he put his ear to the speaker, he couldn't hear even a whisper of the constant static that should always be there even when the radio wasn't speaking.

A cold sweat ran down his spine.

"Corporal...Hey!"

Automatically he gave it a few good shakes. Kieli looked beseechingly up at him, but he didn't have anything to comfort her with.

After several shakes, he heard a soft snap of static.

"......*Hmm? What? What is it?*" came an absentminded voice from the speaker. When Harvey and Kieli just stared, half-frozen and awkward, the radio went on. "*Huh? No wonder it seemed dark—we're in the hallway! What's a grown man*

doing squatting in the hallway? You're like a kid, always want-
ing to just plunk yourself down wherever you end up." There
came the usual rapid-fire criticism, as if nothing at all had
happened. Getting annoyed, he shoved the machine back into
Kieli's arms.

"Oh, Corporal…!"

Kieli hugged the radio, relief flooding her face. Harvey
stood up and backed a few steps away. Evidently it had just
been a loose connection somewhere, or something. "Damn,
he pisses me off," Harvey grunted. Then he sucked in a harsh
breath. Maddeningly, his hand was shaking slightly.

This happening right after the Corporal's weird out-of-the-
blue talk at the party had made him lose it a little, if he was
honest.

"For heaven's sake, what are you two fussing about?"

And now the radio who'd caused all this trouble was the
only one talking on a different page, as if it was totally clueless. Harvey ignored it and made for his own room, determined to grab his cigarettes and get the hell out of this place.
Go on a walk or something. He just knew that if he didn't
have a smoke soon, peace of mind was going to become physically impossible.

"Jeez, and it's late, too. Go on, Kieli, get to bed. Tomorrow's
the big wedding party, you know. It's gonna be a busy day."

… Wait.
What did he just say?

Harvey stopped walking with one foot through the doorway. After a moment frozen in that position, he turned jerkily

back toward the hallway. Kieli raised her head with equally jerky motions. Their eyes met over the radio in her arms.

Tomorrow was the party—?

You're fine now, right…?

She'd watched the ghost band say that as they disappeared and had seen double, the friend she'd parted ways with two years ago overlapping with them in her mind. A girl with blond pigtails and a red coat, saying with a bright smile and a bright soprano voice, *You'll be fine without me now, Kieli,* before she disappeared.

No, I wasn't *fine*, she protested in her heart, all this time later. *Why would you say something like that and then leave me? It makes no sense that I'd stop needing you just because I met Harvey and the Corporal.* Kieli loved all of them. They were all among her very few treasures. There was no one she didn't need. So why did God take away those treasures one by one after she finally found them?

And was God trying to snatch the Corporal out of her hands this time?

She'd asked him over and over again, wondering if it was some kind of misunderstanding, but the Corporal really didn't remember that day's wedding party at all. From what she could tell, he remembered everything up through two days ago, and then time seemed to have stopped for him. There was the bad connection to think of, among other things, so the next morning they talked to the bar owner, and got the address of a junk shop on the edge of town whose owner did general mechanical repairs. They took the radio and set off. Harvey was back to his usual self this morning, wearing his usual "This is a pain in the butt" expression as he came with her, but Kieli thought he'd been just as shaken as she was last night.

The store was a disordered jumble of display shelves and baskets and drawers crammed full of tools and mechanical parts. There were some old radios, too, though none as old as the Corporal.

The shopkeeper had opened up the radio on his worktable, and was currently investigating its insides. "Oh, wow, this thing is in bad shape! Sure, it's old, but it seems too thoroughly beaten up for it to be age alone... The circuit board's really on its last legs. It's even melted in a few spots. How have you been using it that got it like this?!" he blustered, sounding half-impressed and half-flabbergasted. She thought she could hear a little blame in there, too.

"*He's* the one who's too rough on it," Harvey responded, clearly taking exception to his tone. Kieli doubted the shopkeeper understood what he meant, though. She was sure the way she and Harvey treated it had contributed to the problem, but it was easy to see how overusing a destructive shock wave like the Corporal's would melt a few of the inner workings. Kieli felt pretty positive that radios weren't designed to release shock waves.

"Can it be fixed, sir?"

"Well, it's so old... My shop doesn't deal in parts from that era. I don't think you'll be able to get any in the towns in this area. Practically speaking, I'd say the easiest thing would be to buy a new radio…" The shopkeeper swept his eyes over the used radios for sale on his shelves, and then looked back down at the Corporal-radio with a sharp eye, as if mentally estimating its value. "Well, it is quite the antique. I'll give you a good price for it as a trade-in. What do you say?"

"N-no thank you!"

Sensing the Corporal was in danger, she grabbed his strap and Harvey's hand, and fled the store.

Harvey was the one to mention the northwestern mining district. There were three main mineral deposits on this planet that still managed to provide resources for the people to some degree: the ones in the far south mining district that supplied Westerbury, the southwestern mining district that made up part of the South-hairo continent, and the northwestern mining district that lay west of the capital. As for the eastern part of the planet—the mineral deposits in the Easterbury region had been tapped out, and the area largely laid waste. Easterbury had been the site of the War's final hard-fought battles, after all.

Of the three remaining mining districts, the northwestern one was the oldest. Apparently it actually contained the remains of an older mine where people found relics of the high-level civilization before the War. There, they might be able to get hold of some radio parts. "I'm only saying there's a *possibility*, though," Harvey waffled. "You want to go?"

"Yeah…but what should we do about Beatrix?" Of course she wanted to go, but on the off chance that Beatrix tried to contact them while they were away from the border town, they would miss her message. On the other hand, staying here fretting wouldn't necessarily bring any developments on that front, either. At any rate, they couldn't easily decide; they looked at each other pensively for a while, and then ended up just dropping the whole line of thought.

"Maybe it's like what you'd call dementia," the bartender mused thoughtfully when they told him about it back at the bar. Harvey perched himself on a bar stool and crossed his legs, sighing in agreement.

"He said the capacitor's in bad shape and some of the circuitry's not working because it's worn through. And if *this* is the result, it means the Corporal's spirit has grown totally dependent on this beat-up radio's circuit board, and they're functioning in synch. So I guess it's basically like his brains are turning into a senile old fart's."

"Who are you calling a senile old fart?!"

The radio jerked violently on the countertop, clearly enraged at being treated like an old man. No matter how carefully they explained what the junk shop owner had told them, the Corporal kept insisting that he wasn't one bit broken down. He didn't seem to be aware of his memory loss.

"I ain't kicking the bucket for a good while yet! I've got enough bones to pick with you to last another fifty years, easy!"

"You don't even remember you said that same thing yesterday, do you?" Harvey shot back, massaging his temple and looking fed up. His expression didn't change as he slumped against the low back of the stool and looked up at the ceiling like he was giving up on the whole conversation. When he noticed Kieli watching him anxiously, though, he straightened up a little as if embarrassed.

"I-it'll be okay, won't it...?" she ventured, forcing a smile. But Harvey only looked away as if it was too hard for him to answer. With no more outlet, the smile turned stiff and unconvincing. She gulped, and asked hesitantly, "What will happen to the Corporal if the radio breaks down?"

Harvey's gaze stayed fixed on nothing in particular. In a voice deliberately stripped of all emotion, he said—

"He'll cease to exist, I guess."

There was nothing to say to an answer like that. Kieli and the bartender listening nearby both fell silent, and there was a strained, awkward pause that went on for several seconds.

It was the radio itself who attempted to snap them out of it.

"*Hey, quit being stupid, you jerk! I told you, I'm fine!*" Then it shouted in an overenthusiastic voice, "*Kieli, I'm fit as a fiddle! Just look at this!*" and unleashed a shock wave at the wall, completely ignoring the bartender shouting at him to stop. The bartender went pale, and gasped something about how he'd catch it from Yana later.

Luckily for the bar, the shock wave didn't turn out to be that strong. All it did was scorch the wall a little. In fact, the radio was the only one really affected; the recoil sent it tumbling off the counter.

"Oh, Corporal...!"

Kieli hurriedly squatted down and picked it up off the floor. When she examined it to see if it was okay, she discovered that it had apparently knocked one of its connections loose again, and wouldn't respond to her.

"Again?" Harvey sighed exasperatedly from somewhere overhead. He'd said before that the way to fix old things was to kick them. (She'd heard that from her grandmother, too—it seemed to be an old saying.) So Kieli tried shaking it like Harvey'd done the previous night, and then gave it a few light whacks with her hand.

Eventually the static started up again and the Corporal's familiar voice gave a sleepy grumble.

Kieli sighed in relief.

"Corporal, are you all right? I get that you're full of energy, I promise, so just don't be reckless, okay…?"

"Hmm? Where am I?" he asked blankly. Her relief turned into foreboding before she had a chance to enjoy it. *Don't tell me he's lost a day's worth of memories again…* Kieli hugged the radio to her chest and darted a glance up at Harvey from her position on the floor.

He frowned back as though he was a little worried, too. Turning around in his chair to face them, he asked, "Corporal, do you know what day it is?"

"What day?" the radio echoed. There was an odd pause.

"Wait…who am I?"

"Huh?!" Harvey squeaked, sliding half out of his chair. "No—hey—hold on, say that again," he demanded in a reedy voice.

The question he got in response was even blanker: *"Hmm? Oh…who are you again?"*

Kieli listened to this disjointed exchange in silence, frozen in place there with the radio in her arms, unable to make any sort of response.

She was seized by a terrible sensation: she was holding the radio to her, clutching it tightly to her with both hands, and yet it felt as if something were being torn out of her arms.

❦

"I can't believe you're going away so suddenly…" said Yana. She was standing at the bar entrance to see them off, her eyes downcast as if she was feeling lonely already.

Kieli gave a polite bow and said, "I'm sorry." Her shoulder bag bobbed along with her.

Yana didn't know about the "talking radio" yet, so she couldn't go into detail about why they were leaving. Yana's expression said she didn't like the situation, but she didn't try to force any explanations out of them. Instead, she set about gathering up supplies and putting together a packed lunch at top speed, which she pushed firmly on Kieli. She really was like Suzie. "Write me. Stay in touch, okay?"

"Yes, ma'am!" Kieli said, accepting the cloth bundle full of bread and cheese and preserved foods. And then her heart was bursting with so much guilt and gratitude it stopped up her throat, and all she could do was nod over and over.

"You sure you don't want me to take you to the station?"

"Nah, this is fine."

The voices of Harvey and the bartender talking drifted to her from a little way off. *"Are we going somewhere?"* asked the clueless radio hanging from Harvey's hand along with his backpack. The two men sighed in unison.

"Kieli. Let's go," Harvey said briefly, shifting the backpack to his shoulder and turning toward the station. He set off at a fast pace and showed no sign of waiting for her to catch up, so Kieli shoved the parcel of food in her bag in a panic and left the couple seeing them off with a hurried "O-okay, bye!" and one last light bow of her head.

The rusty radio and the back of the lanky redhead blended right into the cityscape covered in its thin layer of fossil-fuel smog, and for just a second she was afraid she'd lose sight of them completely. She shifted her shoulder bag behind her and took off after them at a run. For the first time in three months, here she was in her travel outfit: big shoulder bag, duffle coat, and the shorts that gave her freedom to move around easily. She'd dragged her travel boots out from their storage spot under the bed, too. Winter's frosty air caressed her cheeks as she ran. Maybe it was just her imagination, but she thought she could smell a whiff of spring on the breeze.

There was only a short distance between her and her companions, but for some reason they felt horribly far away. Kieli upped her pace so she wouldn't get left behind. *Don't let me be separated from the people I treasure. Don't let me lose sight of them. Please, don't take anything else away from me*, she prayed silently—to whom, she wasn't sure.

It was the final winter of her sixteenth year—and another journey was about to begin.

CHAPTER 2

AS THE TOY SOLDIER WEEPS

The young arms clutching the doll were nothing but skin and bones, and the skin was yellowing with jaundice. The air around them was thick with the stench of bile and shit. "Captain, we're the only survivors...from our unit now...Our food and water supplies...are exhausted..." The scratchy voice mumbling to the doll carried feebly to his ears along the yellow sand piled on the ground. The captain being addressed was a tin soldier in uniform.

The monologue abruptly ceased, and hollow eyes rolled slowly up to meet his.

"Do you have any water?" The child lifted one hand a little from the ground and reached weakly toward him. He didn't think the kid could have been even ten years old yet, but those eyes were the cloudy yellow of an old man's.

He thought for a moment, then drew a metal flask out of his practically empty backpack. He started to toss it over before realizing that the kid probably didn't even have the strength left to open the lid. So instead he opened the lid himself and pressed it into the child's hand. Giving the water felt kind of hypocritical, considering it would probably only buy the kid a few more hours of life. But when the boy's tiny hands brought the flask up to his face, and he put his mouth to it and drank in audible gulps, he looked as if he were savoring a small taste of happiness. Water spilled over, dribbling over his cracked lips and down his cheeks to form a dark gray patch on the parched ground. The thirsty ground seemed almost like a part of the thirsty boy.

When he took his mouth away from the flask, his speaking voice was closer to normal, as if he'd come back to himself.

"You're not one of the charity people, huh?...I mean, even they don't come here anymore. If you stay here you'll get infected and die. Didn't you know that...?"

"I know," he said, accepting the flask back and sitting down next to the kid. He leaned back against the crumbling wall of blocks. They were on a perfectly ordinary roadside on the edge of town. Still, when he looked at the cityscape he couldn't sense any of the vitality of the people living their desperate lives there. A thick, putrid smell had settled onto the piles of sand and dust around them.

Looking without much thought at the corpses lying along the other side of the road, he brought the flask to his own lips. The kid squeaked in surprise. He drank from the same place the boy had, unconcerned. Now the boy was watching him with something like wonder, dull eyes open wide, but eventually he murmured, "You're weird..." and let his cheek fall limply back to the ground again.

"Aren't you scared to die? I am...Hey—I'm going to die soon, huh?"

False comfort wouldn't do the kid any good, so he just nodded. "Yeah."

"Huh. You don't talk like the charity people."

"......?" He shot the kid a questioning look. The kid turned back to the doll in the soldier's uniform without raising his cheek from the ground. He began casually moving its tin arms around, speaking as if to the toy and not to him at all.

"They all say, 'There's nothing to be afraid of. God is calling you to be with him.' But you know what? I think it's a lie that

God's world is a world of happiness...I mean, it's full of people who hurt real bad and died looking all nasty, right? Sick people, people who died in the War. That's who lives there. Mom died of the sickness too, but I know even if I go to God's place I won't be able to find her. See, before she died she got so skinny, and she was such a funny color, you could hardly tell her apart from the others...That's why I'm really scared to go someplace where everybody is like that..."

The words broke off for a moment, as if the boy was exhausted from all the talking, and he heaved a dispassionate, resigned sigh that didn't suit his age at all. Then he finished in a voice that was almost a sigh itself:

"But I'll be just the same as them soon..."

The wind blowing in from the city stirred up the yellow sand at his feet just slightly, leaving in its place a new rotten smell. He drank another sip of water to try to wash down the smell where it stuck in his throat. It tasted just like the air: yellow sand and rot.

"...Want me to tell you how to not die?" he whispered softly, casting a sidelong glance at the doll in the kid's arms, and at the time, he didn't feel particularly interested or think particularly deeply about it.

That was a long time ago now. Still, looking back on it, it wasn't so long ago at all.

"Kieli, hurry up."

The bell signaling the train's departure echoed up and down

the platform. People seeing their loved ones off and people who'd been reluctant to say good-bye all started picking up bags and hurrying them onto the train. Gazing out the window, he could see a girl running up from the direction of the station and dashing into the train car at the very end of the line of passengers. The clamor of the bell cut abruptly off, and after a beat the scenery out the window began sliding gently by, leaving the platform and the station behind.

Around the time they made it past the platform completely, the somewhat flushed girl entered the car through the connecting door.

"H-here are your cigarettes," she said, panting. "These are the right kind, right?"

Harvey accepted the pack with a simple "Thanks." He didn't really think he'd ever explicitly told her his brand, but she'd gotten the exact one he always smoked.

"Sheesh, I can't believe you didn't notice you were out until the last minute! Next time buy them yourself."

"Yeah, sor—"

"*You just need to be thoughtful enough to buy him spare packs. Problem solved,*" cut in the radio coldly before he could finish. Kieli made a miffed noise, glaring sidelong at it where it sat by the window and looking steadily more displeased. And then when she began to lower herself into her usual spot in their set of facing seats, the radio said in a scathing voice, "*Know your place, girl. A servant never sits down without the master's permission.*"

"What?!"

"Okay, okay, you can sit down. Just sit down," Harvey interceded tiredly. Kieli pulled a sour face and plopped down violently into her seat. As he was searching his pocket for something to light the freshly bought cigarette in his mouth, thinking things had finally quieted down, the radio burst out with another ridiculous criticism. *"Hey, give him a light. Honestly, you're completely thoughtless."*

"…Harveeyyyy, do something!" Kieli entreated, giving him a reproachful glare. Harvey couldn't muster the will to keep playing peacekeeper, though. He looked away from her and lit his cigarette for himself. *I'm not making him say that stuff, you know!*

He leaned his head against the windowpane, sick of it all. When he gazed outside, relying on his good left eye, the criss-crossing rock ledges marking the fault line that cut through northwestern North-hairo towered in the distance.

They'd fixed their destination as the northwestern mining district that supplied the capital. This was the second day of their journey along the railroad stretching out of North-hairo to the west. The mining district they were heading for was on the other side of that fault line to the north, but coming from North-hairo the rock ledges were in the way, and they had to travel far west to get around them. There was actually a direct route there from the capital, but going through the capital was a no-go for obvious reasons, so their only option was to go the long way.

Harvey'd told his information broker to keep looking for clues about Beatrix before they left the border town, just in case, and given instructions to contact the bar if he found anything. Their departure had been pretty sudden, sure, but he'd been getting tired of staying in one place (and he wasn't keen on getting in the way of any newlyweds, either), so he'd intended to leave anyway. This had actually been good timing, in a sense.

There was no guarantee that they'd be able to fix the radio in the northwestern mining district. He hadn't decided on his next step after that yet, but he could figure it out a little at a time during the trip…

What was really pushing his limits right now was this situation.

"What's the matter, Master? You keep sighing," asked the radio, puzzled, after yet another smoke-filled sigh of displeasure. In stark contrast to the verbal abuse it heaped on Kieli, the radio addressed him with ridiculous politeness. Shuddering at the chill crawling up his spine, Harvey said, "Cut that out. The 'Master' thing."

"What? But why?"

"Because I said so. Just call me by my name."

"Your name…So, 'Mr. Harvey'?"

Harvey swallowed his drag of smoke the wrong way and almost choked himself to death. *Wait a second, you* can *say 'vey'!*

At first he'd thought its bad wiring had blocked off all access to its memories of the past—but thanks to God only knew what kind of memory mix-up, out of nowhere the partial-amnesiac radio had started treating him as its master. Considering that it meant he wouldn't get nagged all the time, he initially thought this might not be so bad. That naive idea was gone in one minute flat. Getting chewed out would be a hundred times better than this disgusting feeling as if a pack of centipedes were crawling around in his stomach.

"Corporal, are you sure you're not doing this on purpose?"

Right: meanwhile, Kieli was fed up for a very different reason. Glaring at the radio with an enormous scowl on her face, she added, "If you're not, maybe another shock will bring you back to normal. Maybe I should try dropping you." The dangerous look on her face as she grabbed it and lifted it overhead made Harvey think she might actually be serious. The radio screamed.

"Cut that out! Cut it out, you stupid girl!"

"What did you just call me?!"

"…Kieli. Cut it out. It'll be hell if he gets any weirder," Harvey intervened, simultaneous headache and chill and heartburn making him listless. Kieli pouted and said "He started it!" before grudgingly putting down the radio.

Yes: as for how Kieli was being treated…the radio seemed to think she was some sort of handmaid. The radio's normal attitudes toward Kieli and himself had flipped 180 degrees. Their loudly arguing voices pierced his temples, and he bent his head away from them, unthinkingly crushing the end of his cigarette between his teeth. Given the situation, you'd have thought the atmosphere on their journey would be more somber. What the hell was with this surprise turn for the ridiculous?

"Where did this whole 'Harvey is our master' thing come from, anyway?"

"Where did it come from? What, do you want to hear the story of how the master and I met? It's a touching tale that

leaves both the listener and the teller in tears, believe you me. It all started years ago, when a scoundrel of the blackest dye captured me and brought me to the gambling house to bet me on a card game. Now, during this game there were some accusations of cheating, and a brawl broke out. The man who lent me his aid in my hour of need was none other than our master."

That never happened, Harvey mentally shot back, but he didn't have the energy to say so out loud, so he pointedly ignored the whole thing. But then the next thing he heard was, *"He made a dashing entrance, shot a card at the villain that lodged itself in the dead center of his forehead, and then—"*

"Stop making up lies! I don't have any embarrassing moves like that," Harvey denied immediately. There was no way he was letting *that* go. He was pretty sure one of the radio plays the Corporal was so into—probably one of the hard-boiled private-eye ones—had gotten mixed up with the truth in the ghost's mind. The part about how they'd first met at a gambling house was weirdly on target, so apparently he didn't have complete amnesia; his mind was just scrambled to high hell because his wires were shot.

The radio yammered on at Kieli about his logic-leaping delusion. Glancing at it with his eyes at half-mast (there was so much wrong with their conversation that he didn't even know where to begin anymore, so he just left them to it), Harvey abruptly realized something.

I get it . . . so that's why I remembered that kid out of the blue after all this time. That was the town where I met the Corporal. Although "encountered" is probably more accurate than "met" . . .

* * *

It was a town completely saturated with the stench of death.

All the places to house the sick were full to capacity or beyond, and the dead had littered the roadsides like trash.

He didn't remember exactly when he'd developed it, but at any rate, by that time he'd definitely been in the habit of visiting a gambling house when he was feeling down. Normally he hated noisy places. Mysteriously, though, he felt no aversion to the clamor of gambling houses. Maybe it was because the crowd noise and the low lighting hazed with tobacco smoke built a wall around him and concealed him more than they did anything else.

It figures I wouldn't get infected . . .

Holding his cards in both hands, Harvey sighed dejectedly. The other men circling the table grinned at his expression. At the dealer's signal, each player spread his hand out on the table. A "free city" flush, a bishop's staff and cruiser full house, and four swords—as the men showed their cards, the various onlookers cried out in excitement or disappointment. The man with the four swords gave Harvey a demanding look. He was the only one left to show his cards.

" . . . Five judges," he announced, setting them down. Four-swords Man immediately turned purple and started shouting, and before he knew it the others had joined in.

"Hey, what's with that?!"

"That's not playing fair!"

"What's unfair about it?" Harvey asked calmly as he collected his winnings.

At that, his opponents all started bitching under their breaths, looking sour. "Don't pull that gloomy face for no reason, dammit!" "God, I'm going home. Nothing left in my pockets tonight." One by one, they got up from their seats. It wasn't until then that Harvey even realized his expression had been that gloomy.

But I went all the way out to that "quarantine area" or whatever, and just look at me...

He watched the other men walking away from the table out of the corner of his eye, leaving him all alone to sulk as he stuffed his collection of banknotes into his pocket. He'd been playing without really thinking, and now he'd won a little too much and there was no one left to play with. *Oh, well.* He'd made enough cash to get him to the next town, and although he'd only just gotten to this one, he'd already finished his business here. *Might as well just leave today.*

Harvey'd half-stood up from his chair when something was plunked down on the table in front of him.

He blinked and looked down. It was a small, extremely shabby-looking radio with a round speaker—a short groan escaped Harvey's mouth before he could think to stop it. He couldn't tell exactly what it was at first glance, but there was a strange presence bound to that radio. Blinking one more time, he raised his eyes to see a thinnish man he didn't recognize standing across the table from him with a stiff, fake smile on his face.

"Would you play a round with me? With this as the stakes."

"Huh? I don't want it," said Harvey, eyebrows drawing together.

But the man stubbornly kept pushing: "Come on, please? I know it doesn't look like much, but it's antique. Worth more than you'd think. If you win it, you can just sell it off right away. I think you'll get a pretty sweet price for it."

It sounded to Harvey as though the game was just an excuse. Obviously what he wanted was to foist the radio off on him. He glared suspiciously. "...What is it you want?"

The man paled, looking frightened, and darted a glance at the radio. "Well, the truth is he asked me to do it. He said he wanted me to give it to you."

He asked you to? "Who did?"

"Um, well...p-please! Please take it! Think of it as a favor to me!" he babbled rapidly, not even attempting a pretense about gambling or whatever anymore. Then he shoved the radio forcibly into Harvey's hands and disappeared into the noisy crowd.

...What the hell was that all about?

The man's behavior had been blatantly suspicious, but it'd be a pain in the ass to chase him down and make him take the damn thing back. Harvey looked warily down at the radio that had been forced on him. It was old and very old-fashioned-looking; he could see signs that the round speaker had broken off and been reattached at least once. A leather strap was fastened to the right end of its rusty lead-gray body. It *looked* like the transistor kind, but most likely it wasn't the same technology people used now. No sound was coming from it even though it was switched on, so maybe it was broken, but he'd definitely been right: he could feel some sort of presence from it. *Memories? Lingering sentiments?...No, it's something with a little stronger of a will. A ghost possessing the machinery? Can't tell whether it's dangerous or not, though...*

Harvey hesitated a bit, but in the end he only sighed. *Oh, well, whatever.* He stood up from his chair, the radio dangling from one hand.

At the time, "danger" was a matter of indifference to him anyway.

There was known to be an epidemic in this town. An area on the outskirts of town had been designated as the quarantine area, and the sick as well as those suspected of infection were kept isolated there. There was an asylum, technically, but it was well past capacity; the patients stricken with high fever and jaundice overflowed into the streets, and most of them died in a few days without ever receiving any treatment.

Or at least, he'd heard that he could find such a place there, and so even though he hadn't been actively wishing to get infected, a sort of vague interest in whether he *would* had made him visit...

But apparently he couldn't die from infectious diseases.

He didn't *think* he longed to die, exactly, but he found himself feeling pretty disappointed for someone who didn't. Without realizing it, somewhere in the back of his mind he must have been looking for a way to die via convenient "force majeure."

The main street that led to the train station had a decent

amount of foot traffic, along with the attendant commotion. The quarantine area had been downright gruesome, but the urban area removed from it was operating more or less normally. Not prospering, no, but at least doing well enough for him to make his travel expenses at the gambling house.

A sudden thought made him stop on his way to the station and change direction, abandoning the main street for a back alley lined with comparatively sketchy-looking shops. It was too early for the sun to set, but there was no one out and about on this street. It was dotted here and there with open stores, but about half of the businesses had gone under, and their buildings had fallen into disrepair.

Harvey was just setting out in search of a secondhand shop where he could sell off the radio when he sensed someone behind him.

Using his peripheral vision to look around, he found a figure watching him from one street corner. Something that looked an awful lot like a military cap caught his eye. Even though he knew there wasn't a single army left on the planet anymore, reflex set him on instant alert. But—

A kid?

No, the head was tiny; too small even for a child.

He wondered about it, but he didn't change his pace. The presence behind him kept following him at the same pace as well, not too close and not too far away. And there was something else: a strange sound trailed behind Harvey's follower. A sound like something dragging along the dusty pavement.

What to do?

Harvey pondered a little bit as he walked, and then

abruptly changed directions to slip into a nearby alley. He ran straight through it at a sprint, came out into the street at the end, and promptly veered down a different alley. Down that alley by way of the fire escapes on an abandoned apartment building and out the other side—then around another random corner, and then one more again—and then he stopped in his tracks and leaned against the wall of the nearest building, watching the alley entrance he'd come through. There was no sign of anyone following him.

I guess they gave up?

That was good enough for him. He didn't actually care why he was being tailed. As long as they were gone he saw no reason to put any further effort into it. *Whatever's going on here, it's going to be a headache for someone. The best bet is to get out of town on the first train.* He'd been planning to sell the radio, but it looked as though he'd just have to keep it until he got to the next town.

But just as he was about to start walking again, he heard a faint crackle of static from right nearby.

A short burst, then silence for a moment, and then a steady stream of it, accompanied by what sounded like some sort of rhythmic music. A little startled, Harvey lifted the radio dangling from his hand up to eye level. Sure enough, the choppy, static-filled sound of string instruments was coming from its round speaker. What surprised him, though, was that the radio could play at all, not the fact that it had started playing *by itself.*

The air around him swirled toward the radio and condensed, and in the very moment he sensed potential danger an invisible blade shot out of the speaker straight toward him.

"Gah!"

He managed to jump back just in time to dodge the brunt of the surprise attack, but the chunk it tore out of his cheek as it flew by was no laughing matter. The blast of air crashed into the oil shop behind him hard enough to knock down the wall. Hunks of concrete and scraps of iron frame rained down on the narrow alleyway, blocking the entrance and his only escape route. Keeping his back to the wrecked wall, Harvey cursed under his breath and put some distance between himself and the radio before they squared off for their fight.

The radio had fallen near the alley entrance; now dark green particles of noise were swarming like flies in the air above it. Each little blip moved along its own orbit, painting a blurry, monochrome picture he could nonetheless recognize as a human form. It was a painfully thin man wearing what seemed to be a soldier's uniform. While the rest of the noise-filled image just looked like a dark shadow, two points of sharp green light gleamed where the man's eyes should have been beneath the brimmed cap pulled low over his forehead.

"That's some way to greet a guy you've never met before," Harvey said as he wiped his bloody cheek on his sleeve. If anything, he felt a little impressed. He got it now: when the terrified-looking guy at the gambling house said "he" had said to give the radio to Harvey, that "he" had been referring to *the man himself.* Harvey didn't remember doing anything to make the soldier bear him a grudge, but the soldier obviously had some business with him. He must have just grabbed some random guy and threatened him to get him to fob off the radio on Harvey.

"'*Never met*'?!" growled the soldier in a low, staticky voice—which came from the radio's speaker in time with the movements of the noise-cloud's mouth. They were the first words he'd spoken. Evidently Harvey was dealing with a ghost that was using the radio as a medium to anchor itself in the living world. In response to the growl, the hunks of concrete scattered around them began to shake, and then to rise off the ground as if pulled up by strings.

"*Ah, so that's how it is. Yeah, I guess that makes sense… Guess you've killed hundreds, maybe thousands of people in cold blood, after all. Guess you wouldn't remember the face of every single foot soldier you wiped out. Me, on the other hand…*" Static filled his voice until it was almost unintelligible, and the radio's pitches started to warp in resonance with the rise and fall of his emotions. First they surged up high, and then they tumbled low again.

… Wait a second.

Harvey's vision swam violently.

What's he talking about? What's he trying to say to—

"*I've never forgotten your face for a single day!*"

At the soldier's roar, all the concrete pieces suspended in the air flew at him like an artillery barrage. He couldn't even react. He took a direct hit, and slammed back against the rubble that used to be a wall with the concrete right on his heels. To top that off, the impact brought a shower of iron—the skeleton of the roof?—down on his head.

Harvey crawled out from under the rubble, coughing, but a chest-crushing pain shot through him and knocked him over. On the next cough he spit up a black glob of blood. He immediately shut out the pain, but until the wounded parts of his body started regenerating themselves, he wouldn't be able to stand up. *"What's the matter, Undying? Don't tell me peace has made you soft?"* a scratchy voice jeered somewhere beyond the veil that seemed to lie over his senses. *"So, with the War over you let yourself get cocky, and you've been living a nice comfortable life for the last eighty years, eh? Ha ha, must be nice to be you."* The little laugh was spat scornfully, and accompanied by another flying hunk of concrete that hit Harvey in the shoulder and knocked him over onto one side.

Did he just say that I...wiped him out...? Harvey wondered, cheek still glued to the ground.

A reel of all the images Harvey could remember began to unroll in the back of his mind, each scene flashing by fast enough to make him dizzy. With an abstractedness that was kind of odd, considering, he wondered which one this was. *There's the ones I shot to death, the ones whose throats I cut with sabers, and the ones I stabbed in the back with bayonet guns...and then there's the ones we mowed down with armored trucks or whatever, and there's no way I could remember their faces, plus I was never the one driving.* Was the noise-cloud's face really somewhere in there? He had the feeling none of them had been this soldier, but then again, now that he thought about it, he also got the feeling all of them had worn this soldier's face. And the more he thought about that, the more the faces of all the ones he'd shot and the ones whose throats he'd cut and the ones he'd stabbed in the back really did all look the same in his memory.

When he blinked the past out of his eyes, he realized that

at some point the rubble had stopped attacking him. Harvey had been letting his gaze roam vacantly along the ground; he lifted it a fraction to see the noise-cloud soldier floating above the radio giving him a look that made him almost expect to hear teeth grinding.

"*Why aren't you dodging?*" he asked in a low, furious voice, as if it pissed him off that Harvey wasn't putting up any resistance.

They glared at each other for several seconds in silence.

…And then for some reason Harvey found himself laughing. His own laughter struck him as even funnier, and then he couldn't stop—he pressed his forehead into the pavement, shoulders heaving, and tried to bite back the guffaws, but they still vibrated in his throat.

He was in luck. He hadn't managed to die from disease, but here was another chance, right here in the same town. Maybe it hadn't been the epidemic that had made him wander this way. Maybe he'd really been drawn by *this*. Apparently his trip here hasn't been wasted after all.

After the laughing spell passed, Harvey gave a drained sigh.

"Go ahead. I won't dodge. Do it."

Instantly, an aura of powerful malice swelled up around the radio. "*Don't you make a fool of me, you bastard!*" The radio's speaker had ballooned outward into a dome shape, and the high-powered shock wave shot toward him right along with the soldier's roar. The warping of the air made the scene before Harvey's eyes ripple like water. He didn't think or feel anything in particular as he waited for the wave of air barreling toward him to hit.

"Hey, Mister," he heard a voice say. A young child's voice.

And then something very small popped out of the shadow cast by the mountain of debris. A tin doll in an army cap...a tin doll—

—gripping a child's emaciated corpse by the hands and dragging it along the ground.

It approached Harvey casually, unguarded, and got blown away by the shock wave. It crashed into the rubble, corpse and all, with an incongruously mild cry of surprise.

After a brief, dumbfounded moment, Harvey tried to jump to his feet. "Wait—just wait a second—" He couldn't quite stand up, though, so he crawled over to pile of rubble on all fours, intent on rescue—and then found himself momentarily confused about *which* one to rescue. Doll and corpse alike lay with their limbs splayed every which way, looking so literally like broken dolls he could hardly tell which one was the real doll anymore, but on second look the corpse's skin had been torn to ribbons like an old rag by its trip along the pavement; if anything, it looked less human than the doll.

"Mister...Mister..."

At first Harvey couldn't tell where the voice was coming from, but a tug on his arm made him look down. The tin soldier's hand, not the kid's, was gripping his sleeve. As the doll called *mister* in a somewhat clumsy child's voice, its tiny hand tugged again and again at his sleeve.

"Look, I did just like you taught me, and it worked! I really didn't die, just like you said. See, isn't it great?" the uniform-clad doll with the grim expression said, laughing innocently.

Like I taught you...?

What did I—he only had to start the thought before he realized what he'd done.

That's right; he had said that. He'd said, *Want me to tell you how to not die?* He hadn't been serious, in particular. He'd just been talking; he'd never thought the kid could really do it, but he remembered saying it, then, to that child: *All you have to do is possess something when you do die.*

I wonder if I can do it right.
Beats me…It'd probably work better to use something you know really well. Like that doll.

That was all Harvey'd "taught" him; then he'd left the quarantine area without even sticking around for the kid's last moments.

A "way to not die"? That wasn't any way to not die. Your own tattered body is lying there right in front of you. Did the mind of the child, who'd walked here dragging his own corpse behind him like a substitute doll, just not grasp what was happening?

"Hey, Mister, will you take me with you? I told you my mom died of the sickness, right? So I don't have anybody now. I'm glad I didn't die, but I don't have a home to go back to." The doll's hand on his sleeve yanked his shirt down with unnatural strength, strength he couldn't have imagined from its small size. An innocent smile was plastered on its tin face, but something almost reproachful flickered in the wide toy eyes.

"You're the one who taught me. It's your responsibility. So you'll take me with you, right…?"

Harvey could see the child's face overlapping the doll's. The child's face in death, wasted away and jaundiced, both eyes fallen out. Harvey shuddered. Just as he tried to pull his hand free, a chunk of concrete hit the doll full in the face with a dull *clunk.*

"Huh?" said the doll, in a bizarrely cheerful voice for someone whose tin neck was snapping in half until its head hung upside down. Harvey thought he saw its eyeballs roll fully around.

"That hurt…." The doll began to cry, goggling upside down at him.

With a start, Harvey turned around to face the radio's noise-cloud, careful to shield the doll. "No! Stop. Wait a second!"

"You're saying that now?!*"* it raged. The shock waves kept coming, slamming into the wall until the entire thing collapsed and began to bury everything around it. His vision was cut off by rubble and dust, but he could hear the doll's voice—no, the child's?—no, the doll's?—sobbing in his arms that it hurt.

"Sto—" Still ducking on the ground with his arms protectively encircling the two small bodies, doll's and dead child's, Harvey raised his voice and addressed the wall of rubble still crumbling over them. It was all he could think to do. "Stop, please! *Please!*"

He hadn't screamed for all he was worth like this in a long time. He hadn't pleaded with anyone like this *ever*, as far as he could remember. He couldn't say himself why he was this desperate when it was meaningless to protect the already dead anyway. Was it his guilt for having told the kid something irresponsible? Maybe that was part of it, and maybe logic had nothing to do with it, really; probably he was just doing this because he saw a kid in front of him hurting and crying.

After a little while, he noticed that the shock waves and the rain of debris had stopped. The angry shouts and rumbling static he'd heard from across the debris were gone, too. It was eerily quiet, except for the occasional dry sound of shifting rubble around him.

Slowly, Harvey lifted his head. The pile of iron framing and concrete on his back slid off to either side of him.

"It hurts…it hurts…"

He looked down at the crying doll in his arms and started to lift it up—but its neck had wrenched right apart, and the second he moved it, its head rolled off and hit the ground. "It hurts…! Am I gonna die after all, Mister? I got out of dying before, and now I'm gonna die after all?" The half-crushed tin head looked up at him imploringly. Maybe the headless tin body still had some kind of power left; its arms reached unsteadily into the air and tried to grab at his clothes.

"Hey, are there any more ways not to die? You know another one, don't you, Mister? I bet I can do it right again. Tell me…please tell me…"

Harvey swallowed, grinding his molars hard. He couldn't even bring himself to grasp the small hands trying to cling to him.

After some hesitation, he said, "I'm sorry…"

That short apology was all that came to him. He couldn't

think of anything else. No soothing white lies, no excuses, no consolation; nothing.

"Aw, there's nothing else?" murmured the doll, sounding disappointed. Its hands plopped back down to the ground as though they had no strength left. They sent up tiny, really tiny, little clouds of dust. Harvey couldn't confirm it or deny it. He'd never known any ways to begin with. He'd rather the doll rail at him, ask *Why did you lie to me like that in the first place?!*, but it only gave a dispassionate, resigned, very un-doll-like sigh.

"Oh...I guess that's that, then...But I'm really scared to go to God's world..."

The scratchy voice faded steadily into air white with mineral dust.

After that the tin head just stared empty-eyed into the sky, and didn't say anything else.

He dug a grave for the child and the doll in the quarantine area's public graveyard. They called it a "graveyard," but there were no neat lines of gravestones; it was only a place for crude, rough-and-ready interment of the epidemic's many victims. Harvey buried the small body and the even smaller body together in one corner of it. There was no shovel or anything, so he used a random piece of broken glass he'd found nearby.

Afterward he bent his knees in front of the pile of dirt. He didn't offer any prayers to anything, but he did offer a brief moment of silence. He'd clenched his right hand hard around the piece of glass without realizing it. When he opened his fist, the tip had cut deep into his palm. He pulled it out and stood it in the ground in place of a tombstone. The wound on his palm started to close after not too long.

"Okay." Harvey stood up from the grave site and addressed the radio he carried. "Thanks for waiting for me. Want to restart the fight?"

The radio gave a snort. *"No way,"* it turned him down flatly.

Well, he hadn't seen *that* coming. "Huh? Why not?" he asked, baffled.

Spewing a few dark green particles of noise from its speaker, a low voice answered, *"A guy with no will to live isn't worth killing."*

He heard himself give a deeply frustrated "Aw…," but he was at a loss for real words, and nothing else followed. Somehow he felt as though his entire existence had just been rejected, or more that he'd been denied the right to even breathe, and yet apparently that wasn't enough, and the radio wasn't even going to kill him. "What should I do now, then?"

"Like I care. Figure it out for yourself." Remorselessly dismissed, just like that.

Harvey was silent for a while, nonplussed. He heard a train whistle off in the distance. The wind blowing in from the wilderness ruffled his hair and brought with it the smell of dry sand to replace the thick stench of rot that hung along the ground.

"…I have a grave in Easterbury," a disgruntled voice said from the speaker after quite some time had passed. Harvey greeted this abrupt change of subject with a listless "Huh," and there was another period of silence.

"You've got time on your hands, don't you?"

"Yeah, I do."

More silence.

As Harvey wondered vaguely whether that train from before was going east or west, the radio started spitting out progressively more irritable static. Tilting his head a little, he said, "Where in Easterbury?"

He started walking, the radio dangling from his hand.

How many decades has it been since I've gone back to Easterbury? he pondered in one corner of his mind as he walked. It would be a pretty long trip from here. *By train, or on foot?* There wasn't any particular need to hurry, but it seemed that his brand-new partner had a pretty short fuse.

You're not gonna take me with you, Mister…?

Harvey felt as if someone was calling out to him, and he turned back, just once. A skinny kid was sitting with his knees pulled up to his chest next to a bloodstained glass grave marker, hugging a tin soldier. He gazed reproachfully at Harvey for a time, but then:

Oh…I guess that's that, then… And he heaved a dispassionate, resigned, very unchildlike sigh, and faded slowly away as if becoming one with the glass.

…I'm sorry, Harvey apologized silently as he left the meager glass-shard grave marker behind.

The rhythmic clacks of the train wheels and the thin smoke from his cigarette streamed away behind him on the wind. The noise of the train was loud when there was nothing between it and his ears, sure, but it struck Harvey as a *peaceful noise*, and he didn't find it unpleasant. Come to think of it, for some reason he'd never had a problem with ambient noises like the rumbling of a train or the clamor of a gambling house.

Eventually being treated as the master had gotten too creepy to stand, and he'd escaped to the deck. Now he was leaning against the guardrail, enjoying the wind and having a smoke. When he was all by himself like this, letting his mind wander and puffing on a cigarette, he could almost believe that the world had always been a peaceful, problem-free place.

His bangs had gotten a little long; they tickled his nose as the wind blew them about. *My hair's getting annoying...* In the act of shaking his head to get rid of the offending strands, he accidentally lost his cigarette in the wind. "Ah—" He gave a plaintive cry and turned around, but after a moment's dance on the wind like a flower petal, the white stick disappeared into the distance. There'd still been a lot of it left, too.

Harvey gave up on smoking and let his gaze roam the slowly unrolling scenery of the wilderness in the distance. The cloudy right half of his vision lightly overlaid the left. It was still rough enough to focus on things at close range that it gave him motion sickness, but if he looked into the distance it didn't feel so wrong, even if his vision itself wasn't that good.

He idly wondered which way was east.

I still haven't managed to keep that promise, have I...?

They should have parted two years ago at the mine in Easterbury, but instead Harvey'd ended up dragging him from one corner of the world to the other ever since, making him worry all the time...and now here he was breaking down, and he couldn't even leave the radio anymore. Harvey thought if he'd tried a little sooner, he could've separated the Corporal from the radio and let him rest in peace.

Oh.

In that moment he realized: now that things had come this far, did they really need to force the radio back into working order? Dead people were supposed to fade away, weren't they? It hadn't occurred to Harvey to take that kid with him, and he still didn't think he'd been mistaken not to. And he thought it was only right that the ghosts at the bar had disappeared after seeing the bartender off down his new path in life. And yet—*How long do we intend to keep the Corporal pinned to this world?*

"Ugh..."

He sighed disgustedly at himself. *Talk about a shitty thing to realize. If I hadn't had that thought, I wouldn't have to worry about this stuff...for that matter, I just lumped Kieli and me together as "we," but maybe I'm really the only one who needs to get his act together here.*

"Harvey?" broke in the girl's voice all of a sudden, catching him with his expression totally unguarded. His face abruptly froze. When he schooled his expression and turned around, Kieli's face was peeking out from around the connecting door.

"You were gone so long I got worried. What are you doing?"

"Nothing, just looking around outside, letting my vision adjust," he answered, just as he had once before. He looked away from her. Inside, he thought with a little contempt, *You've got a nice convenient excuse whenever you want to be alone now, don't you? Not that she won't see through it right away.* Kieli looked every bit as unconvinced as he'd expected, but he pretended not to notice. She didn't press him any further; she merely closed the door and came out onto the deck with him.

"Where's the Corporal?"

"I left him sitting on the shelf. He was being way too bossy."

Kieli's pout as she grumbled this was so entertaining that Harvey couldn't help laughing a little. He wondered if that was what he always looked like when he was fed up with the Corporal's lectures. "Sheesh, you act like it's not your problem. You're enjoying being 'Master' a little bit, aren't you, Harvey?" Kieli said, looking even more cross.

"No, no, of course not. I hope he goes back to normal soon. Yeah." He recited this speech in a deliberately unconvincing monotone, and then since he was already distracting her, he went ahead and got himself another cigarette. The blatantly suspicious glare she gave him hurt as though it was physically boring into his cheek.

Kieli sulked at him for a while, but eventually she just clucked her tongue in annoyance and looked away, coming up to stand next to him and lean on the guardrail, too.

"I hope he gets better soon..." she murmured quietly to the

ground below them, her voice carried away behind them in no time by the same wind stirring her long hair.

"…Hey, Kieli," he began, pretending to gaze off into the distance even though he couldn't really see that much. Kieli looked up at him and blinked. He started to go on, but then he hesitated with his mouth half-open around his cigarette.

After a little thought, he ended up saying something completely different. "I need a light."

He glanced at Kieli out of the corner of his eye. She looked confused, as if she was trying to work out what that meant. After a beat she seemed to get it, and fell speechless. Then:

"See, you really *are* enjoying it!" she accused him indignantly. He started to smile and take it back, but before he got the words out he realized he was about to lose his cigarette in the wind again. "Ah—" He was going to seriously grieve if he lost *this* one. He hadn't even lit it yet!

Luckily he managed to reach out and grab it at the last moment. Somehow after that he ended up staying in that position with half his body leaning out over the railing, just letting his gaze wander the horizon.

"I wonder if Easterbury's that way," he said, half to himself. Gripping the back of his coat, Kieli craned her neck to peer up at his face.

"Harvey…what's wrong?"

"Mm. Ah, it's nothing."

She looked worried, so Harvey shrugged it off with a casual "I guess that was a weird thing to say."

He guessed maybe it was far behind them, a long, long way southeast of here. There was no way he'd see even a shadow of it from here, obviously; there were only the gently rolling hills of the wilderness on the horizon. The gradually curving train tracks stretched out beyond that horizon. *So, these tracks go all the way to Easterbury, huh?*

I want to ask you a favor—

The radio's words echoed in the back of his mind. *—When I break down and stop working for real, take me to Easterbury. To that grave at the mine.*

Would he end up going to Easterbury before too long? He didn't know whether that was the right thing or not, though. Which choice came the closest to the right answer—?

Harvey's conclusion was postponed for another day, and only the sounds of the wind and the train's wheels made it to the distant east, left behind as the train itself headed ever westward.

CHAPTER 3
THE TRAVEL-LOVERS OF CAR NINE

The seat closest to the aisle, facing the back of the train.

From this spot, which had been firmly established as hers at some point without them ever talking about it, Kieli kept a sharp eye on the copper-haired man sitting kitty-corner from her, in the seat by the window facing the front of the train. He was casually letting his eyes roam the scenery outside, chin propped in his hand and head leaning on the windowpane. He hadn't moved from that position in a while. After a few minutes, he abruptly lifted his head from the glass, easily rearranged his long legs, and reached a hand into his coat pocket.

He got a cigarette out and into his mouth, movements easy and familiar even with only one hand now, and as soon as it was in position Kieli promptly held out a lighter in front of him.

"Here. Go ahead," she said with deliberate nonchalance. Harvey pulled back for a moment, shocked. But when Kieli calmly clicked the lighter and brought the fire to life without moving, he brought the tip of his cigarette in close and accepted the light with an extremely conflicted expression on his face. Kieli grinned to herself. *That's payback for before.*

"Well, look at that! You're finally starting to get thoughtful."

At this tolerably impressed assessment from the radio by the window, Kieli shrugged lightly and smiled. "Aren't I just?"

It was the fourth day of their journey. At first she'd reacted every time the radio had tried to order her around, but once she'd started humoring it, things had gotten reasonably fun. She actually thought this might be fun, as long as it lasted only until they got to their destination. When you got right down to it, the Corporal was the Corporal, and he and Kieli were on the same wavelength a lot of the time, particularly about things to do with Harvey.

Harvey himself was the only one out of step with things, in fact. He took the next puff on his cigarette with an expression on his face as though he'd just bitten a lemon.

"You don't have to be thoughtful about *this*. Why do you even know how to do it, anyway?"

"Because I helped out a little bit at a bar Beatrix worked at," Kieli answered easily. For some reason Harvey inhaled the wrong way and choked on his smoke.

"...You're kidding, right?" he pressed in a weirdly raw voice after he'd rescued his fallen cigarette.

"No, it's true. It was only a little bit, though. It was pretty interesting," Kieli said as she pocketed the lighter she'd bought at the station. Harvey clicked his tongue in a really pissed-off way and then started mumbling invectives under his breath. She caught only a few snatches, including one that sounded like *When I find that woman, she's dead meat.*

Kieli almost never saw Harvey react like this; it was so entertaining she couldn't help laughing—which made his coppery eyes narrow and look even more disgruntled. She stifled the laugh when he glared at her.

She felt a little better now, somehow. When they'd left the parish border she'd been so uneasy, and she'd prepared herself for a more heavy-hearted journey, but whatever the circumstances might be, the three of them were still together. *Being depressed won't help anything. I'll just do what I can, as well as I can.* Once she put her doubts behind her like that, the somewhat out-of-the-ordinary relationships between the three of them seemed like a new, fresh experience, and she started to feel strangely as though she was redoing that fall two years ago when she'd met Harvey and the Corporal for the first time. The old days when Kieli was at the boarding school, and Becca was still with her. She'd met Harvey at Easterbury station, and she'd boarded his train thinking she'd tag along with him just for the length of the Colonization Days holiday, but that had been the beginning of a long, long journey. She and the Corporal had opened up to each other relatively quickly, but she and Harvey had gotten along awkwardly at first; he wouldn't talk to her much, and they didn't know each other very well yet…but she'd felt as if each discovery she made about him brought them a bit closer.

Every little thing had sparkled for her, every little thing had excited her, and she'd wished their journey would never end.

She was certain that feeling hadn't changed, even now.

As Kieli stepped out of the restroom car and out onto the deck, she remembered that reaction of Harvey's and started laughing to herself all over again. She happened to meet the eye of a male passenger she'd come across on the deck at just that moment, so she tried to smooth it over with a polite smile and nod, but the smile came out strange and stiff. The man did return her greeting, but he gave her a funny look.

This is really embarrassing…

Kieli hurried away, flushing. However, when she was

about to step through the connecting door into the next car, she heard something like a moan behind her. She took her hand off the lever and turned back to the deck, only to see that same man curled into a ball on the floor where he'd stood.

"Um…"

Kieli hesitated a little, but she couldn't just leave him there, so she walked back up to him. When she stooped over to check on him, she saw that his bent back was heaving and his breathing sounded strained.

"Are you all right?"

"It's nothing, I'm just a little train-sick…" the man answered in a feeble voice, lifting one hand a little. He didn't look up. Kieli scratched her head for a few moments, unable to decide whether she should tell a conductor or try to find someone in his party to help him. Hesitantly, she reached out to at least rub his back for him, but he cut her off with a wave. "I'm fine now. Thanks."

Then he stood up under his own power, although he didn't look too steady on his feet.

"What car are you in? I can walk you back there, if that's okay."

"Oh, I'm in the same car as you."

Kieli couldn't quite understand what he meant right away.

"…Um, do you mean Car Nine?" She and Harvey were in Car Nine.

"Right, exactly. That one." The man nodded, so Kieli ended up just sort of naturally accompanying him back to Car Nine.

"Are you on a trip?" the man asked her amiably as they

walked down the aisle of Car Eight. He'd been quite sick just
a minute ago, but now he seemed all better.

Wondering what had been the matter with him, Kieli nodded with a vague smile and an "I suppose so." They were on a
trip, technically, but it wasn't for the sort of lighthearted reasons that come to mind when you think of a "trip."

"I see," said the man, beaming. "So am I. I'm here with my
daughter. You see, we both love going on trips."

"Right…"

"Do you like to travel?"

It was a casual question. Kieli thought about her answer a
little before she gave it. "… Yes, I do. Sometimes I even think
it'd be nice if I could ride the trains forever."

She found herself smiling, just a teeny bit wryly, but honestly, nonetheless.

Their conversation brought them all the way to Car Nine.
When she pulled the lever and opened the door, a funny feeling gripped her for just a moment, as if she'd stumbled into
the wrong car. She checked the plate over the door, but it
clearly said Car Nine. Kieli tilted her head in confusion.

"Papa!" cried a bright soprano voice as a girl ran up to
them from a set of facing seats near the middle of the car. She
flung herself at the man, who greeted her with a smile. "Here
we are. Thank you very much," the man told her, taking a seat
with his daughter. They were in the set of seats just behind
Kieli's. Apparently they'd been sitting right nearby the whole
time.

"Thanks!" called the girl, waving with her father. She
looked to be a few years younger than Kieli. As Kieli waved

back and smiled, she thought that the bright hair divided into two pigtails on either side of this girl's head reminded her of Becca somehow. She went back to her own seat feeling satisfied at having helped someone, even if she hadn't done too much.

Harvey was smoking with his elbow propped on the windowsill. He glanced up at her and said, "Took you long enough. What were you doing?"

"Hmm? Oh, nothing much," Kieli answered vaguely, taking her usual place kitty-corner from him. Harvey returned his gaze to the window, not looking particularly interested. She hunched her shoulders, feeling just a little bit miffed that he'd asked her what she was doing and then not bothered to press her when she didn't answer.

"*Herbie*," called the radio by the window.

"*Harvey*," Harvey corrected as usual, glaring peevishly at it.

"*History homework is right up your alley. Even more so if it's Church history—you could tell her more than she'd ever want to know. You should just help her already.*"

"You're kidding. Why should I?" Harvey retorted immediately, scowling. Listening to them, Kieli thought *Oh, right. Technically I'm on this trip to write my Church history report.* Considering that this fact directly concerned her, she should really have realized it before the other two did.

Reports are such a pain… When she thought about when Colonization Days would end and she'd have to go back to the boarding school, she started to feel a little gloomy.

Damn the woman, making Kieli work a job like that…

Cursing mentally, Harvey jabbed the butt of his cigarette into the ashtray by the window with uncalled-for force. It made him seriously want to track her down and give her a piece of his mind. Though at the same time, since he couldn't imagine he had a chance against her in a verbal argument, he also got the feeling that his "piece of his mind" would end with her getting the last word.

He'd just put out his cigarette, but a long sigh escaped him like exhaling smoke.

He'd considered, as one of his options, leaving Kieli in Beatrix's care again when they found her and setting out for the capital on his own. As a pretty attractive option, in fact. But since they hadn't gotten a single lead on Beatrix's whereabouts, he hadn't been able to really make a move since they'd come back from Westerbury, so the trip to the capital was on hold. It made him impatient, but on the other hand he suspected he was half-relieved that he wouldn't have to leave Kieli behind until then. *Am I using Beatrix as a convenient excuse to put off dealing with my problems…?* When he thought about that, he felt himself sinking subtly into self-loathing.

"Master, you keep sighing lately. Is something weighing on your mind?" asked the radio propped more or less right above the train's fixed ashtray. Stupid question, asked in a stupid voice. Feeling a migraine coming on, Harvey gave an even deeper sigh.

"Right now what's weighing on my mind is you."

"What?! I'm making you worry, Master? This is horrible—I have no choice but to atone with my death…!"

"Seriously, you're already dead." The offhand jibe was all Harvey had in him; he didn't have the energy to deal with the Corporal anymore. He leaned his head heavily on the windowpane. He was so used to the view of the gently sloping wilderness that it just slid past his eyes without making any claim on his brain. The scenery practically looked static, and the more he stared at the boring sight, the more all his synapses threatened to come to a halt, too.

And then far off in the distance, at the very edge of his field of vision, he saw a great swaying shadow in the sky above the northern fault line.

Harvey lifted his chin from his hand and squinted. His right eye went out of focus and blurred the image, so he concentrated on the vision out of his left and looked closely.

What is that, a tower...?

Something that looked like a man-made, spired structure was gently wavering in the sand-colored smog that drifted through the air. He was fairly certain there wasn't a town there. Gradually other passengers in their car noticed it too, until a group of them were plastering their faces into the window glass and peering excitedly. Was it a mirage...?

Fzzsh...

Suddenly he heard an alien static crackle from the radio's speaker.

"...Did you just say something, Corporal?"

"Hmm?"

The radio's blank response was infused with a static Harvey hadn't heard until now. When he focused his attention and listened, although it was almost too faint to make out, he realized the static had a fluctuation to it like a new wavelength. A fluctuation with dynamics that sounded like some sort of music. "Where is that signal coming from?"

"Huh? I'm only picking up the same frequency as usual…"

Harvey didn't quite trust the radio's response, but evidently a different signal was interfering slightly with the guerrilla station's frequency.

Something struck him. He returned his attention to the shape above the fault. The other passengers were still gazing at it, whispering excitedly. *A towerlike building, radio waves broadcasting music on the guerrilla station's frequency— radio—tower—* Strings of words ran through his head, tugging at his mind.

From this car the angle was all wrong for him to see the tracks ahead of them, but he was pretty sure they were getting close to the next station. *Maybe I'll try getting off for a while…*

It was then that he realized something.

"Hey, where's Kieli?"

"She never came back from the toilet, did she? For goodness' sake, where could that stupid girl have wandered off to?"

Harvey was already standing up by the time the radio finished its invective (which was exactly the type that normally would have been directed at him). *"Are you going to search the bathroom for her, Master?"* Ah, good point, he thought, sitting back down. There was still some time, and she'd probably be back by the time they pulled into the station.

Harvey leaned against the window again and gazed at the faraway floating tower. It would mean an abrupt change in their travel plans, but if his instincts were right (and for better or worse, his gut feelings were hardly ever wrong), it was probably worth spending a little time looking into that thing.

"Um, hey. Harvey, have you noticed that there's no God in the Church?"

"What are you talking about? Have I *noticed*...?"

As Harvey brought the lighter to his cigarette, he gave her a funny look. He didn't deny it, though; rather, he seemed to be wondering why she would be asking about something so obvious. Kieli automatically brightened.

She continued enthusiastically. "Do you know why that is? I think this planet was too far away, so He went back home..."

Before she could get very far, someone was standing by her seat. She looked up to see a man in a high-collared dark blue uniform standing in the aisle. "Oh." She hurriedly pulled a ticket out of her school uniform pocket and offered it to the conductor. The conductor leaned over and peered at the ticket, then smiled as if to say "You're okay." Kieli smiled bashfully back at him. *Come to think of it, wasn't it my child-hood dream to be a conductor?*

For some reason she felt nostalgic all of a sudden, and her eyes started to sting with oncoming tears. She couldn't think what had brought the feeling on, though.

"Want a cookie?" said an innocent voice, and someone held out a paper bag to her from overhead with a little rustling noise. When Kieli cut off her train of thought and looked up, the girl from before who'd been sitting in the seats behind them was leaning out over the backrest, peeking into their seats. The girl in twin pigtails, who looked a little like Becca.

She was holding the bag of cookies in both hands and grinning, so Kieli smiled at her and took a cookie. "Thanks."

She could hear the girl's father's voice from the other side of the backrest saying "Stop it, that's dangerous," but the girl paid no attention to him, happily seesawing back and forth on her stomach. "You want some too, Mister?" she asked Harvey, untroubled.

"No," Harvey refused flatly, without even lifting his head to look at her.

"Grumpy! No fun!" the girl declared with extreme bluntness, and then stuck her hand into the bag and fished out her own cookie. Kieli couldn't stifle a giggle. She really *was* like Becca. Before she could help it, her thoughts turned to a future that had never happened: she was sure if Becca had come with them on the trip, it would have been lively in just this way.

"I love traveling! I've been traveling with Papa forever," the girl informed her as she munched on her cookie.

"Yeah, I like it too," Kieli answered with a smile, and brought her own cookie to her mouth.

"How long have you been on the train?"

"Huh? Um…"

She'd been about to give an offhand answer, but for some reason only fuzzy numbers were coming to her, and she couldn't reply right away. *Wait, when* did *I get on?* Kieli racked her brain for several seconds, but by then the girl had changed the subject to herself without listening to Kieli's answer.

"*I've* been riding it for about ten years, I think."

"Huh," murmured Kieli, but she was privately impressed. The girl couldn't be more than a few years past ten from the looks of her, so she must have started traveling when she was really little.

"Hey, will you be my friend?"

"Sure, if that's all right with you."

They'd probably end up being friends only until they got off the train, but Kieli'd felt drawn to this girl who looked like Becca, so she agreed gladly. The girl screamed a delighted "Yes!"

"All these people are my friends, too. We all get along."

The passengers in the other seats started to gather around them too, bringing all different sorts of refreshments. They struck up conversations with good-natured smiles. It was sort of cozy, like they were all old acquaintances.

"I love traveling, too. I've been riding for just about fifteen years now."

"Well, I've been traveling for over twenty years."

"Trains are just wonderful, aren't they? I could ride for decades and not get tired of it."

Kieli looked around at all the passengers falling over one another to brag about their travel experiences (actually, it seemed more as though they were just saying how long they'd been on the train), and though she smiled back at them, she was starting to feel a little spooked.

She shot a diagonal glance at Harvey that said *Aren't these people a little strange?*, but Harvey actually spoke up and said, "Me, I've been traveling for eighty years," looking perfectly at home. Kieli knew that, of course, but... It felt as if she was being left out of the group, with nothing to do with herself. This time she darted a quick look toward the radio at the window for help.

Outside the window, a white platform and a station house were coming into view. She felt somewhat relieved that they were reaching a station, until—

Huh?

—instead of slowing down, it felt as if the train was *speeding up*, and they shot past the platform in no time. It was no abandoned station; she'd seen people ready to greet arriving passengers, and people who looked as if they were waiting for the train...

Something was definitely strange here. Kieli got up and started to step into the aisle, but the girl grabbed her by the shirt. "Where are you going?"

"What's the matter? I thought you liked traveling, too. So you can just keep riding forever."

"Traveling is so much fun. It makes you wish the journey would never end."

"If you stay here, you can stay on this fun trip forever."

"Come on. You won't go anywhere, will you? You said you'd be my friend!"

More passengers came up to her, clamoring one and all for her to stay. By this point every single passenger in the car was surrounding Kieli in a throng. Behind the smiles of the people she'd thought were so cheerful, Kieli glimpsed madmen. "Harvey!" she cried, turning back to their seats for help, but Harvey was serenely smoking his cigarette as he regarded her distress. If anything, he looked confused.

"What's wrong? Stay on the train. Don't you want to travel with me forever?"

Kieli shuddered. Before, she'd thought something was off, but now she *knew*. Harvey would never say something like that—and for that matter, this Harvey had a right arm. Why hadn't she questioned that until now? This wasn't the Harvey of now. This was Harvey from when she'd met him two years ago in Easterbury. She should have known from the fact that she was wearing her school uniform that something funny was going on, but until this moment it had seemed only natural.

"You can't get off now. We were sucked into this place ten years ago. Come on, stay with us. We're not lonely if we're all together…"

The train hurtled faster and faster, and each patch of scenery out the window was gone almost before it appeared. The girl and the other passengers grabbed at her clothes and hands, and Kieli lurched this way and that as they pulled, calling with all her might for someone who wasn't here.

"HARVEY!"

Where did she go?

Harvey was at a total loss. He hadn't figured she could get lost *inside the train*. As he looked left and right, standing stock-still in the center of the platform where he was in pretty

much everyone's way, the hurried flow of passengers disembarking and passengers boarding branched in two around him like a river hitting a sandbar, and then merged together again once it was past.

Kieli still hadn't come back when they started approaching the station, so he'd searched every car from front to back for her, but he hadn't been able to find her anywhere. Meanwhile the train had pulled into the station, so he'd grabbed their belongings and gone outside, just in case she'd gotten off the train before him. But no matter how hard he scoured the platform and the ticket gate with his eyes, she was nowhere in sight. The train parked alongside the platform was restlessly belching out steam as if it couldn't wait to depart.

Guess I'll search inside one more time…

He got back on board, taking just the radio with him, and started walking back from the front-most car just as he had last time, but somewhere around halfway through the train he started to feel as if maybe this wasn't the way to find her after all. Still, if "this way" wasn't right, he naturally had zero idea what else to do. He was so far at his wit's end he was starting to actually feel impressed—how could anyone possibly get so neatly lost on a train, where there was nowhere to go but in a straight line?

"*You know, Master, the train's going to leave pretty soon.*"

"I know, but…"

When he came through the rear deck of Car Eight and into Car Nine something suddenly caught his attention at the edge of his field of vision, and he came to a stop.

"……?" Harvey walked a couple of steps backward, coming back out onto the deck again to stand in front of the connecting door. For just a split second, he felt something off, as if he was seeing double. His right eye had taken a beat to catch up with his left and let their two images overlap, so at first he thought maybe that was what was causing the feeling, but no; the quality of this "offness" seemed different.

He squinted intently up at the door, but the harder he looked, the more it seemed to elude him, slipping out of his peripheral vision so that it was impossible to grasp what it really was.

"Sometimes the clearest way to see the unseen is with the unseeing, huh?"

A voice piped up behind him out of nowhere. A boy's voice, a bit on the high side, with intonation that betrayed an accent he'd never heard before. Sensing something like malicious hostility, Harvey's brain automatically kicked into high alert.

He spun around only just in time for his peripheral vision to catch a shadowy form fleeing nimbly out of sight. Immediately, he launched himself half-over the railing of the deck, but it had already disappeared without a trace into the gap between the train and the platform. *What was that…?*

Whoo-oo-oo!

The piercing scream of the train whistle started up, heralding their imminent departure. Light gray steam belched out of the exhaust pipe as if to tell him he was out of time. Harvey tore his attention away from the suspicious figure and turned back to face the connecting door again, but he was at just as much of an impasse as before; he still couldn't figure out what had felt so off.

The clearest way to see the unseen is with the unseeing…?

After a moment's thought, he experimentally covered his left eye with his hand. With his good eye blocked, everything in eyeshot abruptly turned sketchy. He looked up at the door again using only the unreliable vision of his right eye.

There before him loomed a door so old-looking it was uncanny. Every last inch of it was covered in red rust. The stench of rotting flesh began to waft toward him and mingle with the thick smell of rust, leaving Harvey momentarily transfixed. He gulped. When he looked up to the top of the door, he saw the words "Car Nine" engraved in a scratchy, antique font on a metal plate as horribly rusted as the door itself. It was *the door to a car that wasn't supposed to be there.*

"Can you see that, Corporal…?"

"Yes, Master. I just saw the same thing you did."

Quit it with the damn "Master" thing, Harvey grumbled internally, winding the radio's cord around his wrist before setting his hand on the lever of the door, which was coated not only with rust, but also with some viscous, sticky substance he couldn't identify. He paused for just a moment, and then with no further hesitation pulled the door open with one yank.

For all he'd imagined exactly this, he still sucked in a little startled breath when he laid eyes on the interior of the car. The walls and ceiling and even the seats were crawling with the same dense red rust as the door. In any normal circumstances, the long car stretching before him would have been rotting in a corner of some dump for decommissioned vehicles long ago. He didn't see anyone sitting in any of the seats; instead a crowd of people had concentrated together in one section of the aisle. Looking around above the heads of the shorter passengers, he caught sight of the girl he was looking for in the center of the throng.

"Kieli!"

Within the group, every member of which turned toward him in concert, he glimpsed a certain face that shocked him to the core. *Me—?* Yet even as he stood gaping at it, the face crumbled apart until the figure looked like a poorly made clay doll.

Pestered and pulled at from all directions, Kieli turned a near-tearful face at him. Harvey forced his way through the outer circle of the crowd and reached out his hand. Kieli reached out too with all her might from in between the people surrounding her. When her hand brushed his, he gripped it and pulled her forcibly out of the middle of the mob.

"Harveeyyyy!"

Kieli leaped at him; he caught her to his chest and, for lack of any better ideas, launched into stream of abuse.

"What's wrong with you, just wandering into another weird dimension *again*—?!"

"No, you can't take her away!"

A little girl clutched at Kieli's clothes—at least, you could call her a girl, but her face was plainly that of a corpse. Half-rotten skin darkened to an earthy brown, all the flesh gone from its cheeks, no eyes in either socket, and a void yawning black as night behind the round eyeholes and the gaping oral cavity.

"She's going to stay here forever. She said she wanted to ride the train forever!"

All around the girl, the other passengers stretched out their hands toward Kieli. Harvey turned around to face the exit, careful to shield Kieli, but the moment he laid eyes on the connecting door, it melted as though it had been doused with acid, fusing with the rusty wall.

Now come on, why don't the both of you stay here forever? Stay with us on our never-ending journey...

The passengers began to flock around them, all entreating them in dull, monotone voices and wearing vacant smiles on faces the color of dirt. Maybe the lingering sentiments of the ghosts had gathered together to carve out a niche for themselves within some tear in the fabric of reality; whatever was going on, it seemed that inside this space that should have been impossible, they could manifest physically. In short, they were being mobbed by a pack of dead people, and it was making Harvey himself shrink away now. "Do something, Corporal!" he yelled to the radio in his hand. But no, even this radio that would've blasted a shock wave at them any other time was panicking. All Harvey got was a squawking clamor of *"Gah, stop it. Stay away from me. You're creepy! Get away!"* Had the Corporal forgotten about his shock waves along with everything else—? Now was definitely *not* the time for it, but Harvey found himself getting dizzy. *You're so useless...*

The train careened onward at an unnatural speed. Harvey darted a sidelong glance at the scenery shooting past out the windows and cursed. But then:

Whoo…

His ears picked up a faint, faint sound just barely in hearing range, and intuition kicked in.

He reached out his arm as far as it would stretch through a gap in the horde to open the closest window. The outside wind whipping by stirred the hair on his head and the stale air inside the train car.

"Kieli, Corporal, we're jumping!"

"Huh?"

"Huh?!"

Before the other two could grasp what he was about to do, Harvey lifted Kieli up by the torso onto the window frame and flung himself out the window, half-pushing her along ahead of him.

The wilderness scenery had been tearing by at breakneck speed; tossed right into it, Kieli screamed, and the radio screamed right along with her. Harvey gathered them both into his arms in midair. After only the briefest of flights he was slammed into the ground; he made a controlled landing and rolled a few times. The hard concrete did bang up his shoulders and back some, but the impact was nothing compared to what it would have been at the speed his sight had gauged.

The walls of the train cars glided by bare centimeters from where they lay. When Harvey heaved himself into a sitting position with a sigh, the last car was just clearing the end of the platform, and the train pulled away from the station with one last loud whistle.

"...Hmm?"

Kieli, who had been clinging to him with her eyes squeezed tightly shut, hesitantly raised her face and started looking around them in openmouthed bewilderment. A group of people in the middle of the platform were watching them, wondering what the matter was. Harvey also heard a few whispers of "Where did they just come from?"

"Sir, you must know that's dangerous!" bellowed a pale-faced man, running up to them. He looked to be the stationmaster.

Harvey's eyes met Kieli's—she was obviously still dazed—and they sighed and shrugged in defeat.

The two of them (plus the radio) had been sitting on the very edge of the platform.

They got a harsh tongue-lashing from the stationmaster, but fortunately the train had departed on schedule anyway, so they were released after about half an hour with no more punishment than that, and with a series of apologetic bows (from Kieli; Harvey just looked moodily off to one side and refused to apologize at all), they put the station office behind them.

"I got royally chewed out. I got unjustly chewed out when I didn't do anything wrong. And it's your fault."

As soon as they left the station house with their belongings, Harvey immediately lit the cigarette he'd been holding off on during their chewing-out (his one concession) and started complaining. When Harvey was really mad he was more likely to stop talking altogether, so Kieli didn't think he was that angry, but her "I'm sorry" was contrite anyway. "Ugh, and the Corporal is completely useless." *"I'm a-ashamed of myself, Master…"* The radio sounded crestfallen, too.

There was a high fence that started next to the station house and ran along the train tracks. Leaning her hands lightly on the chain links, still a little groggy, Kieli looked through the fence toward where the tracks disappeared on the horizon. She couldn't even see a trace of the train's belching trail of steam now, let alone the train itself. The ghost car carrying the dead was probably riding along with it, in some chink of reality on that train.

Never, ever stopping, no one able to get off, no choice but to continue their never-ending journey…For decades, for centuries, maybe even for eternity.

The girl's face sprang up in the back of Kieli's mind. *I couldn't be friends with you after all. I'm sorry. I can't afford to ride in that train car with you forever. Because we still have a destination to get to on our trip.*

But if we didn't have a destination, if it were okay to go on a carefree trip forever…

"…Were you thinking you didn't want the trip to end?" Harvey murmured out of the blue. He was leaning against the fence and smoking, still looking disgruntled. Kieli kept her eyes on the tracks and didn't answer. But she didn't deny it either, which went a good way toward confirming it in the end.

She liked to travel. She liked riding on trains, and visiting all kinds of cities and places, and absorbing the feel of different atmospheres dyed with the emotions of the people who lived there, or of the people who had once been there. And most importantly of all, as long as this journey lasted, they could stay together—that's how she'd always thought about it. Unconsciously she was always worried that something would be lost when the journey ended.

If we didn't have a destination, if it were okay to go on a carefree trip forever... Could that train car have been reflecting a warped version of her own desires?

"Never-ending journeys aren't all they're cracked up to be, you know," she heard Harvey mutter quietly next to her. That familiar low, gravelly voice that rumbled in his throat a little, speaking in unemotional, offhand tones.

Kieli tore her gaze away from the tracks and turned to look up at the tall man standing beside her. But Harvey ended his speech there; now he was gazing beyond the fence with an *I didn't say anything* expression on his face. Whenever he made that face it meant he was 100 percent uninterested in continuing a conversation, so Kieli turned back to the tracks too, and made no response.

Maybe the train Kieli wanted to ride on forever was a train Harvey was sick of and wanted to get off. She could so easily picture him not even waiting until they reached a station, just jumping out the window all by himself instead, and that terrified her.

Even if I can't make it to the final stop with him, please let me ride with him for as many moments as I can...

The wind blowing along the tracks hit the fence and changed angle, whipping Harvey's coppery hair and Kieli's black hair in two different directions. They gazed off in the distance where the train tracks met the sky, each with their own thoughts...thoughts Kieli was sure didn't quite meet.

THE STORY OF A CERTAIN PRIEST AND
ANOTHER VERY EMINENT PRIEST
LONG BEFORE SPRING

The home he visited was shockingly plain and unadorned. It blended right in with the squalid neighborhood around it, just another house like all the others. It made him bizarrely worried—should a man of stature, one of the direct descendants of the Eleven Saints who made up the Council of Elders and the man in charge of the Church's Preaching Department, really be living in a place like this?

An ordinary residential district spreading from the middle to lower strata of this city called the "capital"—this dark gray city clinging to a slope in the heart of the mountain range. It was a district inhabited mostly by techs who maintained the city's various functions, people who did menial work at Church headquarters, and the like; unlike the capital's central area, which was a forest of steeples jutting up toward the heavens, here relatively small-scale buildings jumbled together willy-nilly, forming a jagged and incongruous skyline.

The rail lines running into the city spread great billows of thick smoke everywhere that must be a nuisance to everyone in the neighborhood. Still, even that smoke disappeared easily into the ash-gray smog ceaselessly rising up from every point of the skyline. Fossil-fuel exhaust pipes jutted out of every single building's walls, and if he tilted his head up even further, he could see that thick piping passed between the walls of each building like clotheslines. It covered the whole sky. It was from this sight of pipes crawling over the whole city like meshwork that the capital took its nickname "the mechanical city." Fossil fuel–based power networks extended to every corner of the capital, with centralized control in the heart of the city, but on the periphery in particular, the pipelines were uncovered and exposed. It made him genuinely feel like a dwarf who'd been sucked into some great machine.

Father Sigri's private home sat in a corner of midtown, at an elevation where you could look down on the overpasses above the railways climbing their way to headquarters.

"I was told to come to your residence…" he explained stiffly, nervous. The man of stature in the Church greeted him in friendly tones.

"Right, come in. There won't be any tea, though—I don't have anybody working for me right now."

"That's quite all right! P-pardon my intrusion!"

A former teacher was someone owed deep respect, and technically Father Sigri was a former teacher from his seminary days. Father Sigri had only an honorary trustee position at the school, and ordinarily had no place teaching a course at all, but for just one year the man had held a special seminar, and he'd been lucky enough to snag a spot.

After he'd picked up the communicator that transmitted to the capital that day the woman came, he'd abruptly changed his mind and decided to consult with Father Sigri, so instead of the Security Forces, he'd called the Preaching Department. It was good timing: Father Sigri had been in the office, so his call was transferred and he was able to speak to the man directly. He'd explained the situation and requested advice, the result of which was that he was re-called from the Church outpost in the boonies back to the capital, bringing the Undying as a thank-you gift for the invitation. Now he was scheduled to assume a new position in the capital this spring. It was like one stroke of good fortune after another after another. Or maybe this was what you called a "godsend."

"Sir, what are your plans for dealing with the…you-know-what?" he ventured timidly as Father Sigri shepherded him up the stairs. Father Sigri tilted his head slightly, looking somewhat at a loss.

"A good question…I'm still thinking about it," he answered vaguely.

He'd been told that Father Sigri would personally take charge of the female Undying and deal with her, but so far he showed no signs of doing anything about the issue. Apparently Father Sigri hadn't yet made it publicly known that he'd secured an Undying, although he couldn't possibly fathom what the man's reasons for that might be.

Father Sigri seemed a bit different now than when he'd been taking that seminar. He'd grown mellow—or perhaps it would be more accurate to say he'd grown offhanded. The Father from back in the day had been a strict priest, and he'd had an ambitious side. Housing an Undying under one's own roof was likely to be one's political downfall; the Father Sigri in his memory wasn't the sort of man to cross such a dangerous bridge.

Was it simply that he was getting older? Still, this great man had been the youngest person in history to join the Council of Elders. Chronologically, he wasn't even an "old man" yet.

"Father"—that title was proof of his stature, accorded only to the highest-ranking clergymen in the Church.

Would you like a promotion?

Two months ago he'd been asked that question, the very first time he'd visited the office after being summoned to the capital. It had come in the middle of their conversation, seemingly out of nowhere. Though he couldn't really fathom what Father Sigri was after, he'd simply nodded. At that, the man had given him a wry smile, and muttered something that sounded like "If you say so...but you know, that might not be such a good thing." Then the Father had arranged a new position for him that would set him on track to promotion in the capital. For some bizarre reason, that conversation continued to stick in his mind.

When they reached the second floor, he began to make out a muffled voice coming from one side of the semicircular corridor. At first it seemed to be one continuous stream of cackling, but soon he noticed that it occasionally broke off on a falsetto shriek. A bewitching female voice...So bewitching he thought that if you listened to it for long, it might make your hearing go strange. When he cast a quizzical glance at Father Sigri, the Father shrugged.

They reached a locked door at the very end of the hallway. Father Sigri unlocked it and opened it into a dimly lit room. There was a woman there, lying facedown on the bed in the center of the room and clutching her stomach.

"Aw, now my stomach hurts! Come on, no more funny stories!" she was saying, pounding her pillow with one fist. She acted as if she were talking to someone right there in the room with her, though there was no sign of anyone there but her, of course. Wailing now with laughter, she rolled back and forth as if she couldn't take it anymore, until she finally rolled so hard her head slid off the edge of the bed. Long golden tresses flowed like silk to the floor.

Lying on her back with her head hanging backward over the edge, she glanced up, apparently finally noticing them. The light from the hallway set her white skin and ice-blue eyes aglow against the gloom, and this was worlds away from the dirty wretch he'd collected in that country town—this was exquisite beauty that momentarily took his breath away.

"Oh, it's you." The woman pointed at him from her position upside down. "I remember you; you're that guy, right? Hey, guy, thanks! I'm so glad you brought me to this place!" He had no idea how to respond to being *thanked* for her capture. As he stood there speechless, she began cackling to herself again.

"The capital is a blast! It's just full of lingering sentiments and ghosts and other weird stuff. I wonder if so much pent-up resentment's piled up here that it just permeates the place. It's got to be the most haunted spot on this planet…Look, there's one behind you right now."

Her voice abruptly dropped into a lower register for the last part, and he whirled around in alarm. There wasn't a thing there, however, but the decorated handrail out in the hallway. *Should've seen that coming…* Apparently the woman found his reaction hysterical; looking more entertained than ever, she burst into another fit of laughter and got so carried away that she slid right off the bed with a shriek. Still she kept right on laughing, prostrate on the floor. Beside him, Father Sigri sighed sourly. "You see what she's been like. I'm a little at a loss."

Ah. Yes, I can see now why he'd be having trouble deciding what to do with her. Abominable weapon of massacre or whatever aside, on a fundamental level she was just a crazy woman.

"I've heard all kinds of stuff from all kinds of ghoulies! Hey, do you wanna hear today's biggest scoop? Do you? Get this: today's biggest scoop is..."

Evidently all that laughing had finally tired her out: she was crawling back up into the bed as she spoke as if it was some huge ordeal, and her voice had gone colorless, descending almost into an incoherent mumble. Still, the fatigue didn't stop her from talking at them. She lay down and placed her cheek on the pillow. Tired, misty blue eyes flickered around the room.

Then she fixed those eyes on Father Sigri's face and said, "Let's just say it's about the wife and daughter you obliterated all record of."

There were a few seconds of odd silence.

It took a bit for his brain to process this revelation, during which time he could only gape at her. After he finally pulled himself together enough to glance at the profile of the man standing next to him, he was left gaping once again. The Council Elder and head of the Church's Preaching Department, the man in charge of every single priest on the planet, had gone still and pale as if he'd seen a ghost.

The woman burst out laughing once again. "Aha! Aha-haha..."

It was a singularly obnoxious laugh, one that grated at his ears. "I never dreamed I'd stumble across a secret *this* entertaining here—I'm a lucky girl! Really, thank you so much for bringing me here! Ahahahaha…" Her hoarse laughter echoed eerily in the shadowy gloom of the bedroom.

Father Sigri was still frozen in place, his eyes riveted on the curious spectacle of the woman whose shoulders were shaking with the force of her cackles. Without moving a single other muscle, he managed to move his lips just barely enough to murmur, "This never leaves the room. Do you understand?"

His voice was stiff, stilted, as if he'd swallowed a rock.

In the Elder's words he heard his own echoing back to him: that day, he'd told the children, "Pretend you never saw this woman." *So even the highest priest there is says the same things as my stupid, ordinary self*, he thought. It almost came as a relief, and yet somehow also as a disappointment.

Facedown and laughing tightly, the woman murmured deliriously, "Heyyy, Kieliiii, I'm waiting, you know…"

According to the calendar spring was right around the corner, but here in the northern mountains, it was still a long way off.

The young priest was scheduled to begin a new job this spring. But before he received his official appointment, he was ordered to play a wholly unexpected role.

CHAPTER 4

A DANGEROUS YOUNG LADY AND A KIND BEAST

The self he saw in the pictures seemed so awfully foreign to him that it gave him an uncomfortable feeling. After all, until quite recently he'd never even imagined the day would come when he'd be in photographs like these. There he was, standing next to the woman who'd vowed to spend her life with him only a few days ago, dressed up just a little more than usual and facing the camera with a nervous smile that was nevertheless so stupidly happy that even *he* wanted to tease the guy wearing it.

"What do you think? They came out well, didn't they?" said that same woman, raising her eyes from the photos lined up on the counter and smiling. They'd been looking through them together.

"Yeah, but I've gotta say they make me feel a little shy."

He gave her a strained smile to cover up his doubts. *Maybe part of my problem is that I feel guilty for being the only one of us to get a happy ending.* But no; thinking like this would only get him yelled at by the leader and the rest of the guys.

It wasn't quite time to open the bar yet. Lazy evening sunbeams filtered in through the windows. The bartender turned his gaze toward the far side of the hall, past the reach of those sunbeams, toward the little stage where nothing was left but some ancient sound equipment. After the night of his wedding party, the four-man rock band hadn't appeared on that stage again. He still stayed behind by himself after closing every night, polishing glasses until bedtime in the faint hope that someone—his old bandmates, past regulars, anyone—would appear. There was a gaping void in his heart, but nonetheless, he suspected that nature would take its course in time and fill up the gap with the contents of his new life. Starting next week, a new band was scheduled to play here. It wouldn't be rock music, of course; they'd be doing something safer. But hey, he was a music lover.

"Here's Kieli. She looks so cute!"

Brought back to himself by Yana's voice, he turned his attention away from the stage and back toward the photographs.

When he looked down at the picture she'd brought to the top of the pile, his heart swelled, feeling warmed and broken at the same time. A girl smiling a little hesitantly in the wreath of artificial flowers and white lace that had been clapped on her head—how could this girl on the edge of seventeen look so painfully much like Setsuri? For all her eyes were modest, her strong will and dignity were plain to see there. They seemed to be an even deeper, more striking color now than when she'd first visited his bar.

The bartender reached out to touch this photograph with far more emotion than he'd felt looking at his own. But when he picked it up, he caught sight of the edge of another one stuck to the bottom of it.

...*Oh God.*

He hurriedly covered it up with another photo.

"Is something wrong?"

"No, ah, no, it's nothing. Well, it looks like it's time to save the rest of these for later and open up the bar," he babbled quickly. Yana gave him a puzzled look, but she soon smiled in agreement. "Yes, let's take our time over them after we close for the night." His conscience twinged. He...he hadn't been married a week, and he'd already hidden something from her.

"I'll go open up," said Yana. After she'd jogged outside to flip the sign, he wiped the cold sweat from his brow and covertly snagged one photograph out of the pile. It was the other picture of Kieli. Her smile was far prettier and more natural than in the first one, but…

The bartender couldn't have stopped the dry, grim laugh from escaping him if he'd tried.

Kieli, sitting primly in the chair, wasn't the only one in the photograph. His old bandmates were clustered around her, leaning forward and clamoring to be in the picture. The vocalist/guitarist, trying to casually put his arm around Kieli's shoulders; the bass player on her other side knocking away his hand and trying to get an arm around her himself, the drummer striking a pose with a stick in each hand, and in the very back, the bandleader holding up his sax.

"Aw, jeez, it turned into spirit photography… that's Kieli for you, huh?" he said wryly to himself. Then he put a hand over his eyes for a moment. *I really was blessed with good friends, and they've sent me off on the rest of life's journey with all kinds of other good fortune. I've got a long way to go yet.*

And then he heard a little shriek coming from outside.

With a start, he hurriedly wiped his eyes and lifted his head to see several people standing in the doorway, crowding Yana back inside. Soldiers in white clerical robes with armor plating, but these were large, muscular soldiers who radiated an extremely intimidating air: clearly on a whole different level from the town's laid-back Security Forces outpost—! All at once the horrific raid fifteen years ago sprang to his mind in full color, as if it had happened only yesterday. His whole body went tense.

"H-how can I help you?" he greeted his rude, unwanted guests in a hard voice as Yana ran to him. He hugged her from across the counter. It looked as though a few more Church Soldiers were standing by outside, but only two of them entered the bar. One of them came up to stand in front of the counter to loom over him.

"Sir, we've been informed that there's a girl working at this establishment."

The mechanical politeness was civil enough, and yet somehow it didn't sound very sincere. This man must have come not from the town outpost, but from the Security Forces headquarters in the capital. The bartender couldn't grasp the situation yet, so he decided to stall for the time being. "I'm afraid I don't quite understand what you're looking for..." But as he spoke, the soldier's eye settled on the photos scattered on the counter. *Crap.* It was too late; a rugged gloved hand was reaching for the one on top. The other soldier drew an old-looking photo out of his breast pocket, and the two of them compared the photos and nodded to each other.

He caught a brief glimpse of that old photo, and the woman in it was—

Setsuri—?

The soldier put away the photo again while the bartender was still standing there bug-eyed, and gestured to the one left in his hand of the raven-haired girl in the wreath of artificial flowers.

"Where is this girl now?" he said. He'd gone from the former polite attitude to something like cross-examination, but his tone was still just as mechanical—to the point where the change didn't even worsen the bartender's impression of him. A tense silence fell on either side of the counter until, after a long pause, the soldier brought out his trump card. "We've checked into this place. If you refuse to cooperate, we'll be forced to take steps."

Yana stiffened uneasily, her eyes wide. The bartender hugged his wife's shoulders tightly with one arm and ground his molars together. She didn't know about the old bar, or the raid. He hadn't wanted to get her caught up in the whole thing, and he hadn't thought it would cause any problems for them anyway.

If you refuse to cooperate, we'll be forced to— If he refused them, he'd lose the peaceful life he'd only just—finally—begun. If he cooperated, though, he'd be betraying two people who had trusted him enough to tell him their circumstances and seek refuge with him.

Harvey, Kieli…

For the past few days he'd been dwelling on one painful question: why was something always lost in exchange for anything new you gained? This world was truly finely balanced. With some irony, he thought, *Maybe there really is a God living on this planet. An ever-so-fair-minded God with an outstanding sense of balance.*

From the moment she'd seen this city's skyline, she'd had the feeling it had reminded her of someplace she'd been before; she just couldn't remember where.

It was a relatively developed city for such a remote part of North-hairo parish, with well-maintained buildings and streets. There was a decent amount of traffic on the main street, too. Three-wheeled taxis with enormous cylindrical fuel tanks on top whizzed by, gushing exhaust and noise. From what she'd heard, a certain wealthy family who maintained an estate here had been investing money in the city for a long time.

"Oh, I know. It's Toulouse."

Something about the mood of this place reminded her of the "witch-hunt town" of Toulouse, which had been flourishing as a tourist destination despite its location far from the center of Westerbury parish. They even had the same geography: they were both framed by a gently sloping wilderness on one side and an intricate network of steep rock ledges on the other.

"Too loose?"

" 'Toulouse.' We stopped there while we were traveling with Beatrix, you know?"

She'd thought of it as an established fact when she said it, but the only response she got from the radio was a blank silence. *Oh, right.* When she remembered their situation, she felt a little glum. "I guess you don't remember Beatrix either, huh, Corporal…The two of you were buddies, you know."

"Mmm?" Kieli kind of liked this more untroubled Corporal, but moments like this made her long for him to get better quickly and go back to normal.

As she walked unhurriedly along the main street, she tried explaining the blond, blue-eyed woman to the radio.

"You see, Beatrix is an old friend of Harvey's, but she's selfish and she lives however she likes and she talks big and she spends money like water—really, I don't know what to do with her! And she can't cook or clean, either…" She'd just said the first things that came to mind, but replaying them in her head, Kieli realized they really didn't sound flattering. Surely there was *something* else she could say. She knit her brows and thought for a moment.

"But you know, she's a good person…and she's really beautiful."

She couldn't help smiling at the memories.

Suddenly the *honk-honk-honk* of someone leaning on a car horn filled her ears. Kieli realized with a start that she'd been about to cross the street without looking. Shrieking, she tried to backpedal, but her heel slipped and she fell down right in the path of a car. Brakes squealed shrilly against the pavement, and the vehicle came to a stop just before it would have crushed her toes.

That was close…

She stayed sitting on her butt on the shoulder of the road, too petrified to move for a while. Her heart was racing in her chest.

"Oh, I'm so sorry! Are you hurt?" a female voice called down from the car parked scant centimeters away. Slim and pale legs descended onto the shoulder of the road. Kieli's heartbeat still hadn't quieted down when she raised her eyes to see a beautiful lady with waist-length hair tucking up the hem of an expensive-looking dress and climbing out of the backseat—though in Kieli's personal view, she wasn't quite as beautiful as Beatrix. The car she'd been riding in was as high-class as her clothes. On the surface it was similar to a three-wheeled taxi, but it was longer, and the rear seemed to have a set of elegant facing seats in place of the standard backseat. A large man Kieli guessed was her private chauffeur climbed out of the driver's seat after her.

For a split second her nose detected something off, but the soft scent of perfumed oil wafting from the woman's hair soon banished whatever it was.

"I'm fine. I only fell because I was so startled. I'm the one who should apologize to you for not looking where I was going."

It looked as if the driver was about to help her up, so Kieli hastily declined and started to get up herself, but just then an arm seized her from another direction and yanked her upright. "Kieli," muttered a voice overhead. When she craned her neck to look up, the familiar tall, redheaded form was standing there looking down at her. The tone of his next words didn't change in the slightest, but she thought he probably was worried.

"What's wrong?"

"I almost got bumped into, but that's all. I'm not hurt," she hastened to explain. Harvey appeared skeptical, and turned to regard the driver and the young lady in the dress with eyes that weren't hostile, but weren't exactly friendly, either.

The moment the young lady saw Harvey's face, she cried, "Oh!" and her eyes went round. Before Kieli could blink, her whole face lit up. "Please, I'd love to invite you to my house for tea, if you would be so kind," she said, reaching out to grip Harvey's hand and more or less shoving Kieli aside in the process. Kieli blinked, stumbling.

At this abrupt request from a total stranger, Harvey's "not exactly friendly" attitude visibly slid to "unfriendly."

"No thank you. Kieli, let's go."

He brusquely shook off the slender hand touching his, turned his back, and began striding away. "R-right," Kieli agreed, rushing to chase after him. He was walking fast; she had to jog to catch up. When she managed it and took up walking diagonally behind him, she turned her head to look back. The young lady they'd left behind was still standing stock-still in front of the car, gazing at them. Eventually, though, she addressed a few words to the driver and disappeared back into the car.

"Didn't you think there was something strange about that woman?"

At Harvey's gruff voice, Kieli turned back to look at him and tilted her head to one side.

"Not really; why?"

"What about you, Corporal?"

"Ah, she was quite fine-looking, wasn't she?"

"…All right, then," Harvey tossed carelessly over his shoulder, withdrawing the topic without even turning around. He was directing his feet toward their inn.

"Could you see the mirage?"

"No," he answered flatly. He'd gone out to the outskirts of town today to have a look at the mirage.

It was two days ago now that they'd disembarked (through the window) at the station closest to where Harvey said he'd seen a towerlike mirage from the train. Apparently the mirage Harvey and the radio had seen had started appearing in the sky above the rock ledge across from town about a year ago, and all the townspeople were talking about it. But they said you could see it only once every few days, and not on any sort of regular schedule, so now they were staying here for a few days waiting for its next appearance. It seemed as though Harvey'd had some ideas of his own about that mirage. It was nothing unusual for Harvey to summarily change the route of a journey (whatever he might say, Harvey was pretty stubborn when he got a hunch about something), but since she couldn't rely on the radio to grill him about it this time, Kieli was even more strapped for information than usual.

Just as she was looking up to check his profile diagonally in front of her, he abruptly stopped walking and swiveled his head to one side. "Did you notice something watching us just now?" By the time Kieli managed a flustered "Huh?" while trying not to trip, Harvey was already bursting into a sprint in the direction he'd gazed.

"Harvey?!"

Harvey's back was retreating down an alleyway; Kieli took off after him, but in no time he was too far ahead, and she lost sight of him. When she emerged from the alley and into the next street she couldn't figure out which way he'd gone, and she was at a loss. Happily, though, before long she made out a redheaded figure wandering back up the street.

"What did you find?"

"Nothing," he said, but he was still darting his eyes this way and that, looking unconvinced.

The radio asked in a worried voice, *"Say, Master, are you maybe feeling a little tired?"*

"Yeah, and you're not helping," Harvey snapped in a way that left no possible response. Kieli privately thought he might really be a little tired. That hadn't been his usual curtness; she'd sensed more bite to it. She hardly ever heard that tone coming from Harvey's mouth. Normally the radio was the hotheaded one, and yet now it felt as if Harvey was on edge, as if he was being more impatient to make up for its complacency.

"Hey, Harvey, we're not in too much of a hurry, so why don't we take a little break here before we go on…?" Kieli ventured tentatively. She wanted to fix the radio as soon as possible, of course, but she sort of got the feeling that Harvey was in an even worse state, somehow. Coppery eyes glanced sharply at her. She was pretty sure that if he'd used that tone with her it would have hurt a lot, so she'd felt a little apprehensive as she asked, looking up through her eyelashes. After a pause, Harvey was the one to break eye contact, and then he smacked his own cheek lightly with his left hand.

Dazed, Kieli wondered what that behavior was all about.

"Yeah, I guess… Sure, why not?" He was back to his normal slightly uninterested voice. Sighing, he said, "Thanks. Sorry." She thought he was probably directing that to both her and the radio. Then he took the hand he'd struck his cheek with and ruffled her hair. Its ingrained tobacco scent gently tickled at her nose.

Caught off guard by this gesture he hadn't done much lately, Kieli felt a sudden sting of tears and promptly ducked her head to hide her face. While she pretended to wipe some sand off her coat, she gazed at the tips of her toes and thought, *What a mess.* Usually she could stay calm and composed, but every so often when she let her guard down she felt like crying. Sometimes she accidentally remembered the fact that she didn't see a single good thing to look forward to after this.

I really do wish the journey would never end…

That night she dozed off in the middle of writing a letter and had a bizarre dream.

An indistinct white figure stood in the middle of a dim space. She knew, vaguely, that it was somebody she knew, but when she tried to look closely the person's face blurred, and she couldn't tell for sure who it was.

Whoever it was stood staring down with tousled hair and eyes fixed on a corpse lying on the ground—head crushed in, body so mangled Kieli couldn't even tell if it was a man or a woman—while gripping a blood-spattered ax. Thick, red-black blood dripped—dripped—dripped down from the tip of the broad wedge-shaped blade. The person's clothes and face were equally plastered with blood, but no attempt was made to wipe it off; the figure just stood there placidly gripping the ax. Kieli was thinking, *I just did what anyone would do. I didn't do anything wrong.* He tried to take *something precious from me. I was only protecting what was mine.*

All of a sudden it was Kieli herself holding the ax. The iron handle of the ax she gripped was so heavy she thought it might wrench her arm right out of its socket, and strangely warm when it should have been cool. The warmth came from the still-wet blood clinging to it. The ax got heavier and heavier as she held it, but she couldn't let go of the handle, so it dragged her arms down until they stretched in a weird, slithery way toward the ground.

It should have been frightening, but for some reason Kieli felt perfectly calm, thinking the same thing *she* was thinking. *I didn't do anything wrong. I was only protecting.*

Kieli—

When she looked up at the sound of her name, there was a person standing in front of her. She could tell now that it was definitely someone she knew, but she couldn't recognize who it was. She couldn't recognize her, and yet she could see the expression on the individual's face with crystal clarity; something sticky clung to those familiar cheeks, and eyes that Kieli couldn't place scrutinized her as if near tears.

Why do you look so sad…? Kieli didn't know what was wrong, and so she just looked up, still brandishing the ax.

Just as the person's mouth opened to say something, the dream dissolved.

Kieli woke up with her face planted on the side table of her room at the inn, gripping the pen in her hand almost hard enough to break it.

...She wasn't holding an ax. When she fumbled her stiffened, cold fingers open, there were nail marks imprinted deeply into her palm.

What an awful dream. I wonder what that was about.

First things first: she pulled herself together and finished writing the letter, her hand still a little numb. The next day she set off for the post office just as Harvey was coming back from whatever walk he'd apparently gone on early that morning, so she left him at the inn. The letter was to the bar on the parish border, and she took the opportunity to report their change of travel plans, too. She'd wanted to write a letter to settle her feelings and cheer herself up anyway. And after she had that thought, she realized that without even noticing it, she'd found a place she could send a letter to anytime she wanted. In exchange, though, lately she'd stopped writing letters to Becca that she never planned to send...Most people might think that was the normal thing to do, but it still made her feel a little lonely. Next time, she'd write a letter to Becca, too.

I've got to hang on and do my best...

She was the only one here with both a sound mind and body. She couldn't let herself feel blue. Telling herself the dream was probably just groundless fears, she forced it to the back of her mind, mailed her letter, and left the post office.

She walked down the post office steps with her shoulder bag clopping against her side and came out on the main street at the bottom, where her eye caught sight of a car passing by on the other side of the road. Longer and classier than a three-wheeled taxi—it was the car that belonged to the young lady they'd met yesterday. The car was gone before Kieli could get a good look through the backseat window, but maybe she was riding in it right now.

The next time she left the inn, she asked the doorman about the girl as they exchanged greetings. Apparently the young lady was so famous there wasn't a single person in town who didn't know her; the doorman understood whom Kieli was talking about as soon as she described the car. He explained that the young lady was the current head of the family investing so much money in the town. There had actually been a male heir, but there'd been some kind of trouble and he'd left home, or something, so his younger sister had inherited the family fortune.

True, it was rare for a woman to be heir to such a prestigious family, but there was something that nagged at Kieli even more about the whole thing. According to the doorman it had been more than ten years since she'd taken over the family estate, and yet the lady had still looked quite young to Kieli. About Beatrix's age, going by appearances. *Could she be a woman Undying like Beatrix?* she mused, and then immediately dismissed the idea. If she were, surely Harvey would've noticed right away.

I wonder why she wanted to invite Harvey over all of a sudden yesterday.

Kieli puzzled to herself for a moment.

She couldn't have a crush on him, could she...?

She looked in the direction she'd seen the car heading. Faint traces of its thick fossil-fuel exhaust still hovered along the surface of the pavement, showing the path it had taken.

Kieli doubted it meant anything, but technically that was the same direction as their inn.

It probably doesn't mean anything, though, she repeated to herself firmly, even as she unthinkingly began to lope back toward the inn.

There was a faint, dully colored bruise on his left wrist. It was shaped almost like a set of fingers.

What is this...?

He held up his hand in front of him and stared at it for a while, but it was becoming too much of a bother to think about it. He let it drop back to his side and straightened out the cuff of his sleeve, which he'd tugged up with his teeth. Without a right arm, even trifling movements like these were slow going. Harvey rolled over and lay facedown in his bed, burying his face in the dusty pillow and feeling somehow drained. The end-of-winter air, still crisp but pleasantly, refreshingly so, streamed in through the window above him and ruffled the hair on the back of his head, bringing with it the smell of smog and the noise of the city.

Evidently the mirage hadn't shown up today either. He wanted to get another look at it and confirm what direction it was in. And then there was the other issue that wouldn't stop bothering him: the issue of the voice he'd heard for a moment at the station and the form that had escaped into the gap between train and platform. And that feeling like discomfort that he'd had when that woman touched him yesterday, the one he just couldn't explain the reason for—there was such a confusing jumble of things going on in his head that he couldn't tell anymore what he should think about first. Or maybe he was overthinking things, making them more complicated than they had to be?

Why was he so impatient to take care of all these different things at the same time, anyway? All it did was make him brood too much all at once and make him tired and pissy, until he almost took it out on Kieli and then *she* ended up worried about *him*. Pathetic.

This is all the Corporal's fault...

Harvey turned his cheek against the pillow and glared resentfully at the unconcerned radio sitting on the windowsill. Any other time that radio would have butted in with *"There you go again, thinking in circles about complicated stuff and not getting anywhere,"* and Harvey would've gotten sick of the whole thing and just stopped thinking about it. But no, now there was nobody to put on the brakes, so his thoughts had gotten so snarled up that there was no untangling them anymore. He was actually starting to think that maybe in some sense the Corporal's insufferable nagging had acted as a tranquilizer for him.

Harvey dragged himself upright and half-crawled to the window like a lazy animal, reaching for the radio.

He grabbed it by the cord and suspended it out of the third-story window. It seemed like a good way to vent his frustration.

"...Master, do you have something against me?"

"Not particularly."

Dangling his arm out the window and letting the radio swing in the breeze, Harvey propped his chin on the sill and looked down below. Their room was only on the third floor of the inn, so it wasn't all that high up. From here he could take in the street beneath them. This town was no Westerbury, but there was still a fair amount of traffic. His right eye's lag had cleared up quite a bit in the last few days. If nothing else, he didn't get dizzy anymore.

He was mindlessly watching the pedestrians go by when he noticed someone watching him from across the street.

That gaze—!

"*Wah, Master, I'll fall! I'll fall!*" shrieked the radio. Harvey realized that he'd abruptly stuck his upper body out the window, and the radio was in serious danger of getting flung away. By then it was already too late: the owner of the gaze tore off in a single bound, disappearing into the alley behind it. The glimpse Harvey'd caught was of an all-black creature, and he had the impression it had run on four legs. *Was it... an animal?*

That took him enough by surprise to momentarily delay his reaction, but after a beat he slid out of bed and burst out of the room. He ran down the stairs, impatiently hanging the radio around his neck one-handed, bolted past the cheap hotel's cheaply paid doorman standing at the entrance with about as much enthusiasm as his salary warranted, and came out into the street.

Which way did it go? Harvey turned in the direction he'd seen the shadowy figure run off, and was just starting to cross the street when a vehicle pulled up on his right, announcing itself with the sound of a clamorous fossil-fuel engine as it appeared out of the edge of his vision, just where a bit of a blind spot still lingered. He threw himself back into the shoulder of the road just in time, but—

What the—?!

The driver turned and, of all things, headed straight *for* him! He couldn't avoid it in time; he ended up pinned between the car's front bumper and the wall at his back. While he'd reflexively shifted the radio to spare it the brunt of the damage, Harvey himself took a heavy hit to his side. At the same time, the short, abrupt squeal of brakes sounded practically right in his ear, close enough to rattle his brain.

The part of his brain that worked automatically without his conscious thought immediately determined that his injuries weren't fatal, but they were sure enough to impair his sight and hearing for an instant; he heard a disturbingly excited female voice say "Oh dear, how awful!" but it sounded fuzzy and distant (*"Oh dear," my ass! You were blatantly aiming at me!*).

"Carry him quickly, Job!"

"Hey! What—?!"

Pinned between the car and the wall, Harvey couldn't move. Hands yanked him roughly free and he was tossed over a man's broad shoulders like a sack of potatoes before he could put up any resistance. The same sort of discomfort he'd felt from that woman yesterday tickled at his nose. Now he finally realized what had made him uncomfortable—this was unmistakably the stench of rotting bodies.

Harvey was tossed on the floor of the car's backseat, where

he hit his back hard. He was ready to spring back up in a heartbeat, but a metallic *clang* made him jolt. When he looked up, his left wrist was bound in an iron manacle attached to a thick chain. The other end of the chain was fixed to a seat leg. "What the hell are you—"

"I finally get to see you!" It was that same woman from yesterday, throwing her arms around him as if to cut off the violent struggle Harvey was seriously contemplating.

The *next* thing she said, though, he reacted to.

"Brother! You came back to me!"

"Huh?!" he blurted. He had to admit, it came out as more of an undignified screech than anything else.

"When did he leave?"

"About fifteen minutes ago…I think…"

She'd run straight back to the inn, but neither Harvey nor the radio was in his room. So she'd tried asking the doorman at the entrance, but all she got was that vague, dubious answer.

Where could he have gone? He could have at least left her a message telling her where, or even just a couple of words scrawled on a napkin, but as usual, those little considerations were completely off his radar. Nonplussed, Kieli turned around and left the inn again without even putting down her bag. She figured she'd try looking around the neighborhood a little, just in case.

"……?"

After she'd walked for a while, she realized that something was following her. At first she thought it was just her imagination, but when she stopped and glanced behind her, *it* stopped short too, maintaining the same fixed distance. It was an animal a little larger than the average dog, with short black hair. It looked like a dog, yet Kieli had the distinct feeling it wasn't one; she couldn't figure out what it was, exactly.

Does it have some business with me . . . ? Not that she wasn't skeptical about the idea of a dog having "business." She was deliberating whether to approach the doglike thing when a commotion suddenly started up around her.

"It's the mirage!"

"I can see the tower!" cried voices from somewhere in the distance, and the flow of people on the streets all turned in one direction as if pulled by an invisible magnet.

The mirage . . . ?

Maybe Harvey and the Corporal had gone to see the mirage. Yes, that sounded right. Kieli was about to set off running that way too, when a cry sounded behind her.

Not a human cry—something very much like a dog's howl. She turned to see the animal being kicked as it tried to weave its way through the legs of the crowd. The man who'd kicked it merely said, "Where did this thing come from? Little piece of shit could hurt someone," and began to hurry on, leaving it there on the ground. Kieli was just turning to go back to it when it leaped up and immediately sank its teeth into the man's shin.

The man cursed loudly as he shook his leg free, and for a short time the attention of the crowd shifted from the mirage to them—which was when Kieli saw something incredible.

The animal landed nimbly on its feet, and its lips pulled

back, mouth suddenly gaping open from jaw to ears. Closely packed sawlike teeth rimmed a mouth that was green like rotten meat; abnormally overdeveloped canines dripped with saliva. The animal launched itself into the air and latched on to the man's arm with those two varieties of sharp teeth, sending a spray of tiny beads of blood into the air like fog. Everything from the elbow down was wrenched off.

The man collapsed to the ground, one arm just a stump now, and rolled around there, blabbering deliriously words that didn't even manage to become screams. The first truly scream-like scream came from the mouth of a nearby woman who probably didn't even know him. Panic spread from there until people began running in all directions from the spot where the animal had landed, just as if someone had dropped a bomb there. Kieli herself had been rooted to the spot with horror; now, pushed along by the crowd, she stumbled into motion too and started to run mindlessly.

That was—that was—

Her brain was half-numb, and she couldn't quite get it to work. The sight of that animal just now, its mouth greenish as if its cells were rotting and falling off in clumps, made a series of similar images flash through her mind—the monsters in Gate Town's underground waterways, Christoph when she'd met him in Westerbury, and Joachim. *Is it like they were?*

After someone passing her from behind knocked her off balance and almost made her fall, Kieli turned down a side alley to escape the chaos of the crowd. She kept running for a while, looking over her shoulder periodically to make sure no one was following her, until at last her legs faltered and she came to a stop, clinging to the wall for balance. As she put a hand to her chest and tried to catch her breath, she checked the alley behind her one more time. It looked as though she was the only one who'd come this way. The screams and pounding footsteps of all the people faded into a distant roar that bounced off the walls of the gloomy alley.

Just when she returned her gaze to her own surroundings with a sigh of relief, a dark red droplet landed with a slow liquid *plop* on the gray pavement before her. Kieli gasped and tried to back away, but she found she couldn't move. Petrified, she stared in terror at the puddle of blood forming right in front of her boots. When she forced her head to tilt up, frozen neck muscles creaking, that doglike animal was balanced catlike on top of one of the exhaust pipes along the alley wall. Blood dripped steadily from the severed end of the human arm in its mouth.

It casually dropped the arm right in front of her, and with a strangled cry, Kieli managed to back away at last. Somewhere in the middle of her retreat she plopped down on the pavement and couldn't stand up again. She thought she could see the arm lying in front of her boots, still twitching slightly. She felt bile rise in her throat.

The animal that alighted across the arm from her gave her a blood-soaked grin—at least, she thought it was grinning. The corners of its mouth pulled back all the way to its ears to reveal a glimpse of its slimy green mouth.

"Here. Your friend can have this. It's gotta be inconvenient having one."

The creature spoke. Its intonation was a little weird, but it spoke, in human language.

"Undyings can just stick on body parts, even ones that don't belong to them, and the nerves will pretty much hook right up. Pretty convenient, huh?" it continued, giving a single wag of its tail (although its body was doglike, its tail was long and thin like the tail of a mountain lion she'd seen in a photograph once) and contorting the corners of its gaping mouth into what Kieli thought was probably another smile. When it closed its mouth, it went back to more or less looking like a dog. Kieli stared at the baffling animal standing before her eyes in openmouthed amazement, still sitting on her butt on the ground.

It could speak in words, and it seemed fairly intelligent, too. And by "your friend" and "Undying" it could only mean Harvey. Which meant it was saying that it must be *inconvenient for Harvey* to be missing an arm, so it was *offering him a new one*. If she set aside the fact that it had torn a man's arm off with its teeth (although she didn't necessarily think that was an issue that could fairly be set aside), maybe this animal didn't pose an immediate threat...?

"Are you...um...a dog?"

It was only when Kieli heard her voice come out scratchy that she realized her throat was dry. The animal seemed offended.

"How rude. What part of me makes you think of some *mongrel*?"

Kieli wasn't sure how to answer that question. It was built like a medium-sized dog, and its long-nosed face looked like a dog's, as long as it kept its mouth closed. The pointy, triangular ears and short, jet-black fur made it look like one of those slender breeds of dog, too. On the other hand, the hair around its neck, which was longer than all its other fur and stood stiffly out, and the slender tail with just a poof of hair at the end reminded her of a mountain lion. The expression in its eyes—they were mismatching shades: one amber and one a dark brown—was oddly human, and as it continued to regard her she grew uncomfortable.

…All in all, though, Kieli still felt it was more like a dog than anything else. After observing all its features and considering them, she only ended up at the same conclusion; she was at a total loss for a response. Eventually the animal said "Eh, whatever" in a sulky voice, and leaped nimbly back up onto the pipe again. Though it was a lot bigger than a cat, it had a catlike way of moving without making a sound. Kieli was getting more and more confused about what kind of animal it was.

"I know where your friend is."

"What?!" Kieli cried, taken by surprise at the unexpected subject change. "You mean Harvey, right?! You know where he—" She leaned forward eagerly only to snatch her hand back in a hurry when she almost touched the fallen arm.

Mismatched brown and amber eyes gazed down at her from the pipe, and the animal made a rumbling sound in its throat with another probably-a-smile.

"He's a pretty interesting guy. A little old to be getting kidnapped, isn't he?"

"Is this the place...?"

Facing the back gate of the estate's cracked border wall, Kieli hunched her shoulders against a chill that had nothing to do with the evening breeze.

On the other side of the gate an old mansion stood against the sky, where sunset's copper glow was beginning to melt into blue-gray. She'd been told the mansion belonged to a distinguished family that brought wealth to the town, but it looked awfully run-down for such an important estate. The border wall and the walls of the mansion itself were riddled with fine webs of cracks and liverwort. There wasn't a single plant in the garden that you'd expect to find in a place like this. Even the iron gate before Kieli's eyes was so completely covered in rust that she was afraid if she touched it, it would come loose and just fall down.

According to what she'd heard from the doorman this morning, about a decade ago—in other words, not long after the newest family head had assumed that position—there had been a natural disaster. An earthquake had opened up a fissure at the northern end of town, and several mansions like this one had been destroyed. That was exactly where they were right now: the northern outskirts. Of all the grand homes, this one alone had miraculously escaped destruction, and the female head of the family still lived here to this day. But apparently there wasn't a single other occupied house anywhere nearby.

Still, Kieli's impression was the opposite of what she'd

heard: vague though the feeling was, she thought *this* was the house where she couldn't sense a living presence.

The sight of it made her flinch more than a little, but she gulped and pulled herself back together.

"Did Harvey really get carried off by that woman?"

"Yep," the beast answered lightly, and jumped easily to the top of the wall. It balanced all four limbs adroitly on the narrow surface and began to walk back and forth along it, perhaps scoping out the interior of the estate.

"Climb on up."

It said this as if it were the easiest thing in the world to do. Kieli gave the animal a slightly envious look as she nodded. They'd circled the whole estate, following along the wall; the front gate was far too tall for either of them to imagine Kieli climbing. This servants' gate in the rear seemed surmountable, but certainly not *easily*. It was like when the creature had brought her an arm it had torn off of someone: it meant no offense, but the way it showed her consideration left something to be desired. Was that because it was an animal?

The moment Kieli placed a foot on the rusty gate, it screeched loudly. White-knuckled with fear, she did her best not to make any noise as she scrambled up; when she reached the top she straddled the gate and surveyed the grounds inside.

On the other side of a barren, empty space Kieli wasn't sure she could properly call a "garden" stood the crack-riddled walls of the estate. They had a really creepy air about them. All the visible windows were dark gray. Scraps of once-white curtains hung in a few of them, but no light was on in any of the rooms. Kieli started to wonder whether Harvey was really in this place after all.

She swung both legs over the gate and jumped down into the estate grounds. She was just pulling her bag back up to her shoulder and pondering her next move when suddenly a voice behind her asked, "Who are you?"

Kieli's heart leapt to her throat. She hadn't sensed anyone there at all. She turned around stiffly, trying to get her heartbeat back under control, and discovered a long-haired woman in a beautiful dress that looked out of place in the wild garden. Out of the corner of her eye, Kieli glanced up to the top of the wall, thinking, *She found us right away!*, but the black animal had already disappeared into hiding, abandoning Kieli to her fate. *Traitor...*

All of a sudden coming face-to-face with the mistress of the manor like this had her feeling rattled, but she held her head high, told herself she'd come here for an honorable, aboveboard purpose (though technically, scaling the gate and sneaking in kind of tossed the "aboveboard" thing out the window), and stated her business.

"Um, I heard that Harvey—I mean, the man I was with yesterday—was here."

"Oh, you," said the lady, sounding as if she had only just now remembered Kieli's face. Evidently she really hadn't taken any notice of Kieli at the time.

"Did you come to bring him back with you?"

"Yes...I did," Kieli confirmed cautiously, disconcerted. The lady tilted her head for a moment as if she was pondering this, but then she offered Kieli a gentle smile and said, "Yes, he's here. Come in." She started walking, leading the way back toward the mansion. It was such an unexpectedly normal welcome that it temporarily knocked the wind out of Kieli's sails, but then she snapped out of it with a start and began jogging after the lady in the dress.

The mansion was as devoid of light as it had seemed from the outside. The air inside was chilly, and in it she caught a faint smell like spoiled food. The lady of the house lit a candlestick to light the way and led Kieli down a gloomy corridor. The feeble candle flame made the walls and ceiling flicker into view around her in a way that made it hard to judge their distance from her, making her feel even more uneasy being here all alone. The clacking of the lady's high-heeled shoes and the rustling of her skirts; the clomping of Kieli's boots and the rhythmic thumping of her bag—the sounds of their progress through the deathly quiet mansion echoed eerily off the walls.

Unable to stand the silence anymore, she addressed the back in front of her. "Um..."

Facing forward and continuing to walk, the lady said without warning, "Say, would you give him to me?"

This stunning question came casually, in the same offhand manner someone might say *Can I have your doll?*, and Kieli's feet stopped in place without her conscious order. "Huh?" she squeaked. The candle's circle of light and the dress she was following pulled farther away into the darkness, so she hurried to catch back up, flustered.

"Um, what do you mean by that?"

"You should. He's my brother."

"B-bro-ther…?" Kieli asked falteringly, the word so alien that her tongue fumbled it. The lady calmly kept walking, paying it no mind.

"I knew it from the moment I saw him. I'm positive he's my brother reincarnated. So give him to me. You don't mind, do you?"

"Wait, but Harvey's not a thing. It's not an issue of 'giving' or 'not giving'…"

The lady whirled abruptly around to face her for the first time.

"You're saying no?" she asked, tilting her head to the side adorably. Her confusion was plain. Kieli lost her nerve for a moment at that, and fell silent. Then:

"I-I'm saying no…"

The moment Kieli answered, she was shoved hard in the shoulders. "Huh?!" Taken off guard, she stumbled into a door in the wall—which promptly opened, sending her sprawling shoulders-first into the dark room beyond. She heard the sound of the door closing behind her and sat up in alarm. "What— Please, let me out! Let me out!" She felt around for the knob and seized it, rattling it back and forth, but the door didn't budge.

"No, no, you mustn't get in my way…" came the lady's voice from just beyond the door. It lilted like an innocent child's voice singing a song, interrupted by giggles.

"You mustn't get in my way…because if you do, I'll have to kill you…"

Kieli had the sudden illusion that the thick iron door rippled like a thin piece of cloth for just a moment. It felt as if someone's slightly foul-smelling sigh washed across her face. She took a step back from the door, shuddering.

High-heeled footsteps and the sound of swishing skirts withdrew into the distance. Kieli was pinned in place for a time with her eyes glued to the closed door, unable to move, but when the sound of footsteps disappeared she was released from her paralysis, and she tore her gaze away from the door to look around her. The only thing visible was one dim, lonely ray of twilight shining down on the far corner of the room, hardly enough to see anything but itself by. From the way sound echoed she could guess that it wasn't a very large space, but other than that, she couldn't tell anything about her surroundings. There seemed to be a window where the light was leaking in, but it was high up on the wall, and when she peered closely at it, she saw that some unknown party had nailed a board over it to block access.

When she started to feel around her for anything she might be able to use to escape, Kieli realized with terror that a whitish, humanlike form was lying at her feet.

She looked downward and inspected it carefully: there at the bottom of the darkness, a facedown figure in a pinafore like a maid's—she thought it was a woman, but the head was so thoroughly crushed in that there was no way to tell from the face. Some kind of mushy substance lay scattered on the floor around it.

"What's wrong?" said a voice out of nowhere.

The lady of the house stood in the center of the room, bathed in a ring of pale light. How long had she been there? Her long hair was disheveled, both her face and the dress she was wearing were greasy with the blood of her victim, and she was brandishing with both hands a great ax dripping with gore.

"Brother, what's wrong? Why are you looking at me like that…?" she asked in confusion, tilting her blood-soaked face to the side endearingly.

"You're blaming me…? It wasn't my fault; it was hers. After all, she was about to toss out my ring right along with the laundry. I know she meant to take the ring. She wanted to get in our way. I just know it."

As she calmly explained this, she walked closer, dragging the bloody ax behind her. *Shnnk. Shnnk.* With each step came the heavy sound of it scraping along the floor. Kieli backed away in horror, but after only a few steps her shoulders hit the wall.

That dream— This is what that dream was about.

As she realized this, something made a creaking sound overhead. The lady's form blurred sideways and dissolved into static as though the noise had erased it, and at her departure the darkness around Kieli softened slightly.

Kieli's eyes traced the wall upward. Her chills hadn't disappeared yet. When her gaze reached the window, she saw that the boards nailed over it had been snapped apart from the outside, and the color of the night outside was streaming in. It was still brighter than the room, if not by much. A long, thin black face suddenly popped up against the backdrop of the twilit sky, one amber eye gleaming eerily, and she'd opened her mouth to scream before she realized.

"Oh!"

An amber right eye and a dark brown left eye: it was the black beast. Relieved, Kieli ran up to the wall below the window. "I was afraid you'd run away…"

"I found him. That way, over there," the animal said cheerfully, indifferent to Kieli's emotional state. It indicated with its eye for Kieli to come outside. Which was all well and good, but the window was high out of Kieli's reach. The animal didn't quite seem to understand that, however. She turned and looked around the room again, but it seemed to be an unused storeroom or something; all she saw were a few odds and ends piled up in one corner. Nothing that she could use to stand on.

When she looked up at the window through her lashes and made a display of her distress, the animal appeared to notice for the first time that Kieli couldn't climb up. It blinked both eyes. Then it scrunched its long nose as if in deep thought, and after an amazingly sulky-looking grimace, it grumbled, "Dammit, I can't believe this," drew its head back outside, and thrust its rear end through the window frame instead. That long, thin tail just like a mountain lion's on a body that was otherwise pure dog dangled down to her. Kieli gratefully took hold of the end of it to use as a rope. When she gripped it tight and pulled, she heard a strangled groan overhead.

Kieli climbed up the wall with her feet, using the tail as a handhold, and let out a little sigh of relief once she'd gotten her upper body onto the window frame and dragged up her shoulder bag after her. The tail fled from her the moment she let go. When she looked down from her position half-in and half-out of the window, she saw the animal's back; it was scratching its claws against the ground for some reason, writhing. "I'm sorry; did it hurt?" she whispered. But the animal shook its head without looking up. Apparently pain wasn't the issue. Maybe it had tickled.

Kieli transferred her gaze to the wall below the window. There was a little mountain of loosely heaped fossil fuel like brown coal at the bottom, maybe for heating. She thought she could probably slither down from here onto it.

"That way. You can see it from up there."

The animal lifted its head unsteadily, as if exhausted, and pointed with its nose toward a point off in the darkness. Across an open space that she guessed was the courtyard, though it was as barren and empty of plant life as the back garden had been, Kieli could see a smallish building that must be some sort of detached cottage. A faint light bled from one of its windows. So, one of the building's rooms was apparently occupied.

The lighted window seemed almost as small as a postage stamp from this distance, but when she squinted she could make out a redhead sitting against the wall inside.

"There he is…!"

You got "hit by a car and kidnapped"? What are you, a little kid? Honestly… She was heaving a half-worried, half-exasperated sigh when the hem of a long dress appeared from the side of the room, and someone came to stand in front of Harvey. It was the lady.

Kieli's heart gasped, and then she froze up completely.

Within the square of the window, the lady drew up her skirts and knelt on the floor before Harvey. Her two white hands reached out to palm Harvey's cheeks, and her face drew in close—

Wh-wh-what is she…?

But before Kieli could see what happened next, a great shadow loomed in front of her, cutting off her line of sight. The chauffeur that had been with the lady when they'd met her yesterday was standing beneath the window, brandishing a large ax with both hands. Kieli jumped down onto the coal pile just in time. The very same moment she slid down to the ground, there was a great metallic clang as the thick wedged blade slammed into the window frame with enough force to send vibrations through the air that Kieli could feel. The rust on the window frame exploded into fine mineral dust that filled the air.

The animal launched itself off the ground and sank its teeth into the chauffeur's neck, but the chauffeur didn't seem to think anything more of it than Kieli would of a fly buzzing in her ear. He just shook it off harshly and lifted the ax to swing at Kieli again. *He's not hurt—?* "He's only a moving corpse," the animal explained as it landed lightly on the ground next to her. It continued to expound, though Kieli was fairly certain they didn't have the time: "The woman's been dead a long time. You noticed her smell, right?"

Kieli was in no state to answer. She rolled out of the path of the chauffeur's blade with no room to spare and scurried away on all fours as fast as she could. A great crash of impact sounded behind her, followed by a clanging roar that reverberated in her ears until she couldn't hear anything else. The ax flew out of the chauffeur's hand and came careening toward her, turning end over end and grazing past her dangerously closely before it lodged itself in the ground.

Only the first gasp of the scream made it past her throat.

She felt all the blood drain from her face, and all of her strength went with it, sending her crumpling to the ground. She couldn't make her legs stand up again. When she turned her head nervously to check behind her, she found the chauffeur buried under the collapsed coal pile, kicking his legs up and down like a mechanical toy.

Harvey didn't hold back at all. He used all the force he could muster to kick the woman bringing her face close to his. It sent her flying.

Reeling, she fell against the table behind her, knocking the candleholder onto the floor. The candle flame that had been illuminating the room went out, and the faint twilight beaming in through the window became the only thing to see by. That suited Harvey fine, since low light was easier on his eyesight these days.

The woman sank to hands and knees on the floor as if grief-stricken. Eventually she lifted her head and gave him an almost offended look.

"Brother, why are you treating me so coldly?"

"Don't give me that 'why.' Take this off." When he yanked at the manacle around his left hand, it was promptly yanked right back with a jangle of the heavy chain. The other end of the chain was tied to a round metal fitting in the wall, meaning Harvey couldn't move away from said wall.

"What? No, I can't do that!" said the woman who'd shackled him and confined him here, without a trace of shame. "If I take it off, you'll run away! Didn't you say you loved me, Brother? And yet you ran away and left me...I'm never letting you go again."

She crawled toward him, her long hair trailing along the floor. Harvey shuddered at the sight. "Stay away from me!" He made to pull away from her, but his back was against the wall, so he tried to scoot sideways—but she cut off his path by putting a hand to the wall beside his head. *Somebody help me!* he cried in his mind. It sounded pretty close to a whine, actually.

Harvey remembered hearing something about the younger sister taking over the family because her brother had left; he didn't particularly sympathize with this brother or anything, but he could sort of see why. Anyone exposed to this girl's nutty expressions of love would probably want to run away. The fact that she even had manacles and chains and iron rings in the first place already put her squarely in the "freak" category.

"Where's your ring, Brother? Those matching rings are our treasures! I know you have it on you somewhere. I could tell right away." Mumbling nonsense, she put one hand down the collar of his shirt and started fishing around. The sensation of cold fingers slipping underneath his clothes sent goose bumps rippling over his skin.

"Hey, stop it!"

"Come on, where are you hiding it? Over here?"

This time, Harvey's cry wasn't just in his mind. "Wah!" He kicked her off again with all his might. He plastered himself to the wall, breathing hard. Now he really did feel in danger, at least of a certain sort, and he was starting to get chills. He seriously wanted to get out of here pronto.

"Oh, Brother, what am I going to do with you…?"

Harvey was sure he'd kicked the woman hard in the stomach, but she sat right back up again without seeming hurt, and started crawling back toward him, undeterred. He made a last-ditch attempt to pull his left hand free from the manacle. All he got for his trouble, though, was a shower of rust falling down on his head. The chain and the ring in the wall were both corroded, but not so much so that he could break them just by yanking on them.

Just as the woman's arms were twining around his neck again, a metallic vibration like the gong of a great bell echoed somewhere nearby.

"…Goodness, what could that noise be?"

Harvey directed a silent thanks to whatever it was for at least distracting her attention temporarily. It had sounded as if it was coming from outside. *The courtyard, maybe?* After a few seconds' pause, there was another noise like a pile of heavy luggage falling over.

"Perhaps it's another intruder…? Wait just a minute, Brother. I'll be right back. Job? Job, where are you?"

Evidently the unfamiliar word was the name of that hulking chauffeur with the superhuman strength. Harvey watched her disappear out the door calling for her driver, grumbling at the back of her retreating dress that she didn't have to ever come back for all he cared. Once he felt her presence exit the hall, he heaved a deep sigh all the way from the bottom of his lungs.

Give me a break... He slumped back heavily against the wall and let his head droop. The chain prevented him from lowering his left arm; the ring above him creaked and rained another scattering of rust on him.

He was in what seemed like the parlor of a detached cottage. The hallway light seeping in through the doorway and the faint light from the window dimly illuminated the room. In its center stood a table and a chair that were pointlessly large and expensive-looking, but apparently very old too; the ornamental carvings on the legs were worn almost completely away. There was an equally expensive-looking fireplace on the far wall, but it was covered in a thick layer of dust and fossil-fuel ash, and showed no signs of being in use. It was plain that there had been no living residents here for a long time.

At any rate, he wanted to escape now, while he had the chance, but...Harvey cast a hooded glance at the radio set neatly on the table.

"Do something, already."

"To think you had such a beautiful younger sister, Master! I'm afraid I'm a little disappointed in you. I never took you for the kind of man who'd just run away and leave his own sister like that."

"......"

The Corporal had been out to lunch all day, so he was no help at all. Whose side was he on, anyway?

He'd been jangling the manacle for a while now, more to vent his feelings than out of any attempt at escape, and his next tug wore through the skin of his hand, making blood well up there. The bruise he'd noticed on his wrist this afternoon hadn't quite healed yet, either. Harvey had remembered a little while ago that it was from when that woman had grabbed his hand yesterday.

He'd also noticed a ring set with a blackish stone on her left ring finger. The stone's pull was faint due to its small size, but he could sense a fossil-resource-based magnetic field from it very like the one he'd felt at the park in Westerbury. Harvey guessed that stone was somehow providing the energy to keep *that corpse* in the condition it had been in at the time of its death. Still, while he'd known that crystallized fossil resources could affect the dead, he hadn't thought they were powerful enough to animate corpses. The woman must be sensing the "core" buried in his heart, and that was why she thought Harvey had the matching ring…That thought made him feel even more endangered, in several senses.

Then he picked up a faint squeak, not with his ears but by a crawling on the surface of his skin. Someone was coming toward him from the hallway. Reflex put him instantly on high alert, breath silent and all senses attuned to the slightest movement. After he spent a while staring at the doorway by the light from the window, a dark figure appeared within the door frame, backlit by the dull hallway light.

Shnnk, shnnk…

A heavy sound like grinding stone scraped along the floor in time with the approaching footsteps. The light coming from the window hit the end of the rod-shaped thing the figure brandished with both hands, illuminating the contours of a thick wedged blade. The blade bore down unhesitatingly straight toward his head—

A dull clang sounded just above the crown of his head and, since he was leaning that head against the wall at the time, the impact sent his brain bouncing in his skull.

After a split second's pause that felt like time had stopped, fragments of the concrete wall began raining down on him. When he looked up, still unconsciously holding his breath, the thick blade of the ax was sticking out perpendicular to the wall directly below the ring where the chain had been attached. A beat later, the severed end of the chain belatedly slid down the wall and hit him on the head, too.

"Are you okay?" the figure in front of him said in a girl's voice.

"Yeah...but warn me next time you do that," Harvey griped, shaking the bits of chain and rust out of his hair. Then he tried to stand up, but his legs felt weirdly nerveless, and he had to cling to the wall for support.

"Oh, sorry," the black-haired girl replied in a calm voice as she braced one foot against the wall and violently yanked the ax free. *I felt malice for a second just now... What was that?*

"Eh, whatever. Let's just get out of here. Corporal, we're going home."

"Going home? But isn't this your estate, Master?"

"I'm not the kind of guy who's into getting chained up in his own house."

Just talking to the radio was exhausting. He grabbed its strap roughly, and the manacle and strap of chain still dangling from his wrist made an annoying creaking sound. Kieli hefted the ax she'd pulled from the wall. "Want me to break it off?" "...Nah," Harvey declined. "I'll do it myself later." He kind of got the feeling if he let her do it he'd lose his hand in the process. Kieli dropped the ax to the floor with a clang, looking vaguely disappointed...He was starting to get the distinct sense that the malice he'd felt a little while ago had been real after all. *Why's she in such a bad mood?*

"Harvey, back a few minutes ago...did you really do it?"

"Do what?" he asked, falling back on his old habit of answering a question with a question in the face of her glare.

"...Nothing."

Kieli turned away from him, looking miffed for some reason. Harvey saw a figure move behind her.

"Kieli!"

In the same moment that he automatically reached out and pushed her aside, the woman in the dress swung the ax down from overhead.

A dull sound, accompanied by a heavy shock, jolted the bone of his arm.

As Kieli stumbled from the push, the thick, darkly gleaming blade arced down toward Harvey's arm right before her eyes. She tried and failed to scream. It felt as if her heart would stop.

Gong...

Instead of his arm, the manacle circling his wrist broke in two and fell to the floor with a thunk. The lady of the house *hmph*ed irritably.

"Honestly, Brother... I really don't know what to do with you," she mourned in low tones, shifting the ax back to an attack stance with more strength than her slender arms seemed capable of. She took a step forward. "I see you want to run off with some other girl again. Didn't I tell you I wouldn't let you get away?"

"Drop the 'again'; you'll make me look bad," Harvey retorted, taking Kieli's hand and guiding her behind his back. She could feel a tiny bit of his own numbness through the hand he held. His wrist had been badly scraped up to begin with; now it was darkening rapidly even as she watched, standing out clearly against the rest of his skin. The sight made Kieli shudder. If he'd been hit even slightly higher or lower, he really would have lost his hand. And of course there was no manacle to shield him against the next blow.

She was biting her lip at the awful situation when a black shadow leaped into her field of vision and pounced.

Out of the young lady's mouth came a husky scream like an old woman's. Her arm flailed, swinging the ax around wildly, and attached to that arm was the black animal, biting in hard. "Him!" Harvey shouted in surprise. Did they know each other?

The ax clattered to the ground and slid spinning across the floor, and the animal slid equally neatly to rest on all fours. There was a baffling *KKCHK* sound, and the white, pole-shaped object in the animal's mouth broke in half—the lady's torn-off arm. The animal dug right into the arm and began eating noisily. The sound of bones being crushed, the sound of flesh being chewed, the sound of dripping blood: the discordant trio echoed eerily in the dimness until Kieli thought she would vomit.

The ring the lady had worn on her left hand slipped out of the side of its mouth and fell to the floor with a terribly light, soft sound in contrast to the heavy cacophony filling the air.

"Ah!"

The lady instantly lunged for it and scooped it up with her remaining hand. But in just a matter of seconds, though Kieli didn't know what had happened, the lady had transformed into a wretched shadow of herself. Her waist-length hair turned cobweb-gray, her plump cheeks grew hollow and sunken, and her skin shriveled and cracked like one more wall of the estate. Yet the lady paid no attention to these changes as she gripped the ring and gazed fondly at it, as if she had eyes for nothing else.

And right there in her hands, the stone set in it cracked to pieces. Just like that.

The lady stared at the tiny fragments that were left of it, her withered cheeks stiff with shock.

And then right afterward, the wrist of the hand in which she held the stone began to crumble away. The disintegration swiftly spread from her wrist up to her elbow, pieces audibly crumbling away like a dried-up twig. "N-no...*No!*" As Kieli looked on in dumb amazement at the lady waving the remains of her arm about and screaming, behind that lady, with no warning whatsoever, the fireplace collapsed, sending up a thick cloud of ash. Cracks and rust began radiating out from the wall to the floor and ceiling, as if their change were triggered by hers.

"Uh-oh. Broken, huh?"

The animal dropped the half-eaten arm on the floor with an air of regret, and clicked its tongue (the animal! clicked its tongue!).

"Everybody get moving. It's time to run."

It turned around on its four legs and bolted for the exit, so in her stunned state Kieli automatically followed suit. "Harvey, quick!" When she looked over her shoulder to urge him after her, he turned to face her too, looking startled, but then his face suddenly jolted as he was yanked backward. The lady was hanging on to the strap of the radio Harvey held.

"Gah, let me go!" it shouted, its voice overlain with violent crackles of static.

"Corporal!" Kieli frantically snatched the radio out of the lady's hand.

"Wait, Brother. Help me!"

The radio stolen from her, the lady grasped Harvey's coat instead, and tried to pull him down to the floor with her. Her voice was completely the hoarse one of an old woman now. The flesh of the thin arm tugging at his coat dried to dirt before their eyes and dropped away to expose white bones. "Why? Why are you leaving me behind again…?! Please, please don't leave me…!" Her sobbing voice lost its tone, steadily unraveling into something that wasn't a voice at all.

Seeing the barest moment of what looked like hesitation on Harvey's face, Kieli determinedly reached out with both hands and shoved the lady across the room.

"Don't touch him!" she shouted. Then, surprised by her own words and the voice in which she'd said them, she froze in place. Harvey, on the other hand, seemed to snap back to his senses at her cry; he tugged her by the hand and started dragging her forward, and so she started running. Looking back one more time, she saw the lady stretching her hand pleadingly after them from where she'd collapsed on her stomach in the hallway. She'd raised her head, and Kieli could see that the flesh of her face had turned to dust too, and was falling off in great clumps. Eyeballs that looked like cloudy marbles now dropped out of their sockets and rolled along the floor.

She looked as if she was trying to say something, but her voice wasn't there anymore; soon she was just a skeleton, just bones collapsing to the floor. Only her long white hair and the dress she'd been wearing were left.

When they came out of the cottage, the curtain of night had already descended completely over the outside world. Kieli glanced at that place by the wall as they ran through the courtyard and saw the chauffeur lying there. He'd managed to scramble out from under the pile of fuel just in time to turn into an unmoving white skeleton. Then they were out of the courtyard; they could see the servants' gate across the back garden now. The animal running ahead of them launched itself to the peak of the gate in one jump and transferred itself to the top of the wall, turning back to them as if to urge them on.

"Climb."

Kieli scaled the gate first with Harvey's help. When she landed on the ground on the other side, Harvey tossed the radio over to her. It sailed up in a high arc and then down again, shrieking all the while. While Kieli was hastily moving to catch it, Harvey put one foot to the gate himself and climbed straight to the top in one go. But when he tried to jump down—

"…Huh?"

He abruptly lost his balance and fell in an unnatural, shoulder-first pose. Startled, Kieli ran over to him clutching the radio. "Harvey?!"

"I'm—fine." The look on Harvey's face told her he didn't know why he'd fallen either. He braced his hand against the ground and tried to get back up. Kieli lent him her hand and pulled him upright, then more or less dragged him after her until she stumbled too a little ways from the gate, and the two of them fell on top of each other with a thud, the radio sandwiched between them.

Panting, Kieli sat up and turned around, still on the ground. When she looked up at the mansion on the other side of the gate, she saw that the extraordinary decay had spread all the way to its outer walls. Thin cracks covered the whole building until there were more cracks than there was wall. The progression of the bizarre phenomenon had stopped just at the point where it looked as if even the tiniest breath of pressure could make the entire thing dissolve into sand and come washing down to the ground.

"…*What the hell was that…?*"

"What was it…?"

"Dunno…"

After that one round of empty conversation, they all just

stared up at the gate together, unable to snap out of their stupor for a while.

A lady that had aged and withered as if decades of time had passed at the speed of light, and an estate that had moldered just like its mistress. What the heck had just happened...? Whatever it was, Kieli didn't sense that ominous stench she'd picked up from the lady coming from this estate anymore. The only thing drifting vaguely through the air now was loneliness. Unrequited, distorted emotions—not regrets or grudges or anything like that; just a young loneliness like a little girl crying over being abandoned without even knowing why. It tinged the air around them, and then, little by little, it vanished.

The black animal jumped down from the wall and landed soundlessly by them. It merely stood there on its four legs, not taking any sort of offensive stance as far as she could see, but Harvey gave it an openly hostile look and moved Kieli behind him. Apparently he really did know something about it. Was this animal an Undying too, like Kieli had imagined? (Of a different breed, of course.)

"You're the voice that talked to me at the train station, aren't you? You watched me a few times after that, too. What's your game?" Harvey said in a harsh voice, his tone a full two steps lower than usual. The animal made a sort of shrug, and spoke in human language with its animal mouth.

"It'd been so long since I'd seen an *original* Undying that I got interested, so I was observing you, that's all. I don't mean you any harm. So what's your problem? How about you stop automatically reacting with hostility to everything?"

Its intonation was kind of wonky, maybe because its vocal cords were built differently from a human's, but if Kieli went just by its wording and the actual quality of its voice, it reminded her of a streetwise boy. But the human expressions it formed with its long, doglike face were frankly pretty grotesque. It had a very low adorableness factor, as a dog. Asking someone not to automatically be on guard was an impossible request. Harvey just kept glaring at it, his attitude fixed at "hostile."

Kieli wavered a little, but in the end she timidly tugged on Harvey's sleeve.

"Um, he *did* technically save us," she ventured. Harvey darted a sidelong glance at her and blinked. "…Uh-huh. Yeah," he agreed. He didn't look completely convinced, but maybe he'd accepted that she had a good point, because he visibly dialed down his hostility.

The animal twisted the corners of its mouth up to make a smile. The closely packed sawlike teeth and the four sharp canines peeked out from its greenish mouth.

"Okay then, let's say it's technically nice to meet you. I'm—"
Bang!

A sort of dull explosion rattled her eardrums, cutting off its voice. *A gunshot—?* The animal's body was blasted to one side, the grin still on its face.

Letting out a raspy shriek, Kieli instantly started running over to it. "Kieli, wait—" She shook off the hand Harvey tried to stop her with and got down on her knees beside the fallen animal. Then she leaned protectively over it and took stock. There was a hole right where its hind leg met its torso; blood was welling up from it before her eyes. With no real idea what to do, Kieli just covered the wound with both hands and tried to stanch the bleeding.

She could see the flickering white rays of flashlights across the dark road. She could hear voices talking to one another: "That way." "There it is." "It has friends!" Narrowing her eyes against the light behind them, she saw that a group of about ten men had appeared from around the corner of the estate's outer wall. They were armed with what looked like shotguns, but judging by how they talked and the fact that they were all dressed differently, they weren't Church Soldiers. Did that mean they were local men? It didn't take long for things to click: they were out looking for the animal that had bitten off that man's arm this afternoon.

"You're a real fool," said a boyish, streetwise voice with wholly inappropriate calm. Boyish, and yet at the same time the little muffled laugh it gave deep in its throat was like an old man's. It shifted Kieli off of itself and stood up as if nothing had happened. A viscous liquid that looked like coal tar oozed out of the gaping gunshot wound in its hind leg and started covering the opening. *"Core" blood. It really is an Undying—*

"You could've just pretended I was attacking you. I can't believe you actually declared yourself on my side instead...Ah, well, I've gotten real fond of you. Your name's Kieli, right?"

Fangs dripping with saliva peeked out of its smiling mouth. Its dark brown left eye blended into the darkness; only its amber right eye caught the light and reflected it thickly back. As it ambled around to face off against the men with shotguns, it told her, "My name is ____."

One part of the sentence, in which it must have said its name, sounded more doglike than human, and Kieli couldn't make it out.

"In today's language, it means 'Mane,'" Mane supplied, the stiff hair around his neck bristling, and growled like a cat. The skin of his wounded hind leg started to rapidly tear away from where it connected to his torso, and from beneath the mucous membrane swarmed by coal tar appeared a new leg that took the place of the old—a fat leg with hooklike talons, that looked as though it belonged to a giant bird of prey. Did he have the traits of all kinds of different animals—?

The animal kicked powerfully off the ground with his three beast legs and his new bird leg, and went straight for the group of men. A tremor ran through the crowd even as they aimed their shotguns.

Kieli just gaped after Mane for a moment, but then Harvey grabbed her arm and forcibly dragged her to her feet. "Time to run, Kieli."

"But…" She started running down the road with him in the opposite direction from the encirclement, darting worried glances behind her all the while. Without slowing his pace, Harvey turned his head and shouted an order over his shoulder to Mane: "Don't kill them!" Mane, who'd already sprung at the crowd, ducked his head as if to say *Good grief.*

When he returned his gaze forward, he gave a little "Huh?" that sounded like a tire going flat, and before Kieli could process it he abruptly fell flat on his face. He'd shoved Kieli away just before he went down, so her legs got all tangled up and she fell down on her butt in the opposite direction. She picked herself up immediately and crawled over to Harvey, who was still lying where he'd fallen. She peered into his face.

"What's wrong…?!"

"Sorry—my foot just—slipped," Harvey said, as if it were no big deal, but he was curling his body protectively around his stomach with his hand over a spot on his side, and it didn't look as if he could get up. He gave a strange, hitching cough, and spit up a glob of something from deep in this throat that was covered in black blood.

Kieli'd thought that fall from the gate was strange—he must have been sick ever since then; she just knew it. "No! Harvey!" She threw her arms around him; he shoved her off with an elbow in an *I'm fine* sort of way—bringing his hand into her field of vision. When she saw the condition it was in, she doubted her own eyes.

The flesh there was sunken so that the joints and blood vessels stood out strikingly; it was as if it wasn't Harvey's hand at all, and yet those were definitely the bones of Harvey's hand, and she could see where it connected to Harvey's body near his shirtsleeve. *It's just like how that lady changed…!*

"No! What…what is this? Why?!"

Kieli was reaching out to cling to him, scared to death, when someone behind her yanked her shoulder bag hard, tearing her away from him. The townspeople had caught up to them. They bore down on each of them separately to subdue them, cutting off Kieli's view, and the sight of Harvey was swallowed up by the crowd in no time. "Corporal!" She clutched at the radio just as it was about to get taken away from her in the confusion, wrapped both arms around it, and held on for dear life as she scanned the throng for Harvey. She caught sight of a red head of hair through the crowd in time to see a man raise up his shotgun and strike that red head with it. Harvey fell facefirst to the ground; the man straddled him and jammed the mouth of the shotgun between his ribs. Harvey showed no signs of getting up.

"No!"

Kieli's own shriek was accompanied by a scream from behind her. Mane's teeth were sunk deep into the arm of the man who'd been holding Kieli. "Harvey! Don't help me. Help Harvey, quick!" she called at the top of her lungs, pointing toward Harvey even as she stumbled and fell.

Mane alighted on the ground next to her and cocked his head to the side. "Can I kill? It'd be a pain to save him without killing anybody, and it's pretty hard to do."

"Yes! You can kill!"

The next second, Mane was descending on the man holding a gun to Harvey in one leap, baring his sawlike teeth and sinking them into the man's head. Harvey had just found the strength to lift his upper body; the man's skull was crushed in right before his eyes, spattering what looked like bits of brain all round.

While the other men screamed in terror and the crowd began to scatter every which way, Kieli sank nervelessly to her knees where she stood, staring at the almost headless corpse.

Still lying weakly on the ground in front of the body, Harvey stiffly turned his head and looked at Kieli. Something sticky clung to his cheeks, and he looked as though he might cry.

Oh, I was wrong, Kieli realized in that moment.

That wasn't the lady.

In that dream, the one holding the ax and staring at the corpse...

...was me.

An area on the left side of his torso was mummified the same way as his left hand: the flesh was shrunken as if all the moisture had evaporated away at once, and his ribs stood out clearly underneath his too-taut skin. That was where that woman had clung to him before she'd turned into a skeleton, Harvey remembered. He didn't like to look at it, so he smoothed his shirt back down to cover it again. Then he had another fit of coughing.

"Geez, you're a mess," said the black beast that spoke in human words, the unidentifiable creature that'd said that his name meant "Mane" (so Harvey'd decided to go ahead and call him that). His boyish voice didn't sound particularly upset about it.

"The stone's power must've sucked those parts into itself."

"Will he...get better?" Kieli asked uneasily. She'd been watching silently by his side.

"It doesn't look fatal...but I can't say for sure whether it'll heal or not." The beast blinked his dark brown eye and his amber eye, and glanced sidelong at Kieli while deftly turning just one eye to meet Harvey's. "See, this isn't an injury or something; it's his true form," he said, and shrugged in a

strangely human way, regarding them with a strangely human expression.

Then Mane had left, telling them "Wait here" before launching into a four-legged run toward somewhere deep in the gorge. He used protrusions in the rock as footholds, vaulting easily from one to the next, until before long his black form melted into the night and disappeared.

They'd slipped out of town, and now they were camping out by the fault line to the north for the time being. Rock ledges so sheer that Harvey couldn't even see the tops cut in front of and behind and back upon each other to form an intricately winding ravine; he could make out only one of the twin moons, indistinctly visible in one of the thin, irregular scraps of night sky above.

Owooo...nn...

Wind groaned along the rock walls, echoing faintly and sounding very much like a beast howling in the distance.

In the beginning Harvey sat down with his back propped against the rock wall, but before long sitting up straight was too hard, and he doubled over. Probably the stone had taken out part of his digestive organs or something around there, and now they were malfunctioning. He had to say, the fact that this didn't present a clear and present danger to his life meant his body was a pretty crude piece of work. Anyway, he had a feeling it was going to take some time to get used to the uncomfortable sensation that half his insides were made of papier-mâché now.

"Are you okay?"

Kieli peered at him worriedly. He shoved her a little farther away with his elbow. Once there was just the right distance between them for talking, he consciously pitched his voice downward. "Kieli…why did you say a thing like that?"

Kieli was kneeling on the ground with her feet tucked under her now. From the look on her face, she clearly didn't understand what she was being scolded for at first. "That man died, you know. He wasn't a Church Soldier. Just one of the townspeople. He could barely handle his gun." Come to think of it, Harvey got the feeling something gross was still stuck to him, right around the edge of his peripheral vision, so he wiped his cheek off roughly on his sleeve.

Kieli shifted a little, looking uncomfortable. Evidently she understood what he was saying now. She pouted and defended herself, though, even if she did it in a soft, cowed voice. "But," she argued, "it was to save you, Harvey. That makes it self-defense, you know."

"I—" Harvey's voice choked up before he could finish the sentence, and he had to swallow. There was a burning pain deep in his throat that made swallowing rough. "…I don't want you saying things like that. For my sake or not." He knew that he was imposing his own selfishness on her by saying this. He did get that. He did get that he had no right to talk when he'd killed so many people himself. Nonetheless, he didn't want Kieli of all people to have those savage feelings. "Promise me you'll never say that again. Please…"

His voice splintered painfully coming up his throat. He couldn't go on any further. He stopped talking there and watched Kieli's face. He'd figured she'd agree, but Kieli stubbornly shook her head without looking up. Clenching both hands into tight fists on top of her knees, she said quietly and rapidly, "I…I don't mind killing a person or two if it's for you."

Smack.

Harvey reflexively slapped her. The radio couldn't let *that* pass by without intervening. *"Master…!"* He—he hadn't hit her that hard, but the fact was that he *had* hit her. Kieli put a hand to her cheek, looking stunned. Harvey was even more stunned by what he'd done than she was, though.

"No, Kieli, I didn't mean to hit you—"

He could say that all he wanted, but it didn't change reality. He was just making excuses. When he leaned forward with that same hand to touch her cheek, Kieli flinched back, maybe expecting him to hit her again. That reaction was so heartbreaking that he instantly snatched his hand away. In the same instant Kieli popped to her feet, bag and coat whipping out around her, and took off running in a random direction.

"Kieli, wait…"

Harvey tried to go after her, but he fell over again before he'd quite managed to stand up. Swearing quietly, he used protrusions in the rock to help himself to his feet and began tottering after her with one hand on the cliff wall for balance. But Kieli was gone, vanished somewhere among the criss-crossing rock ledges. She did have the radio with her, but he couldn't depend on it in that state—if they got separated in a place like this—

BoooOOOOOOooo…

There was a low rumbling sound and the ground beneath

him began to shake enough for him to lose his footing and almost fall down again. The rock walls on all sides vibrated until he could feel the tremors reverberating in the pit of his stomach.

What the…?

A narrow beam of light similar to a searchlight's shone through a gap in the rock walls ahead of him, lighting up the area. Unable to pinpoint the source of the earth tremors, Harvey pointed his feet toward the source of the light and started walking. As soon as he made his way through the narrow gap between the rock faces into the relatively open valley beyond, a great circle of light assaulted his eyes.

The abrupt change from dark night made him dizzy; he shielded his eyes with his hand and peered until somewhere between the phantom afterimages burned into his retinas he could just about make out an enormous shape covering the whole valley floor, with that light like a single giant eye in the center—a structure with rows of great gray wheels on either side fully the height of an adult person; a structure Harvey thought must be a vehicle. He couldn't judge how long it was, since the end of one side disappeared beyond what he could see of the valley, but in both size and appearance it reminded him of the ships that traveled the Sand Ocean. The crucial difference between this and a sand ship, however, was that it was kicking up sand as it *drove along the ground*.

Then he saw Kieli, frozen like an animal in the headlights. When he tried to run up to her, a section of the structure slid to one side to reveal a rectangular tunnel like a hatchway, and someone's arm shot out and grabbed Kieli by the waist. In no time, she disappeared into the wall, leaving only an echo of her scream behind.

"Kieli!

After a moment so stunned that he almost forgot to go after her, Harvey snapped back to himself and followed, jumping through the hatch door just as it closed. It thudded heavily back into place immediately afterward, cutting off the roaring noise and the bright light so that his senses of sight and hearing both felt smothered. The inside of the place reminded him of a sand ship's bottom, too. It was a closed-off, darkish space thick with the smells of iron rust and fossil fuel. A steep staircase stretched out in front of him. He could hear footsteps somewhere near the top: shrill against the sheet metal flooring, but coming in long, unhurried strides. And there were Kieli's muffled pleas for release, too. Harvey put his hand to one wall and climbed up after her, carefully but quickly.

Once up the stairs and through the narrow doorway above them, he came out into the open air again, into a place that was probably equivalent to what you'd call the "outer deck" of a sand ship.

"Whoa," he blurted when he took a good look around the deck in the pale moonlight.

It was less like a vehicle here, and more as though a (very small) city had been constructed right here on deck. A very different sort of city than modern-day ones, though. Before his eyes were rows of structures you would never see in the average city, tall and shaped like smokestacks. Thick pipes stuck out of the tips and sides of each smokestack, crisscrossing each other like meshwork over his head. Here and there columns of white smoke rose into the sky. The sight made Harvey feel exactly as if he'd been sucked into some enormous machine, which automatically reminded him of a certain other place in his memory.

"What? No, no," said a boy's voice from overhead. Harvey looked up to see a beast black enough to be almost indistinguishable against the night sky sitting on one of the pipes all curled up into a ball and looking as if someone had perched him there for decoration. His amber right eye stood out eerily in the darkness.

"It wasn't the girl I wanted you to carry here; it was the man... The girl can walk on her own."

"Let me *go!*"

The owner of the arms that had snatched Kieli, the large form carrying her over his shoulder, had so far ignored her struggles and walked sedately onward. At the sound of the voice, though, it obediently deposited her on the deck. Harvey ran over to her where she'd flopped down on her rear, and shielded her with his own body as he looked up at the unknown figure. When he got a good look at it, his eyes widened. A large, misshapen man with slack green-tinged skin as though his cells had grown and grown and then melted away—it took no thought whatsoever for Christoph to spring to mind—but junk parts and scraps of metal that must be wreckage from some of these structures on the deck were stuck all over its body like poorly made armor, and two or three bent pipes stuck out of its back at an angle in just the same way they were sticking out of all the smokestacks overhead.

"I apo-lo-gize," the figure said in a mechanical voice, and took a step back. About half of its face was hidden behind metal plating, preventing Harvey from reading its expression; that and the lack of any inflection in its voice gave him an impression of emotionlessness.

"I keep telling you, quit automatically being on guard all the time. *That's* way less dangerous than I am," broke in a boyish voice with all the easy inflection his companion lacked. Apparently Mane *was* actually aware that he was dangerous.

This place…

Harvey took in the sights around him. Everything was covered in rust, so old it was a miracle it was still running, and very definitely not made with today's technology. He knew another city existed elsewhere that was very like this one, but even bigger. All the buildings were relics of the pre-War culture's technology, from back when fossil fuels had been plentiful.

"The 'first radio tower'…?"

"Ah, I thought you might know it. It is sometimes called that, so you're right."

When Harvey looked up, he could see a steel tower even taller than all the rest, piercing through the network of pipes that formed a thick ceiling overhead and jutting into the night sky. It was topped with an antenna. This was the truth behind the mirage he'd seen from the train—

It was what, for a while after the War ended, people had called "the first radio tower."

CHAPTER 5

IN THE LYRICS OF AN OLD, OLD SONG...

Once upon a time.

Well, it had probably been decades at most, but from his perspective it had been a long, long time ago.

Once upon a time, he'd had an owner.

That owner had given him a name. It was a word with a mysterious ring to it, with a pronunciation that struck speakers of this planet's language as foreign. His owner had said it was from a verse in an old, old song.

That song, that music, was from a different planet. According to his owner, it was from long before the pioneering era even, from the mother planet.

In today's language, said his owner, *it means "Mane."*

Before that day, he had always hated the strange, stiff fur around his neck. After he got his name, though, he came to like his fur.

In the lyrics of an old song, this is what they called a mane.

Even more than the name itself, he had loved best the voice of his owner when he explained it.

He, his owner, and his owner's helper traveled all around the planet together. Their job was to teach many different people about the pleasures of music, and disseminate many different pieces of music.

But one day, white people with weapons attacked their home.

They resisted, and after a struggle they managed to escape. However, he and his owner's assistant were wounded, and they both died soon after. His owner had a deep wound in his chest, too. His owner's heart had split into pieces, and so he tried giving his dead friends each a piece of it.

In hindsight, that was a very foolish thing to do. Day after day, week after week, he and the assistant writhed in agony as all their blood boiled and blisters swelled and then burst all over their skin. When the agony finally subsided, their bodies were so distorted that it was hard to remember their original shapes.

Out of his right mind and starving, Mane half-ate his owner.

Now you see, normally his owner would never have died from something like that. His owner had what Mane had

thought was a life everlasting. However, with half of his heart gone, for the first time his owner didn't regenerate.

Mane's owner's life ended there, leaving the two of them behind in their new misshapen bodies.

In the context of that life that had already been long enough to fairly call "eternal," his death just came so suddenly and easily, so flatly that Mane couldn't even work up any tears over it.

Puckered skin as if all the cells had boiled, melted, and dried; gnarled and horribly crooked fingers. The armored man's strange hand called up still-fresh memories of Christoph's, and Harvey couldn't help it: it hurt to look at them. The armored man had identified himself as the assistant of this radio tower's late station chief, and although his hands looked clumsy, they were deftly gripping screwdrivers and tinkering with parts of the disassembled radio with an ease born of long practice.

They were on the second floor of the steel tower in the center of the land ship's deck—the radio tower's station office. The room they were in was full of bulky mechanical equipment. Harvey guessed it was one of those "studio booths."

"If I use these parts, I can re-place the worn-out cir-cuit board. How-e-ver," the assistant explained, raising his face from the radio, "I do not think that will hold a-ny mean-ing for you." His words were polite and fluent, but they sounded almost flat, and his voice got thick and mechanical in spots. It made his speech as weird to listen to as Mane's peculiar intonation, in a whole different way.

The assistant's professional conclusion was what Harvey'd more or less expected since learning that the partial amnesia came from a faulty circuit board. The Corporal's spirit was completely dependent on that circuit board now—which meant that even though they could fix the radio itself by replacing it, it wouldn't be able to form the Corporal's character anymore.

"Is there any other way?"

"It's al-so pos-si-ble to keep this cir-cuit board and patch on-ly the bad cir-cuits. But I be-lieve that will on-ly pro-vide tem-por-a-ry life sup-port. What-e-ver we do, this board will be dead be-fore long." At the words "dead before long" Harvey thought he heard someone gasp outside the room, but that someone's presence pulled away almost immediately, so Harvey kept his peace too, and let it be. The man's toneless voice continued. "If I were to give my o-pin-ion...I think it would be best to leave it like this." He sounded mechanical and emotionless, yet at the same time Harvey got the feeling he sensed something surprisingly human behind those words. The man probably *had* been a normal person, to begin with. Listening to him talk, Harvey had gradually figured out that the mechanical way of talking was due to some sort of artificial voice box in his throat.

He couldn't give a decision right there and then. "...Let me think for a little bit," he sighed glumly.

"That's fine. Shall I put it back to-ge-ther for now?"

"Please."

The assistant returned wordlessly to his task.

Harvey peered out the doorway into the hall. There wasn't any illumination in the corridor itself, and the soft glow spilling out of the room painted a dark gray rectangle of light on the floor. A black animal moved slowly within the dimness. His right eye looked once to Harvey, and then the fickle creature turned away as if to say he didn't feel like listening to any heavy conversations, scrambled nimbly up the metal ladder on the wall, and disappeared.

Right beside the door where Mane had just been, a slight girl was standing against the wall, looking down at the floor.

"You understood him, didn't you?" Harvey asked, but Kieli didn't look up; she only held her body stiff, pushing her back into the wall hard enough to make Harvey wonder if she was trying to physically embed herself in it, and kept firmly silent. Although she at least hadn't tried to run away again, ever since the incident (...the slap...) at the mouth of the valley, she hadn't said a word to him and wouldn't meet his eyes. They'd never finished that suspended conversation.

So Harvey brought up a different conversation that he'd suspended in his own mind instead.

"Kieli, I think it's okay to leave the Corporal this way now."

Kieli's shoulders shook, and she raised her face for the barest of instants to give him an accusing glare. But then she looked right back down again and continued to say nothing, so in the end Harvey just went on by himself. He'd been thinking about this ever since they'd been on the train. Knowing it would render this whole trip pointless made him keep freezing during the moments when he could have brought it up, though.

He propped his elbow against the wall over Kieli's head and leaned in, thinking hard and trying to remember what he'd been planning to say as he slowly began addressing himself to the back of Kieli's hair. Probably he was partly trying to organize his own thoughts; to convince himself of them as much as he was trying to convince her.

"Listen...back in the beginning, the goal of our trip was to take the Corporal to his grave, right? The one a walk down the Easterbury tracks, through the tunnel, at that place where you can see the winch tower at the mine. So I know a lot of time's ended up going by, but…" Somewhere along the way his voice had gotten hoarse. Harvey was pretty sure he didn't usually choose his words this carefully as he talked, but somehow his sentences kept getting drawn out like he was making excuses, though for what exactly, he couldn't say. He swallowed, and tried again. "I think…it might be good for the three of us to go to Easterbury together again, and this time we can return the Corporal to his grave like he wanted."

He stopped talking there, and waited a little. Kieli stayed stubbornly silent, but Harvey'd gone into this intending to wait as long as it took to get some kind of response, so he settled himself into watch-and-wait mode. After a while like that, at last she grudgingly opened her mouth.

"…The Corporal can't go away," she said, still glaring fixedly at the tips of her boots. And that was all.

Harvey could tell he just wasn't going to get through to her in this state, and the longer he went on the more he lost confidence that he was really all right with it himself, so in the end he gave up and didn't say anything more.

He wanted a smoke anyway, so he went out onto the deck by himself and took a little walk around the outside of the station office.

"Brrr…"

He knew it was the end of winter, but here in the ravine the air was bitingly cold. The strong wind groaned like a beast howling in the distance, whisking away his cigarette smoke almost too fast to see.

They were making their way through the gorge at a relatively slow pace, but even so, out on the deck the noise of the fossil-fuel engine beat loudly at his eardrums, and the scrape of the wheels against the rocky ground sent vibrations right up through his legs. From here, the only visible sources of light were the round headlight at the ship's prow that illuminated the rock walls along their path and the single moon shining indistinctly through the narrow scraps of sky above. The contours of the smokestack-like buildings making up the mobile radio station, the mass of piping overhead, and the rocky walls of the gorge on either side stood out faintly under their weak glow.

Harvey had heard stories about a mobile radio station that had traveled to towns all around the planet for a little over twenty years after the end of the War, setting up the circuit boards of today's guerrilla radio stations. That was the "first radio tower." The guerrilla stations scattered around their planet today weren't operating in concert as a single station; they were all just operated individually by interested volunteers, and had each built up their own individual histories. But legend had it that if you traced those histories back to their beginnings, you would find that all of them shared a common ancestor in the first radio tower.

However, after twenty years of post-War operation, it had been all but destroyed in a Church crackdown. People said it had managed to escape, badly beaten up, but nobody had seen or heard of it since.

To think that mobile radio station had been hiding in this gorge… "We weren't actually hiding," Mane had explained to him earlier. He said they'd been in a remote area even farther west than the northwest ruins before, but they were moving east little by little, and they'd been staying in this gorge for the past several years. That jibed with the time people in the town south of here said the mirage had started appearing; apparently the light refraction created by the crisscrossing rock ledges made the mirage of the ship appear in a different location than the ship itself, and that had been what started the town talking. When the radio tower came close to the gorge entrance, the mirage appeared and its own radio waves mingled with the local guerrilla station's frequency. That must have been the sound the Corporal had momentarily picked up on the train, too.

According to Mane, the only parts of this place that were in working order were the central steel tower with the antenna and the station office at its base; all the other structures, even the ones that looked intact, were more or less ruins on the inside by this point. Walking around the steel towers, Harvey could see the scars of a vicious attack. Made by Church Soldiers, and most likely ones with carbonization guns—the guns of the Undying Hunters. Maybe on paper their aim had been to crack down on the guerrilla radio stations, but their real goal must have been the fossil-fuel crystal on board.

Mane said this mobile building with the smokestack-shaped towers so different from modern-day buildings at its core was built during the pre-War era. Which meant that while popular belief held that the only pre-War technology still in operation was that of the capital, the mechanical city, there were other specimens here that were still alive and kicking, if only barely. Apparently there was a power reactor with a pre-War fossil-fuel crystal directly below the station office, in what you'd call the lower deck if this were a sand ship. When Harvey directed his attention that way, he felt as though somewhere amid the engine noise filling the deck he could sense something ever so faintly resonating with the core inside him.

He placed his hand on one of the steel tower's supports as he looked up toward the top of it, and then abruptly lowered his eyes to focus on that hand. He glared bitterly at the thin fingers, the prominent joints, and cursed.

...He couldn't believe he'd raised a hand against Kieli, even if it had been a reflex. Why hadn't he been able to say what he thought in words before it came to that?

I don't mind killing a person or two— Harvey thought she hadn't really meant it—probably she was just being stubborn, and she'd blurted it out without fully digesting her own words first. He really believed that. But even so, had she always been so blind to the people around her? She'd always been pigheaded, but most of the time he'd been able to read what she was thinking, and yet now he couldn't quite tell. It was as if an opaque wall had gone up between them or something.

He squeezed his hand into a tight fist. Just as he was lifting it to punch the steel pole in front of him and vent some of his frustration, he heard a mocking laugh from somewhere above his head.

"If you do anything too stupid, you're going to break that hand, you know," a boyish voice said, controlling its laughter. Harvey raised his face, fist still suspended in midair, to see the black beast's shadow looking down at him from midway up the tower. He was curled up into a ball shape with his hind legs twined around the metal ladder, and grinning at him with that dog's face that sometimes made eerily human expressions. From the moment Harvey'd first seen him, he'd sensed something kindred—he could vaguely tell that this beast had a "core" in the center of its torso. It wasn't that he could clearly see it with his eyes, exactly; he guessed it was more like seeing a heat response with a thermoscope. The shape of the heat he could see wasn't a perfect circle, though. It looked like a misshapen fragment.

Harvey clicked his tongue irritably and brought his hand down, then brought it to his left side as he started to cough, doubling over a little. He could feel how wrongly his ribs stuck out even through his clothes. The hand pressing against them was more wasted away than before, too, and all the joints and blood vessels bulged unnaturally.

The beast's earlier words came back to him: *This is his true form*. He figured that was true enough. By rights, he'd have turned into a mummy or something long ago now, or else he'd have gone even past the decomposed body stage and be just a skeleton, like the woman in that mansion.

Glaring sharply up the tower, Harvey changed the subject.

"You got your core from an *original* Undying…isn't that right?"

"Yep. He was the station chief," said Mane, and then added, "He's dead now, though" in a voice that sounded almost disgusted, somehow.

Dead. The beast had declared it so easily, but outside of some really seriously drastic circumstances, there was no such thing as "death" for a normal Undying. Which meant that Undying hadn't been normal. The fact that Mane had a partial core meant the core left in the Undying's heart had to have been partial too—so probably he hadn't been able to rely on his ordinary imperviousness to death in that imperfect state.

...Just like I can't.

"Say, if that girl happens to die before you do, will you give her your heart, too?" Mane suddenly asked, twitching the corners of his gaping mouth into an unpleasant smile. It was a question that didn't even deserve an answer. When Harvey only raised an irritated eyebrow at him, Mane shrugged his shoulders in a way nothing like a four-legged animal, and withdrew it without fuss. "I'm joking." Then he folded his ears, strangely canine in that gesture. Harvey still had questions to ask, but Mane didn't seem keen on a long conversation. With one last grin that was really more ghoulish than human, he withdrew slowly into the shadows, disappearing behind the steel pole.

His final whisper was swallowed up by the engine noise.

"But she might be okay with that idea, you know..."

Harvey went back inside the station office, and was just about to enter the booth on the second floor when he realized he could hear someone's voice coming from the small room next to it. He'd thought she was asleep, so he was a little surprised. When he peeked around the doorway of the unlit room, he saw a camp bed set up in one corner. The black hair of the girl lying in it was escaping out the side of the blanket she'd pulled over her.

"I first met you and Harvey when I was fourteen. I met you at Easterbury station—oh, I was wearing a boarding school uniform. I had an all-black uniform, and black shoes, and a shoulder bag, and a grouchy face. I pretty much looked just like one of those 'apprentice witch' girls…"

Her voice was so soft you'd almost think she was mumbling in her sleep, but it looked as though she was talking to the radio by her pillow. She paid out each sentence slowly, dwelling lovingly on every word as if she were telling a favorite story.

As Harvey listened, he felt as if he really might see that fourteen-year-old girl in front of him any moment. He remembered: an all-black uniform, and black shoes, and a shoulder bag, and a grouchy face—yeah, that's exactly what she'd looked like when they met. *Now that I think about it, I treated her really harshly back then, didn't I?* He grew uncomfortable remembering it, though he realized it was a little late for that now.

"…and then you got mad at Becca for her prank, and you got all violent, and things were crazy."

"Who is this 'Becca'?"

"She was my good friend. She's gone now…And then we got on a train, and went to all kinds of places. We even rode a ship on the Sand Ocean. I remember some sand got inside you, and you were complaining the whole time that it felt all rough."

"Mmm, it's not coming back to me."

At the radio's vague response, Kieli gave a short, slightly lonely sounding laugh. "Oh. Well, you and Harvey got in some big fights sometimes, too."

"What? I would never fight with the master!"

"Ahaha. When you were your normal self, you and Harvey didn't do anything *but* fight! Usually it was just you being angry, though."

"I just can't believe that. Did I hate him, then?"

"No, no. You were always chewing him out, but really you liked him a lot."

"Hey, don't say that in the past tense," the radio protested at once in a staticky voice.

"Sorry, you're right," answered Kieli's voice, giggling. "That's right; you still do. You forgot about things, but you still like Harvey just like before. That's one thing you never forgot, huh?...I'm glad. I'm really glad about that. Thank you..."

Silence fell for a little while. The rustle of fabric sounded in the darkness and then went away again. Kieli's voice started up again, muffled through the blankets she'd buried her face in. "Corporal, please remember...You're fun the way you are now, too, but it just won't do. I'm sorry. I'm sorry for saying this. But the way you are now won't do. Please, please protect Harvey the way you did before..."

Oh, crap.

All at once it was just too much, and Harvey felt something about to snap. He drew back into the shadowy side of the doorway, out of sight. Then he slid down the wall to the ground and put his palm over his mouth to hold in his breath and his feelings both. He'd forced in more air than he could hold, and his lungs we burning. More importantly, his heart hurt...He wished he hadn't eavesdropped.

Come to think of it, her feelings had always been directed straight at him; that had never changed once since she was fourteen. He ought to be grateful, and he *was*, but even more than that, he felt heavy-hearted. Unless she took off her blinders and started to see the people around them more, too, he was pretty sure she was screwed. *I can't be the center of your world, Kieli; it just won't do. I mean, if you stay like this, I wouldn't be able to go anywhere. I'll never be able to leave you behind again. Once I'm gone, what are you going to do?!*

He sat there for a while, holding his head and not letting himself think anymore. He lifted his gaze a little when he heard metallic footsteps approaching. A man's legs stood in front of him: misshapen metal plating stuck to puckered skin.

"Are you all right?"

"...Ah, yeah," Harvey answered, nodding. He started to pick himself somewhat unsteadily up off the ground. The armored man held his arm and helped him stand.

By then, he wasn't hearing any murmurs from the other side of the doorway anymore. When he peeked inside, the blanket was moving up and down to the accompaniment of quiet, rhythmic breathing. He walked softly up to the bed, careful not to make any noise, and looked down at the sleeping face of the girl curled up in her blanket, which she'd pulled all the way up over her nose. Her forehead was wrinkled a little, as if she was frowning, and her cheeks were stiff. It wasn't what anyone could call a placid face.

Faint static bled from the radio at her pillow, and then Harvey heard a subdued voice.

"Master."

"Mm?" It was getting to the point where he couldn't bring himself to care enough to correct the stupid "Master" thing anymore, so he just let it slide.

"Can I ask you to fix me? He can patch the bad circuits, right?"

Harvey transferred his gaze from the girl to the radio, more than a little surprised. He hadn't actually expected a request from the Corporal himself. He didn't have real awareness of his amnesia, and Harvey'd gotten the impression that he didn't have any particular interest in his own repair.

He thought for a few seconds, but for now his opinion was still the same.

"...I don't like the idea." The armored man, who'd been watching silently at the doorway, took over the explanation.

"We would on-ly be ju-ry-rigg-ing them. You would not get much bet-ter. I be-lieve you will last long-er if we don't in-ter-fere."

"I want to remember," the radio interrupted him, raising his voice a bit for emphasis. Kieli stirred in her sleep, so he quickly quieted down, and the rest was low enough to almost get lost in the static. *"...Listen. I don't understand why this girl is tormenting herself so much about this. I listened to her talk-*

ing just now, and frankly, I still didn't really get it. So I can't say anything to help—not 'Don't worry' or 'Cheer up' or anything. I could've said those things before, right? I was more useful before, wasn't I…?"

The radio's voice faded away into the static, and silence fell for a while.

But when you came right down to it, if the man in question said to do it, Harvey had no reason to refuse him.

"…Okay, then," he agreed, sighing.

Then he looked down at the floor and added a mumbled, "Thanks."

"The wind feels so nice…" Kieli murmured as soon as she went outside that morning, and then felt a little dismayed at herself. Apparently whatever was going on, a good night's sleep made a person feel better, at least a little. Well, maybe "feel better" wasn't quite it. It felt more like during the course of the night someone had cut off power to her head, and she was in a daze because her higher brain functions hadn't started back up yet.

I should take a little walk and get my brain in gear. When she left the radio tower with the station office and started walking around the deck, a four-legged black beast padded lightly after her, not too close and not too far away. *Maybe he's trying to be my guard, or something…?*

Kieli turned around a little without stopping, and asked flatly, "Did Harvey put you up to this?"

"Yep," agreed Mane, unruffled. She silently faced forward again. Mane followed her without saying anything either.

A fresh morning wind blew through the gorge, dispelling the yellow-sand smog at the bottom. The mobile radio station was making its leisurely way through the spaces between the gradually winding rock walls. The deck was awash in sounds as she walked: the muffled sound of the engine, so much like a sand ship's, and the sound of wheels scraping along rock, which on the other hand was definitely different from the noise made by a sand ship's screw propellers.

Maybe this whole radio station was one great grave. Kieli couldn't quite say why, but that was the impression she got as she looked around her.

Pale, sandy sunshine filtered down from narrow scraps of sky she could see through the web of pipes above her, faintly illuminating the crowd of buildings that looked like fat smokestacks. Now that she got a fresh look at the place in daylight, she could see that several of the smokestacks had been laid waste in an attack, and that even some of the ones that hadn't were seriously damaged or bore marks that looked like bullet wounds. It must have been a livelier place once, with all of them operating noisily together, but now there was only the smoke rising out of a few exhaust pipes on the roof in the center, where the station office was.

Kieli came through two smokestacks into a slightly more open area. Now the end of the deck was visible in front of her, and beyond that the ravine's narrow, gently winding path stretching on and on, hemmed in by rock walls. A long tail of thick smoke from the exhaust pipes marked the way they'd come. It looked as though she'd come to what she'd call the "stern" if this were a sand ship.

She had let her hair grow long; a strong gust of smog-filled wind sent it whipping in all directions. If she didn't cut it again pretty soon, it would get as long as it had been before she cut it two years ago.

I don't think I want that. Maybe I should cut it . . .

Come to think of it, hadn't she thought that before, and then never gotten around to doing it in the end?

When Kieli got it all back under control and raised her face again, she stopped walking and stood stupefied with one hand still holding her hair down.

Someone was standing on the edge of the deck. It was a fairly elderly gentleman. He was pretty muscular, but he seemed like the gentle sort. Kieli was sure she couldn't have seen him before, but somehow she still felt as if they'd met somewhere. Quite recently, in fact.

And then all of a sudden the man, who had been standing at the stern watching the valley unroll behind them, turned his head. Kieli started, thinking he'd noticed her, when a casual voice behind her called "Hey!" and someone else came running right by her on his way to the man. The newcomer was a much younger man than the one at the stern. He was carrying a bulging cardboard box in both hands and tottering somewhat as he ran. A blackish dog of about medium size scurried after him.

"Welcome back, Chief."

"Yeah, good to see you! Come on, just look at this. I made a great buy today!"

In direct contrast to the old man, who welcomed him in exactly the calm tones Kieli'd expected, the youth bounded over shouting like a child, finally putting the box down in front of his elder, who watched with a wry smile while he crouched down right on the spot as if he couldn't wait another second, and started rummaging among its contents. The man seemed quite a bit older, but from his deferential manner she deduced that the youth must be in the position with more authority here.

Dozens of what looked like flat, square boards were crammed inside the cardboard box; the young man pulled out one after another and showed them off, explaining each one excitedly.

"I got hold of some seriously great songs. Look, there's this one, and this one, oh, and this one, too... I didn't think there were any more copies left, but I guess it's all about knowing where to look. Now, this one here is the last one by a band I really love. Heh, that old guy at the secondhand shop doesn't have a clue what they're worth, so I got them practically free! Man, what a good deal..." He chattered on in such high spirits that Kieli had to grin just watching him.

"Chief, I can't remember them all if you tell me all at once like that. I'll learn them later while we listen to them one at a time," the older man interjected, sounding a little put out, but smiling just like Kieli.

Those were "records"... She recognized them; there was an old record player at the bar on the parish border, too. The bartender had only a few of them, so he didn't use the player that often, though (evidently there'd been lots of them there in the previous bartender's days, but since they were of restricted music, they'd been confiscated).

"And now, the moment you've been waiting for: this is today's top find!" announced the youth dramatically, livening up the party enough for all three of them all by himself as he drew out the final record and thrust it proudly in front of the dog next to him, who'd been watching the whole affair curiously. Naturally, being a dog, the dog only looked confused. It was a mongrel; short-haired overall, but the fur around its neck was thick and stood stiffly out, and his face was long in kind of a goofy-looking way. The twin amber eyes set in its black face glanced about restlessly, trying to look at everything at once.

Kieli was pretty sure the dog didn't understand what was going on, but the youth insistently thrust the record jacket at him and demanded, "What do you think? Pretty great, huh?" as he stuck his other hand into the hair at its neck and started ruffling and scratching. Instead of showing interest in the record, the dog stretched its neck out as if to say "Pet me more!"

"Aw, come on! You're supposed to be happy about *this*! I've been looking everywhere for this, just so I could play it for you. It's a really old song, from back before the pioneering era, even. It's in here—you know, *that* lyric. Remember how I told you about it before? 'In the lyrics of an old song'—"

The image broke up with a *poof* and dissolved.

The youth, the dog, and the man: all of them were gone, and so were any signs that they'd just been there at all. Instead, the tip of the deserted stern hosted a single pale, rectangular stone.

A gravestone...

Had that been a memory stitched into the air at this spot...?

After Kieli had stood unmoving there for a while, her mind blank, she felt something fluffy tickle the back of her hand. Something warm and alive. A strange-looking, jet-black beast with a long coat of hair like a mane around his neck had come silently up to her and sat down at her side on its hind legs, like dogs were trained to do.

"Mane, was that...your owner?"

"Yeah, well. He'd lived all that time, but he was no better than a little kid. That assistant started out younger in the beginning, and before you knew it he'd passed right by him and turned into a proper old man, but *he* stayed a kid on the inside the whole time, never mind the outside," railed Mane with a sniff of his black nose. Kieli wondered if all Undyings were like children, and then had to smile at the thought.

"So, you really were a dog."

"So?! What the heck does it matter what animal I was before?"

Apparently he really hated being treated as a dog (not that she hadn't known that from the day they met). Mane turned his head away from her, miffed. The hind leg that had gotten shot in town was still swapped out for the thick new one with the talons that made Kieli think of a giant bird, and his tail was like a mountain lion's. She had to admit he looked far different now than his original dog form had. "I ate all kinds of stuff and took it into my body, until after a while even I forgot what I started out looking like." When he let his tongue loll out, Kieli realized it was more like a calf's than a dog's: more cylindrical. And it was also dyed blood red.

She turned her gaze back to the gravestone in front of her. Probably there wasn't actually a body buried underneath it, since it was standing on a steel-plate-reinforced deck. This marker had been built even with no body to bury, just to record the fact that that person had been here, once.

"...He was a fool," his boyish voice murmured softly. "He would've been able to imagine what would happen if he put a core into someone else's corpse if he'd thought about it for two seconds, but at the time he didn't even try to think about it."

And then Mane told her a little bit about his past. About when they were traveling around the planet to tell people about restricted music and guerrilla radio stations, and about when they were attacked by Church Soldiers, and about when Mane and the assistant got hurt and died, and his Undying owner was hurt so badly his core cracked. Out of a fierce desire to save Mane and his assistant, Mane's owner had planted fragments of his own broken core into their bodies, hoping it might help. It was only after trying it that it came home to him just what that would do, and he was thunderstruck.

Mane thrashed and writhed at the anguish and the burning heat as if he'd swallowed molten lead. His owner, said Mane, had held him in his arms and kept him as still as he could, apologizing over and over. They went for days—probably many, many days—like that, until at some point Mane blinked awake to see a sea of blood and torn flesh all around him...and that he'd eaten half of his owner's body.

"...Did you resent him?"

"No. I liked him."

It was a forthright, honest answer.

"True, he did something he shouldn't have done. But that didn't matter to me. To me, the only miscalculation was...that he died before me."

After those last few words, Mane suddenly got cross and clammed up, maybe thinking he'd talked too much for too long.

The two of them stood still before the gravestone, and neither spoke again for a while. Fresh morning wind ruffled through the hair at Mane's neck, caressing the surface of the stone as it passed.

A tear rolled down Kieli's cheek.

Mane gave a shocked yelp. One moment she was casting her gaze downward, and the next she'd plopped right down to the deck floor and buried her face in her knees. "What's gotten into you?! Did I say something wrong?!" Mane asked in a panic, the tip of his nose as well as his animal breath tickling her ear as he tried to peer into her face. Kieli shook her head without lifting it.

"I-I wanted to hang in there and do my best, and I tried, but nothing turned out right, and it kind of seems like I just made it *worse*, and we're always just missing or not understanding each other, and...why won't it go *right*...?" Her own teary voice sounded muffled to her between her knees. "It's—it's like the harder and harder I try to, to protect what I care about, the more something keeps going wrong…but, I know I'd regret it if I didn't do anything! I just, don't know what to do anymore…"

"Hey—no, I don't want you crying on me. Hold on, I'll go get your owner." She sensed Mane turn around, about to leave, so she instinctively reached out a hand and grabbed his tail, making him shriek. "Not the tail! Not the tail!" He wagged it violently, shaking Kieli's hand off, but after circling around her a few times looking reluctantly resigned, he sat down in front of her, presenting her with his back. "Here," he said gruffly.

With a choked wail, Kieli pressed her face into the fur of his back to silence her sobs. The black hair there was stiff and wiry at the tip, but once she buried herself deeper into it, it was surprisingly nice and soft near the root. When she wrapped her hands around his neck and clung to him, beneath the lion's-mane-like fur at his chest she could faintly feel the pulse of his stone-fragment heart.

"_____ was," began the station assistant with a word whose pronunciation Harvey couldn't make out. Then he stopped for a moment, appearing to think before trying again. "…That's right, you call him 'Mane.' Then I will call him that, too. I think I un-der-stand now why Mane was in-te-res-ted in you."

"……?"

"You must re-mind him of the sta-tion chief."

"Oh, really…" From the way he said it, Harvey didn't think

he was being complimented. "I wouldn't try putting pieces of my own heart in corpses to see what happened," he argued, scowling, but the assistant just kept on tinkering at various parts with a soldering iron, his eyes cast downward to look at his work, and Harvey couldn't tell what expression was hidden behind his rusty metal plating. He seemed to be making spare parts for the radio by hand.

You must remind him—Harvey figured he'd probably phrased it as a conjecture because he had only hazy memories of the time before his death. Mane, on the other hand, had gained wisdom in the decades since he'd become immortal, transforming into something between monster and man, and supposedly he now had more precise, systematic understanding of his life before death than he'd had when he was just a dog living it.

They were in the studio booth again. Pale morning sunlight streamed in through the large window taking up most of one wall. There was a space on the other side of the window that looked as if it had once been another room, but its walls and ceiling had caved in, and it was completely exposed to the elements. Harvey surmised that it had been what they called the "mixing suite," and that all the equipment here in the booth had originally been over there, but was moved to this side after the collapse. The second floor of the two-story station office held the studio facilities and enough living space to house two or three people. The first floor contained the pilothouse, and down in the hull, functionally the "basement," lived the power reactor and engine, which together were the heart of this mobile radio station.

Harvey found himself once again subtly impressed with the accuracy of his gut. His decision to come looking for this place had been right on the mark. From the assistant's examination so far, the Corporal's radio was apparently even older than they'd thought; if they'd gone to the northwestern mining district as planned, most likely there wouldn't have been anyone there with the necessary parts and technology to repair it.

After the assistant had watched Harvey gaze at the giant sound board covered in countless dials and knobs with an air of great interest, fiddling with the knobs when it struck his fancy, he warned mildly, "I don't mind you touch-ing that, but please don't break it." Harvey withdrew his hand, not feeling confident that he knew where the borderline between "touch-ing" and "breaking" was.

"A-bout that arm of yours..." said the assistant's flat voice as he continued to repair the radio at his worktable. He looked down at the hand he'd just withdrawn. When he turned it palm-downward and fisted it lightly, the bones and veins stood out so sharply it was grotesque. The cause of it all pretty well had to be the ring that woman back at the mansion had had, the one with the fossil-fuel shard—the same moment the stone had broken, there'd been a wave of extraordinary decay that swallowed up all kinds of things in its path.

"The crys-tal used to make that ring was quite old, wa-sn't it? I don't know how many gen-e-ra-tions the fam-i-ly had it for, but if no-thing else, it was made be-fore the War. I had thought there were none ex-tant out-side this ra-di-o to-wer a-ny-more, but..."

According to the legacy of knowledge left behind in this radio tower, the fossil-fuel crystals of the advanced pre-War civilization were of even higher purity than the Undying "cores" manufactured during the War itself, and were spiritual-material objects that wielded enormous influence over things of spirit nature. As time went on, that power, sleeping in the planet's mineral veins, was drained away. Now, eighty years after the War, the mineral dregs that could still be mined had hardly any power left in them. The pre-War crystals, though, had had enough power even to give the dead the appearance of their transient mortal lives.

Hearing that, Harvey could finally see how that woman had been able to maintain her living form even after becoming a corpse. And why she'd started turning back into her true corpse form the moment the ring broke, too.

"You must have been caught up in the 're-bound' when the cry-stal broke. It seems you es-caped a fa-tal wound be-cause the cry-stal was ve-ry small, but if you had been un-lu-cky, you might not be a-ble to main-tain that bo-dy now...I am ve-ry glad it did not come to that."

As the assistant explained it, the crystals weren't particularly destructive, and their power didn't have any effect on normal humans. However, he said, "*To you and me*, they can be deadly." Power working in the opposite direction of that power to keep the dead in their living form: power to restore the normal, rightful flow of time to the departed.

Normal time, eh?

Harvey picked up the pair of clunky headphones hanging off the end of the soundboard and casually toyed with them.

After a few moments, the assistant, who had been focused on repairing the radio during their whole conversation so far, abruptly stilled his hands and looked directly at him. As always, his expression was hidden behind the metal plating, and Harvey couldn't read it.

"I see your 'cry-stal' is in the same state as our sta-tion chief's. I think you are al-rea-dy a-ware of this, but your crystal is ra-pid-ly nea-ring the end of its life span. I do not know how ma-ny more years it will last. It might be that if you were to live a qui-et life, it would last a-round the length of a human life span, but..."

He took a breath, and something in his tone turned reproving.

"You do not seem to be lea-ding the life-style of some-one who will live long."

"......"

Harvey couldn't find anything to say in his defense. He looked away and started messing around to evade the issue, putting on and taking off the headphones; when he risked a glance back, the assistant had already lowered his eyes to his table and resumed his work. He heard just one last murmur: "...Please take bet-ter care of your-self." Harvey got the feeling that it was directed more toward the man's old boss than toward him.

When he climbed the fixed access ladder that began in the station office attic and made his way up the steel tower, he came to a place about halfway up that served as a simple observation deck, boxed in by handrails. The wind was pretty strong, and he hadn't particularly been aiming to go all the way up to the top, so his motivation promptly evaporated, and he decided to take a break there.

After lighting a cigarette with his back to the wind, he turned around again to sweep his gaze over the view beyond the rails. The towering rock wall on either side flowed lazily away behind them, as did the smog spouting from the exhaust pipes on the station office roof, and the smoke of his cigarette, too. Harvey might be only halfway up, but the steel tower was still a fair bit taller than the other smokestacks, so from his vantage point the smokestacks around him and the deck below still looked small.

Sometime after he'd been leaning against the railing gazing at the view for a while...

...*Slam.*

One leg rose spasmodically and kicked hard at one of the railing's supports. The impact set the whole observation deck shaking; the sound and the vibrations might even have made their way to the station office below, but Kieli was outside right now, so there was no need to be careful. Harvey moved to kick it again, but the first one already had his leg hurting, so he changed his mind.

"It's a little late to say that now..." he grumbled to himself, slumping his body so heavily over the railing that anyone watching might half-think he was trying to throw himself over it.

It might be that if you were to live a qui-et life, it would last a-round the length of a hu-man life span...

A human life span?

It wasn't as if he'd been wishing to die peacefully of old age like a normal person, and he didn't think he had the right to, either. The next time he went to the capital, he'd go prepared never to come back—nothing anybody said could change his mind on that now…But what that meant was, he'd be deliberately discarding the option of living and dying like a normal person—the possibility that he might be able to walk through life with Kieli, in the same time as Kieli. If Kieli ever found that out…could he persuade her to accept it?

I can't tell her…

He would go to the capital. That said, he couldn't very well leave Kieli in her current condition, either. This was his fault. He'd pushed their situation to this weird breaking point because he'd been wavering back and forth, unable to make any real decisions about the future.

What is this?! I couldn't die back when I would've been glad to die anywhere, anytime, but now that dying would take hardly any effort, suddenly I can't afford to yet? What the hell am I supposed to do?

He was starting to feel like throwing up again, and not only because of the strange discomfort in his guts.

…No good. I'd better stop. If he thought any more right now, something would snap. He'd actually started thinking that it might be easier if he just threw himself over the railing for real, which was even more worrisome, so he took a big breath, sucked the tobacco smoke into his brain, and forced all the thought to empty out of it.

…dum…

Out of nowhere, a faint sound entered his empty mind. Or

maybe he'd been hearing it all along, and it just hadn't consciously registered.

...dum dum...dum.

Thick static made it hard to pick out the tune, but the wind stroking the back of his head carried an easy melody. When he slowly lifted his hanging head and turned around, a speaker fixed to a support beam above his head was playing music at low volume. Medium-tempo, bass-heavy strains filled the air on deck as they left the dry sounds of string instruments behind them in the wind at the bottom of the gorge.

At the bottom of the deep gorge, with the exit a long way off and the entrance already invisible in the distance even if they'd wanted to go back, the radio station slowly moved along, a tail of ash-gray smoke and the tones of stringed instruments stretching out behind it. Unable to see what lay ahead or behind, they still went on...moving toward some sort of conclusion, whether they liked it or not.

Hearing music start up from somewhere, Kieli lifted her face from where she'd buried it in Mane's back. She'd never heard it before, but the tune felt comfortable and calming in her ears. Mane's ears perked up and he turned them toward the source of the sound, seeming happy, making her realize it was probably the "Mane song." Kieli shut her eyes softly and listened too.

If anything, it was a stumbling melody that didn't really flow that well, like the guitarist was having trouble with his strings here and there. The low key should've given it a feeling of solidity, but for some reason it felt fragile and fleeting instead, somehow.

It definitely wasn't a pretty melody, but somehow it was deeply touching.

"It's a nice song," Kieli murmured as she listened, and Mane answered, "I like to think so," sticking up his nose as proudly as if he'd written it himself.

Where the thin beams of sunlight hit the black hair around his neck they set it gleaming golden brown, just like a real mountain lion's mane. A mangy animal planting its four painfully thin legs firmly on the peak of a rugged wilderness mountain, letting the wind blow through its dirty, tangled mane. Mangy and thin and dirty, and yet its sharp amber eyes at least never lost their vitality; they stared hard at the ground below, searching for prey.

That was Kieli's mental image of the mountain lion, king of this planet's beasts.

Kieli looked upwind at the steel tower that stood above everything around it, where the music seemed to be coming from, and saw someone perched about halfway up. He was facing in the opposite direction of the stern, letting his gaze roam toward the gorge's exit, which must lie far, far ahead yet. Depending on how you looked at it, that copper-colored hair ruffled by the wind looked every bit as much like a mountain lion's as Mane's did. What was he fixing his eyes on, and what was he thinking? From here, Kieli couldn't read his expression—but she thought that probably wasn't just because of the physical distance. She got the feeling that maybe even when they were both looking in the same direction, those

coppery eyes had always been fixed on a different final destination than the one she wished for.

She'd thought they'd traveled together all this time, but
were the destinations they'd been seeing different all along?
Had they been riding on tracks that never crossed? She'd like
to think they hadn't.

*Will we still be journeying together by the time we leave this
gorge? If we are, where will we be going? Will we be riding on
the same tracks?*

Kieli peered intently at a point just beyond the furthest reach
of the gorge that she could make out, and pictured in the back
of her mind the light of the exit that she'd probably see far,
far ahead. A thread-thin beam of light filtering down between
the steep rock ledges towering on either side at the end of the
long, dark valley—it dangled unsteadily from the heavens and
quivered, as if to symbolize her unease about the uncertain
future of their journey.

CHAPTER 6
AS THE DEEP RAVINE'S WIND HOWLS

Kieli soaked a piece of ship's biscuit in reconstituted dry milk and then put a slice of smoked meat on it. Something seemed missing. After a little thought, she tried topping it with canned chickpeas. *Yep, that's a pretty balanced meal, and it looks pretty good too.* Nodding to herself in satisfaction at her workmanship, Kieli set the tin plate in front of Mane. But he snubbed her, looking miffed.

"I told you not to treat me like a dog!"

"But you are one, aren't you?"

"I'm *not* a dog." Apparently he had no intention of acknowledging it. "And I won't die even if I don't eat anything anyway. Your owner's the same, isn't he?"

"But I made it for you…" Kieli muttered dejectedly as she started mechanically eating her own helping, all alone. She tore herself alternating pieces of ship's biscuit and smoked meat and crammed them into her mouth, stopping periodically to take a bite of the chickpeas with a spoon. The biscuit and bread were part of the standard gear she kept in her bag; she'd found the chickpeas sitting forgotten on a shelf in the station office's kitchen.

While they'd been staying on the parish border, the bartender and Yana had been there, so there'd been comparatively regular mealtimes every day. But once off on a journey, if Kieli didn't remember to secure her own food and her own time to eat it, she sometimes accidentally skipped meals. After all, the thought of "eating" just never even occurred to other members of her travel party. There was no one she could have a proper conversation with about the meals themselves, so things like variation and visual appeal fell completely by the wayside, and she ended up simply trying to ingest enough fuel for the day and calling that success.

After a while of letting her hands automatically go through the motions of pouring nutrients into her digestive system, Kieli realized that somewhere along the way Mane had come up beside her and started eating the food she'd laid out for him. When she darted a glance at him, he only shot her a grumpy sidelong look without raising his nose from his plate and continued messily eating. Kieli faced forward again too, and went back to the business of chewing her biscuit. It seemed more flavorful now than before.

Music wafted to them from the radio tower overhead, along with familiar static. It was a different song from this morning's, but it was equally bass heavy, and it made her feel nostalgic for some reason, even though she'd never heard it before.

Kieli was currently having a slightly late lunch on the doorstep of the station office, with pleasant tunes for background music.

I wonder if the expiration date on these chickpeas is okay. Well, either way I'm already eating them. These vague thoughts were interrupted when she saw a lanky redhead walking toward her from beyond the smokestacks on deck. He'd left on a walk this morning just as she was getting back to the station office.

As she watched him with her spoon still in her mouth, he noticed her, too, and gave her a *What are you eating on the steps for?* sort of look. Kieli groped for words for a while, eventually settling on, "Want some?"

Since she still had the spoon in her mouth, it came out more like "Ahnt umm?" Harvey seemed to get the message, though. Still, he gave her only the barest possible response ("Mm? Nah."). Then he passed by her at about three steps' distance and walked into the station office. With his nose in his milk, Mane twitched his ears, but didn't say anything.

Kieli watched Harvey's tall form melt into the dimness indoors with her head cocked to one side. After a little while, though, she faced forward again and resumed her meal. However, the hand transporting food to her mouth got gradually slower and slower, and eventually it stopped altogether.

She hadn't been able to talk right since that stunted conversation last night. *I forget, why are things so strained between us again? I said selfish stuff about repairing the radio and Harvey slapped me...* She put her hand to the cheek he'd slapped. *It didn't hurt, particularly. Actually, Harvey was the one who looked as though he'd been smacked hard then... huh?* As she thought about it, Kieli realized her own thoughts had gone screwy somewhere. The radio wasn't what had gotten her slapped.

Harvey had begged Kieli. Said "please," looking as if he was hurting really badly.

That's right, I did something I shouldn't have.

When she tried to think more about it, her brain froze up. It was as if a piece in the core of her mind was burnt over. That one little section was smoldering; too hot for her to touch. *What is that? I forget, what's behind here?*

She heard the sound of a pile of rubble crumbling somewhere on the deck. *Maybe a wall caved in or something?* When

Kieli scanned the area to check, she thought she saw some-thing black in the shadow of one of the smokestacks for a moment, but it had vanished from her vision in no time, so she couldn't be sure. *Was that just my imagination...?*

While her attention was focused on the deck ahead of her, out of the blue a muffled explosion sounded in the opposite direc-tion, from behind her, and the entire ship suddenly lost speed. "Wah!" Inertia sent her pitching forward as she turned to look. A different sort of smoke, black rather than the usual light gray, rose from the exhaust pipes on the station office roof.

"What—Mane!"

Mane had pulled his nose out of his food to turn and look, too—and then immediately tore off running into the station office. Kieli hastily stood up and followed him. The living area and studio were on the second floor, but Mane passed right by the steps leading up without stopping, and scrambled down the work stairs that ran from the first-floor pilothouse down to the lower deck instead. She'd heard the power room was below the station office.

As she got farther down the steep stairs, clinging to the rail-ing all the way, the air grew hotter and thicker with the smell of fossil fuels, and a clanging machine noise got steadily, mad-deningly louder, until she could feel it right down to the core of her body. Eventually she saw a thick steel door at the bot-tom, slightly ajar. The tip of Mane's tail slipped around the edge and disappeared. As soon as she reached the bottom and peered inside after Mane, a scorching heat and bright amber light assaulted her eyes.

Her impression of the room was that some sort of cylindrical coal-burning stove monster that stretched up all the way up to the ceiling was enshrined there, in the center of a round clearing in a forest of differently sized piping. *That must be the power reactor.* A big man covered in misshapen armor stooped over the controls, adjusting various valves, and Harvey was standing there looking on interestedly. It appeared as though the reactor had malfunctioned somehow, but also that it was back to working again, at least for now; amber light burned behind a glass window there.

Shy of going up to them, Kieli called out uneasily from behind. "What's wrong…?"

"This re-ac-tor is near the end of its life span, too… We'll stop for a while and give it a break," the assistant explained, turning toward her, and then waved her back outside.

"Go on," agreed Harvey, gaze still lingering for a time on the power reactor. So Kieli turned back toward the stairs.

At which point a dry crack sounded over Harvey's shoulder as he was finally taking a step away, and there was a momentary blinding burst of light inside the reactor.

"Get away!" Mane yelled sharply all of a sudden. No sooner were the words out of his mouth than he was leaping forward. Before Mane could get to Harvey, the station assistant was already there in one running step, launching himself in between Harvey and the reactor and shielding his back. At that same instant, a tiny crack appeared in one section of the reactor and a single beam of amber light spilled out.

He heard a heavy *skrunch*ing sound, like scrap metal being crushed in a compressor. In fact, it was literally the sound of the metal plating that covered the station assistant's back being crushed, and it came from right above Harvey's head. For a split second he felt all his strength leave him, and he thought he might thump down to the ground, but at the sound of a girl's half-screamed cry of "Harvey...!" he pulled himself together and checked himself before he could fall. When he looked over to the power room's entrance, Kieli herself had plopped to the ground, white as a sheet. She was shaking hard.

"...Hey, I'm fine. I'm fine. I'm not hurt at all. Mane, go to Kieli," Harvey said in a somewhat hoarse voice, and Mane, who'd been a beat behind the station assistant in leaping to him, went back to Kieli's side.

He looked up at the massive figure of the assistant standing in front of him. The armoring on his back had been crushed out of shape at the sudden radical pressure, and it was corroded and covered with thick rust, as if it had leaped decades forward in time in the space of a single second. The same phenomenon that had happened when the ring broke—a fragment of fossil resource must have exploded inside the reactor. Whatever it was, if the assistant hadn't shielded him, that same level of decay would have hit him full-on.

"This is no pro-blem. It's on-ly my ar-mo-ring. There is nothing wrong with my bo-dy."

The man informed Harvey of his safety in the same mechanical tone as always, and the brittle tension in the room finally eased a little. "The cry-stal is be-gin-ning to break down. We should not stay here too long. The ra-di-o will be fixed to-day, so to-mor-row we will take you to the town a-cross the gorge."

"Right…"

Harvey nodded, wiping a light sheen of sweat from his forehead that hadn't come from the heat. Then he turned to face Kieli in the doorway. She was still sitting on the floor. Mane sat close beside her, and she gripped the fur on his back hard enough to rip it out.

"I'm fine. Can you stand?" He walked over to her, intending to help her up.

"I'm fine, I was just a little surprised, just surprised," Kieli babbled quickly, holding on to Mane and struggling to her feet without him. "I'll be upstairs." Then she turned on her heel and fled up the steps. Although Harvey hadn't explicitly asked him to, Mane resignedly followed her.

The creaking of feet on the work stairs receded into the distance overhead. Harvey thought about going after them, but he thought with a sigh that he probably wouldn't be able to say anything helpful anyway. So he watched her go, and stayed behind in the power room with the assistant. If the same thing happened again they'd be in serious trouble, so it was probably best not to hang out here too long, but something was nagging him. He turned back to the reactor one more time.

He'd been told that this mobile radio station was powered by crystallized fossil resources from the previous civilization, just like the one in that ring, so it did make sense to him in a general way: that decay just now must've been triggered by a crystal inside the reactor breaking down. Which was fine as far as it went, but why did the crystal suddenly break in the first place? Somewhere in the back of his mind it had bothered him how surprisingly easily that ring had broken, too, though he'd begun to forget about it. *I thought "cores" and other high-purity fossil crystals were harder to break than that…*

He put his vaguely formed hypothesis to the assistant. "Does a crystal's strength…have a natural life span?"

The other man nodded as he continued the work of patching the crack. "Yes, it does. It's ex-treme-ly long; com-pared to a hu-man life, e-nough time to call e-ter-nal, but I i-ma-gine that in terms of ge-o-lo-gi-cal time, it's not ve-ry long at all. It seems the old pre-War ones are gra-du-ally nea-ring the end of their lives and be-co-ming fra-gile."

"Is that right…?"

This new information surprised Harvey, but he found himself accepting it remarkably easily. So, even the cores everyone said were permanent power sources met their end at some point. Since his core was already starting to break down anyway, it didn't make much difference in his case, frankly— but either way, some sort of end really had been there for him all this time.

Huh…

He knew it was weird to feel this way, but somehow, he felt a weight lifted from his shoulders.

So there's nothing really eternal on this planet after all.

Gazing at the whole thing from a distance, she thought again that this ship really did seem like one big grave. The tallest part, the steel tower in the center, was the gravestone, and the shorter smokestacks around it, along with all their pipes, were flowers placed there in memory. Stained by the copper color of the evening sky, the crude, rusty flowers quietly standing by their gravestone were pretty, Kieli thought.

They'd decided to give the engine a break until nightfall, so the radio station was currently parked in the middle of the gorge. A rock ledge stuck out of one wall at just the right level, so Kieli had jumped over from the deck and climbed a little way up to sit there and look at the view. She was at about the same height as the steel tower's observation deck. A black beast was lying on a rock a level lower than hers, standing by. Harvey had told him to stick with Kieli, so he was following that order until it was rescinded. Even if the man himself—dog himself?—denied it, he was definitely like a dog in that respect (and a faithful dog, at that). He was keeping watch over her out of the corner of his eye without getting up. When Kieli met his gaze, he gave a pointed, transparently fake yawn. His mouth gaped open all the way to his ears, revealing the green gums, teeth gleaming with viscous drool, and a fat tongue like a calf's…He had a dog's face if he just kept his mouth shut, though.

Kieli shifted position, lifting her legs from where they dangled over the end of the ledge and hugging her knees to her chest tightly to make herself as small as possible. Hours had passed, and yet the core of her body was still shaking. *I'm glad nothing serious happened, but that scared me…I can't stand for any* more *bad things to happen. I don't want anything else to happen.*

For just a moment, she saw something dart across her peripheral vision, and she lifted her head. *Hmm?* Kieli looked in the direction she thought she'd seen it, far behind the stern of the radio station, in the shadow of the rock wall—but nothing in particular struck her eye on the floor of the gorge that was fading from the color of sunset into the slate gray of night.

She'd thought she saw a funny shadow earlier in the day, too. Was she getting jumpy?

As Kieli tried to drive the discomfort out of her mind, Mane's ears perked up where he lay, and he gave a low growl. He was staring in the same direction Kieli'd just been worrying about. A little later, Kieli's own ears caught a faint out-of-place sound. The sound of tires on rock, the sound of engines—

Kieli stood up with a start. Her eyes caught up to her ears, picking out a vehicle in the shadow of the gently winding gorge. Was it a truck? It was still a pretty long way off, but the radio station wasn't moving; at this rate the truck would make contact with them before long.

"Mane, tell the others!"

Mane didn't need her to tell him; he was already running down to the station house so fast he was practically flying. Kieli herself climbed down from her high perch a little at a time with her whole body in contact with the rock wall, darting frequent looks at the ravine behind the station. She could see now that three vehicles were approaching. They were armored trucks painted black to blend into the darkness—Church Security Forces trucks.

She caught sight of Harvey running out of the station house hardly a breath after Mane dashed inside. After peering behind them and getting a visual on the trucks, he ran up to Kieli as she neared the ship. The engine let out a roar as it came back to life, along with vibrations that shook the very air in the gorge. Puffs of ashen smoke rose up from the exhaust pipe. Before Kieli could get all the way down the rock face, the deck slowly started pulling away in the opposite direction from the trucks.

"Kieli, hurry up! Jump down!" Harvey ordered from below. Kieli was still fairly high up, but she summoned her courage and jumped. Harvey caught her to his body just as she was afraid the steadily accelerating ship would glide right past her. By that time the radio station had taken off at a fast clip, billowing smoke. When she looked behind her, clinging to Harvey's arm, she could tell that the trucks had sped up, too. They were clearly following them.

"Get inside, both of you!" called a boyish voice from overhead. Mane's black form was standing on the observation deck. The sun had set, and he was steadily melting invisibly into the darkening sky. Urged on by Harvey, Kieli staggered across the wildly rocking deck into the station office. They entered the pilothouse on the first floor to find the station assistant's armored body darting busily between the joystick and the various control levers, alternately steering the vessel and glaring at the gauges covering one wall.

"Can you shake them off?"

"It's not pos-si-ble. If we in-crease our speed any fur-ther, the po-wer re-act-or won't with-stand it. They are fa-ster than we are. We'll be o-ver-ta-ken in nine-ty se-conds," the assistant replied calmly, still glaring at the gauges.

"Freeze!"

All of them turned around at the order echoing outside behind them. It didn't do them much good, though, since there was no rear window in the pilothouse. The monitors all appeared to be broken, too, so they couldn't see what was going on to the station's rear from here. Further orders thundered through a megaphone at them. *"Stop! We have some questions for you! If you don't halt your craft, we'll deem you a suspicious converted vessel and attack!"*

"Questions?" Harvey muttered dubiously. He and the station assistant exchanged glances, seemingly having a silent conference, and then he said, "Let's stop. We don't know that they'll automatically attack us."

"All right," the assistant agreed, and tinkered with a few valves and control boards, finally pulling down one big square lever with both hands. The entire body of the ship rocked violently up and down. "Please hold on to some-thing." Kieli did as she was told, clinging fast to the doorjamb of the pilothouse and clenching her teeth against the jolts as they bounced along the rocky ground so that she wouldn't accidentally bite her tongue. They gradually slowed down until after one last giant rock back and forth, Kieli could feel the ship come to a stop.

The vibration and thundering roar that had ruled all of her senses died down, and everything around them fell horribly quiet. Still, she stood frozen with her legs braced for impact a little while longer before she sensed an animal walk up beside her on silent paws. Mane was back from his expedition up the tower.

"We're surrounded. I spotted three Capital Security Forces armored trucks. One of them's circled around in front of us."

"The capital sent their own people...? Are you sure it's not soldiers from town coming after us?"

"They're not from town. But hey, either way, all I have to do is eat them," Mane said, sticking out his slimy tongue pointedly.

"I want everyone on board to come out. I'll wait sixty seconds."

The voice over the loudspeaker was coming from a lot closer now. Everyone in the pilothouse exchanged rapid glances. They might have said "everyone," but the station assistant and Mane couldn't very well show themselves; their appearances were too bizarre. That inevitably limited their options.

"I'll go out alone for now."

"What?! I'll come too!" Kieli hastily asserted. She'd taken it for granted that she'd be one of the ones going out. But Harvey immediately dismissed this, with a face that said he took it for granted that he'd be going alone, and that his mind was made up on that point. "You wait here. I'm just going to find out what they want. I'll be right back."

"But, if you're all alone..."

"Wait here," Harvey repeated in a tone that brooked no argument, and Kieli reluctantly backed down, unable to say anything back to him.

They relocated to the studio booth on the second floor,

where the station assistant concealed his large form in the shadow of the glass window looking out over the stern to keep watch over whatever unfolded. Kieli hid behind the pipes sticking out of the assistant's back and peeked out at the deck along with him. In the white light of the armored trucks' search beams, the forest of smokestacks on the deck cast eerily crisp shadows. She saw Harvey's back leaving the station house and walking calmly over toward the stern just about sixty seconds on the dot after the order over the loud-speaker.

There were footholds on the side of the ship; around a dozen armored soldiers climbed up them onto the deck. A man who wore a greatcoat over his clerical robes and looked to be a commissioned officer brought up the rear. He came up to face Harvey, who'd stopped halfway across the deck, leaving a little distance between them. He seemed to start up a conversation about something, but he wasn't speaking over the loudspeaker this time, so their voices didn't carry all the way to them.

"I wonder what they're talking about…"

"I do not know. Mane may hear it from where he is, how-e-ver."

Kieli might be reading too much into it, but she thought his flat voice betrayed a hint of restlessness. Mane ought to have climbed back up the steel tower by now to keep an eye on how things went.

Since Kieli and the assistant didn't know how matters were progressing, minutes crawled by when all they could do was fret. Not much time could have passed, but she felt as if they'd been waiting a hundred times longer than anything a clock could have told them. As it was starting to be too much to bear without losing her head, a reflection appeared on the metal plating of the assistant's back right next to where her hand touched it.

Kieli whirled around, startled, and for just a moment she caught sight of the tail end of a shadowy form crossing in front of the studio doorway.

Mane…?

Maybe he was back from the tower. The assistant was still focusing intently on the scene outside. Kieli moved away from his back to peek out through the doorway into the corridor. All she saw was a deserted hallway lying there enveloped in coarse, grainy darkness. Mane was nowhere in sight.

"Mane…where are you…?"

When she took a step forward, looking left and right, she heard a voice behind her back—no, at the nape of her neck. Right behind her head, a toneless voice lapping up her neck like a lukewarm breeze.

Found you.

"——!"

Kieli instinctively leapt away, immediately tripping and falling forward, landing hard on her knees. When she turned her neck and looked up at the place where her head had just been, a giant sort of jet-black shadow was hugging the ceiling and dangling its neck upside down at her. The head attached to the end of its long neck gaped in a crescent-moon grin, giving her a glimpse of the inside of its bloodred mouth. Everything above that mouth…was nothing but the darkness of the hallway behind it. There was no nose, no eyes, nothing. Viscous liquid dripped from the severed plane of its half-sphere head where the top half had been.

The scream almost ripped Kieli's throat out in its rush to escape her mouth.

After that brief cry, she cut off the scream and took off running down the hallway, still practically on all fours.

That's what I sensed this afternoon, too. I thought I was imagining things, but something really was there. What is it? What is that?! The black presence followed her, crawling along the ceiling like a spider. She half-ran, half-tumbled down the stairs. By the time she realized that she would've been better off running outside from the first floor, she'd already run all the way down to the power room below deck in her blind panic, dived inside, and slammed her whole body against the thick steel door to close it. She seized an iron pipe lying nearby and thrust it through the inside door handle to bar it shut, and walked backward into the room with her eyes fixed on the door. Her throat had gone all funny and she found herself panting raggedly—but it was because of the scream, not the running, she was sure.

She stopped with the power reactor at her back and watched the doorway in the glow of its feebly burning amber light for a while, but there was no sign of anything strange happening.

Kieli exhaled slowly a few times until she got her breathing under control, and let the tension in her shoulders go.

I wonder if anyone noticed my scream... The tension left the rest of her body along with her shoulders, though, and she went limp; she was afraid she was about to crumple to the ground when she heard a noise on the other side of the door. Her body went stiff again for a moment, but it was a sound like something metal dragging along the floor, so she thought maybe the station assistant had come for her.

A little relieved, Kieli lifted her gaze—and her heart instantly froze solid in her chest. From a gap between the steel door and the wall that was so small she could hardly think of it as a "gap" at all seeped a formless black noise that crawled along the wall. The noise grew like thick liquid waste forming a puddle little by little, encroaching on the wall and the door, and eventually it gathered itself together to form a bizarrely long human arm. The hand groped around until it found and grasped the pipe she'd been using to bar the door, and bent it out of shape as effortlessly as if it were a stick of taffy, and dropped it to the floor.

The door handle worked all by itself and the door was pushed open, and the spreading darkness beyond seemed to give birth to another darkness that split away from it, and then the black shadow assumed its human shape again and plodded sluggishly into the room.

What the barely flickering amber light in the power reactor window revealed was a bizarre form, its entire body covered with scrap metal and rubble from the radio tower assembled into crude armor so that it looked something like the station assistant—but with a decisive difference: underneath this armor there was no body. In the gaps between the metal plating, static the color of darkness swirled. And no, it definitely didn't have a head. Everything from the nose up looked to have been bitten off, it was so cruelly crushed in, and particles of noise swarmed like maggots on the surface of the cut.

Found you...

...said the crescent-twisted bright red mouth again.
"Ah...ah, ahh..."
Kieli's couldn't move a single step; she stared wide-eyed at the sight of *it*, gasping meaninglessly. Her jaws wouldn't fit together right to form words. A ghost with its head crushed in—the image of a man in that same state clawed its way up out of that burnt-over place in the depths of her memory and made a bitter accusation.
You're the one who said it.
With a shrill metallic scrape that gave Kieli goose bumps, the ghost came toward her. She couldn't move. *Screech...screech...screech.* Metal plating rubbed against the floor with each step.
"Kieli!" cried a voice out of nowhere at the same time that a black beast launched himself toward the armor, rounding his back and tackling it in midair. The rubble and scrap metal that had shaped itself into a suit of armor came apart and scattered pieces of junk all over the floor. However, the once-dispersed noise quickly gathered itself back together again into a crawling human shape and sucked in the junk around it, beginning to rebuild its armor.
Mane had alighted in front of Kieli; as he assumed an

attack stance, ready to go for the armor again, he swung his tail and thwapped Kieli's legs with it, shooing her away. "What are you standing there for?! Run!" Kieli snapped back to herself and started to run for the exit, but she made it only a couple of steps at most before her legs got tangled up and she landed in a pathetic heap. Her brain didn't manage to form the idea that she had to stand up again fast. Using her hands, she sluggishly pushed just her upper body up off the floor, and turned to look at the re-forming suit of armor.

Suddenly the jammed gears in her mind started turning again, and her thoughts touched the burn deep in her memory.

You can kill! —There was her own murderous voice when she ordered Mane.

I don't mind killing a person or two. —There was her own half-crazed face when she argued back against Harvey.

I didn't do anything wrong. I was only protecting. —There were her own blood-soaked hands dangling the ax as she stared calmly down at the corpse.

That's right.
That's
the person
that I killed.

"I said go! Kieli! Hey!" Mane shouted impatiently as he leapt at the armor again. Knocked back just when it finished standing up, the suit of armor doubled over and lost its balance. With a jarring screech of its metal plating, it tottered and fell against the power reactor.

More or less halfway between the stern and the radio tower in the center of the deck, Harvey faced off against a man who appeared to be the commanding officer of a platoon. The rest of the soldiers remained behind, standing by in front of their respective trucks. Still, even counting all of them together, this wasn't that large a unit; Harvey got the impression the officer had brought only the men in his own direct command. Actually confirming their pursuers' numbers and equipment didn't help him figure out their objective at all. In fact, he was understanding it less every minute. Local Security Forces troops after them for the Mane incident, a raid on the radio station, Undying Hunters on his tail—this didn't quite fit any of the possibilities he could think of at the moment.

The officer surveyed the antiquated smokestacks clustered on the deck with a slight look of surprise, then assumed a determined expression and faced him again.

"How many more people are inside?"

"None."

The officer sent up the trial balloon without any preamble, and Harvey replied calmly and readily. He didn't look convinced, but Harvey'd never believed they'd get out of this without any trouble.

Judging from the number of badges and various other decorations on the greatcoat he wore over his clerical robes, he was pretty high-ranking even for someone in the Capital Security Forces. Still, he didn't have the unnecessarily high-and-mighty attitude Harvey normally associated with that many medals, and he wasn't overly tall, so he didn't come off as overbearing physically either. Something about him sort of reminded Harvey of someone he knew, but he couldn't place who that was.

What the officer came out with when he got down to business wasn't any of the three possibilities he'd imagined: it was something completely outside the realm of anything he would ever have anticipated. "We're looking for a girl. We have information that she's in this area." Harvey merely lifted his eyebrows a fraction. He couldn't readily decide on a response. The officer seemed to interpret his silence as his way of prompting him to move it along; nodding, he withdrew a piece of paper from the inside pocket of his greatcoat. It...looked like a photograph?

"Do you recognize this girl?"

The surface of the photo he held up reflected the search-lights of the trucks. His right eye wasn't completely accustomed to strong light yet, so it smarted as he squinted at the picture. It was all he could do to make out the edge of the photo that was out of the beams' direct path. He recognized this scene from somewhere; it looked as if there was something like stage sound equipment...?

As he quizzically narrowed his eyes even further, all of a sudden an engine drone roared below his feet, and then the floor bucked wildly beneath them.

—?

Feeling as though he might get whiplash, Harvey planted his heels and just managed to hold his ground. The whole deck shook, and the pipes overhead creaked and showered flakes of rust on their heads. For a second the platoon soldiers looked ready to run, but the officer's sharp voice had them tightening their formation and standing at alert in no time.

"What's this about? Cut the power!"

"Don't look at me!"

He couldn't figure out what the hell this was about either. *Did something happen in the power room?* When he turned toward the steel tower where the station office was, he hardly had time to register the belch of thick black smoke out of the previously still exhaust pipes before, with a ponderous tremor of the ground and an even more violent jerk up and down, they began traveling between the rock walls on either side of them. The abrupt acceleration sent Harvey pitching forward. He managed to catch himself with his hand in a half-sitting, half-standing position before he hit the floor. Several of the soldiers standing near the edge lost their balance and went overboard, screaming as they fell.

"What do you think you're doing?! Stop this ship!" bellowed the officer, who'd narrowly managed to stay on his feet and was shielding his head against the rust rain.

"I told you, don't look at me!" The deck bounced and Harvey almost bit his tongue, so he aborted the conversation and looked up to the roof of the station office. A gritty fog-like substance very different in character from the black smoke of burning fossil fuel was streaming continuously from the exhaust pipes. *A ghost—?*

Harvey had a bad feeling about this. He heard the officer's voice calling after him to stop as he took off running, but he ignored it and ran across the shaking deck back to the station office.

When he dived into the pilothouse, he found the station assistant clinging to the joystick.

"What happened?!"

"Some-thing's gone wrong in the po-wer re-ac-tor. We're out of con-trol."

The tone was inflectionless, but the sense of urgency was unmistakable. Looking around him, Harvey realized the girl it should be his top priority to protect was nowhere in sight, and his flesh crawled. "She's in the po-wer room," the assistant told him before he could ask. "Mane went there." His body had turned without his conscious order and sent him sprinting out of the pilothouse before the man had even finished talking.

"Kieli!"

Harvey skidded down the work stairs to the power reactor with a hand on the railing for balance, reaching the bottom just as Mane was dragging Kieli through the half-open door by her clothes. "My tail got burnt," Mane griped when he noticed him. The tip of his lion-like tail had begun to rot, and it was dangling like wilted ivy.

Harvey was momentarily relieved to see that Kieli was safe, but when he ran over to her, she was curled up in the fetal position, unmoving even though she didn't appear unconscious. "Kieli?" He crouched down next to her and peered at her. Her face was as bloodless-white as a corpse's, and she was trembling like someone off her head with distress. Harvey raised his face and looked closely into the power room. The power reactor was warped out of shape, and all around it swirled something black and staticky, diffusing and concentrating intermittently into a human form.

That's—

The specter of a man whose head was half crushed in by enormous teeth clicked instantly with that image still fresh in his memory. The sight of the man's face as he died, his head crushed in right in front of Harvey, burst back to life again in his mind in a flashback so realistic he could even feel the flying globs of brain hitting his cheek and sticking. Bile rose in his throat.

"...ry......I..."

Sounds burbled from Kieli's mouth. Hardly opening her mouth, she mumbled indistinctly, "I said it, I killed you, I'm sorry...!"

"Ki—" The sight of her weak-voiced apologies stabbed him through the lung, and for a moment, he couldn't breathe. —Yes, he'd told her never to say that again. But he hadn't meant to place all the responsibility on Kieli personally like this when he'd said it. The rest of her name caught in his throat. He forced himself to suck in air that burned his throat and lungs, and tried again. Kieli was holding her head and trembling; he gripped her by the shoulder and shook her.

"Kieli, stop it! That's not true; it wasn't you; you didn't do it!"

"I'm the one who bit him, you know," put in Mane in his usual carefree voice, looking puzzled. But Kieli shook her head minutely back and forth on a neck rigid as a clockwork doll's, mumbling over and over about how she'd killed him. "H-he hit Harvey, and shot…So I…I had an ax, and I…"

"An ax?" She was starting to make less and less sense. Maybe she was mixing this up with something else? Harvey brought his face close to hers and said in a strong voice, "What are you talking about? There's no ax anywhere. Snap out of it!" Kieli's aimlessly wandering eyes finally focused and turned to him.

For a few moments she looked at him vaguely, and then her face crumpled and fat, wet tears began to stream down her face. "I'm sorry, I'm sor…"

"Okay, I understand; it's okay. It's not your fault. You didn't actually do anything. I'm safe, all right? I'm right here with you," Harvey soothed, wrapping his arm around her convulsing back as she sobbed out apologies. He didn't care whether what she said was true, whether any of it had really happened; right now he'd force her to listen to him; for now he'd hypnotize her into believing him even against her own will if he had to. "It's not your fault. I'm here." Holding her with his left arm, he pulled her up the stairs. Mane pushed up from below with his back. Working together, they got her up to the first floor.

"We are not safe here. We need to e-va-cu-ate quick-ly."

The assistant came out of the pilothouse and took over for them, easily hoisting Kieli onto an armored shoulder. The whole station house continued rocking violently. The roar of the out-of-control engine and the ship scraping against rock assaulted his eardrums from all directions.

When he started running, eyes racing over the scenery around him, something coarse and warm stroked his ankle.

Warm, and yet it gave him chills. Harvey jerked his foot away, shuddering at the eerie sensation, and looked down. A thin wisp of blackish noise particles hung in the air just brushing his foot. Even more static swelled and swarmed its way up from the darkness of the stairs down to the power reactor. It was in the process of covering the whole floor.

"This way."

Driven forward by the sea of static, they were forced upstairs whether they liked it or not—but in no time the static began to seep through the second-story floor too, so they fled from the station office roof up the access ladder to the steel tower. Mane took the lead, and the station assistant followed with Kieli. Harvey took the rear, glancing down every so often to check his footing. As they climbed, the station assistant right above him abruptly turned his head down to look at him.

Harvey looked back, blinking.

"You are o-ver-pro-tec-tive," he said softly.

"That a problem?"

"No." Something in the assistant's mechanical voice made Harvey think he was making fun of him. The other man coolly turned his gaze back upward. Harvey glared oddly grumpily at the bottoms of the assistant's metal-plated feet until he heard a flat voice above him call down, "Hur-ry, please." He cursed under his breath at the distance that had opened up between them and upped his pace.

...Call me whatever you want.

Supposing that some sort of blame truly did lie with Kieli, if there was a penalty that had to be paid, he'd happily pay it

all himself. He didn't care if he was overprotective; he didn't have the slightest intention of letting Kieli bear this guilt.

The assistant put Kieli down when they got to the observation deck midway up. "Please stay here. I left your ra-di-o be-hind," he said, and climbed down the tower again. When Harvey looked down over the guardrail, the sea of static had overflowed out of the station office and begun to spread across the deck. The sudden appearance of what looked like a swarm of mysterious black insects threw the soldiers into a panic. Soon they were running in all directions, some falling off the edge of the rocking deck, and a few even deliberately throwing themselves off. The officer he'd talked to earlier was calling out this way and that, trying to calm their agitation, but Harvey doubted any of them had experienced this sort of unusual situation before; the command had totally broken down.

"They're coming this way, too."

Mane, who'd climbed a little higher up and was gazing at the whole scene from above, gave this urgent report in an incongruously carefree voice. The noise wasn't just spreading out like water; tendrils of it were starting to crawl vertically up the steel tower, too.

"Kieli, climb! Move your own legs!"

When he put his left arm around her side to drag her with him and his right elbow against the ladder, and began climbing in that extremely precarious stance, Kieli moved with him. On her own power, if slowly and groggily, she placed her feet on one rung after the other. Evidently the confusion in her mind was finally starting to clear. Harvey had a few seconds to savor his relief before there was a ponderous screech of metal that made him want to cover his ears, and the steel tower started to list to one side. A rock wall was careening toward him at high speed right in front of his eyes. The steel tower wasn't falling down: the entire ship itself seemed to have come up on a rock or something and lurched dramatically to one side—before its flank crashed against the rock wall next to it, and the ship was skewered with a blow and a crashing roar. And even that didn't stop them; the radio station careened on through the gorge, out of control, with its side scraping along the rock wall, taking out chunks of it as it went. Clinging tightly to the ladder with his arm around Kieli so they wouldn't be thrown off, Harvey gritted his teeth and bore it out.

There was one last jolt even harder than the rest, and a high-pitched metallic wail echoed above them.

By the time the sound had stopped bouncing painfully around inside his skull and the reverberations had died down at last, the roar of the ship scouring the rock wall was gone too, and everything was so weirdly quiet that he thought maybe he'd busted his eardrums. After a beat of unnatural silence, the howl of the wind blowing through the valley came back to his ears as if remembering itself.

"…We're stopped."

At the sound of Mane's somewhat dazed voice, Harvey peeled his forehead away from the rung he'd been pressing it against and lifted his face, letting go of the breath he'd unconsciously been holding. He'd be willing to bet he'd scraped his forehead up. The first thing he did was check on Kieli, who was still clinging to him, stiff as a board. Then he looked up—his whole field of vision was tilted on its axis—and saw Mane dangling upside down from a steel pole by the talons of his hind leg and swinging back and forth in the wind. He was looking just a tiny bit miserable.

Even farther above Harvey than that, the tip of the steel tower had plunged straight into the rock wall tilted about thirty degrees, and its antenna was pitifully flattened. Here and there fragments of rock broke off and fell down to earth. The radio station had finally come to a stop.

"No, crap, this is bad." Mane turned just his head to face down as he rotated his upper body, got his forelegs around the steel pole, and swore.

When Harvey looked down, he could see something exploding directly below the steel tower, right around where the power reactor was. An invisible shock radiated from the steel tower across the deck like ripples across water. A beat later the blast came, and fire along with it, but before it could spread, the familiar wave of decay on its heels swallowed it up. The network of pipes rapidly collapsed, exactly like shriveling blood vessels, and started rusting over. The static fog that had covered the entire deck was swept up as the decay moved forward, too. It squirmed painfully as it died away. The soldiers who'd escaped being thrown off the runaway ship and were holding on to the tilted deck for dear life stared with dumb amazement at the phenomenon sweeping over everything around them.

Then a stir arose from one section of them. They snapped out of their trance at the sight of a peculiar-looking armored man appearing on the half-collapsed station office roof and aimed their rifles and, efficiently if timidly, set about surrounding him.

"Ah…!"

Harvey could see the radio held up in the assistant's hand, but the decay had already engulfed both metal-plated legs all the way up to his lower back. Rust covered every inch. Though he seemed hard-pressed to even walk, he moved forward one step at a time, apparently to intimidate the soldiers surrounding him, who backed away in fear.

"Stay here. Stay here and hold on tight. Do you understand? Mane, get over here!"

Harvey took Kieli's hands and forced them into a tight grip around a rung of the ladder as Mane descended smoothly down to them. Leaving her in the animal's care, he climbed down the tower. The station assistant noticed him when he'd made it a little lower down than the observation deck. "I'm thro-wing it." He wound up as he spoke, and he'd already pitched the radio up to Harvey by the time the words finished leaving his mouth. Harvey leaned out and managed to catch its strap with the tips of his fingers, and then cried, "Hurry!," waving at the assistant to climb up. But the assistant only shook his head sadly and gestured toward his feet. Both legs of the armor were completely immobilized. They'd become one with the rust covering the roof, planted in it from the ankles down.

"Hang on; I'll be right there."

"No! Do not come down. Please, climb back up quick-ly and get a-way from here."

"What are you talking about?! We're going togeth—"

"No!"

Harvey's leg momentarily froze in the process of stepping down to the next rung. He'd never heard that violent inflection in the assistant's voice before.

And that was when the shot rang out—one of the soldiers fired right at him, more than likely snapping under the strain of all the commotion. Harvey escaped a direct hit, but the bullet scraped just the shallowest path across his shin to rebound against the rung he was standing on, and the heel he'd jerked away midstep missed its footing when it came back down. "Crap—" He tried to grab hold of the rail with his left hand, but the radio it held got in the way and he missed. Losing his balance, he fell backward.

Before he felt the impact of his body crashing into the station office roof, he made impact in midair against something invisible. It felt as though he'd smacked headfirst into a pocket of a different, high-pressured dimension.

KKCHK…

A dull, baffling sound right in front of his eyes, the sensation of something foreign embedding itself in his body—

Half of his field of vision abruptly left him.

"Harvey!"

Kieli screamed when she saw Harvey fall from halfway down the tower. Just as she took her next step, there was a metallic creak above her—the peak of the tower that had stabbed into the rock face broke off and the tower jolted down even further, shaking her grip free from the rung she'd been holding. After the briefest of moments when it felt as if she were floating, she began to fall upside down. "Ack!" "Kieli!" Mane chased after her, *running down the face of the tower* and finally leaping off one of the supports and launching his black body into the air.

"Grab hold!"

Quicker than thought, she reached out in midair and clutched at the hair around Mane's neck. He was curled up like a black cannonball; pulled after him, she plunged even farther down. The wind howled, cutting at her cheeks. The deck got rapidly closer. Meanwhile, Harvey had crashed into the roof of the station office, bounced, and then rolled off and down toward the deck. Mane managed to slide underneath him, dangerously close, and scoop him onto his back.

"—!"

As she clutched Harvey's clothes, Kieli's eyes opened wide.

Two rifts opened up along Mane's shoulder blades, and with a creaking sound, armlike protrusions attached to some viscous membrane and sticky with coal-tar blood thrust out. They spread out wide, membranes unfolding into bat-like wings, and caught the breeze.

"Hold on tight to him!"

Just before they would have crashed into the deck, they got some lift, and suddenly they were skimming just above it in level flight, shooting forward with all the speed they'd had in free fall. Mane's unsteady wings missed streams of air over and over. Each time Kieli and Harvey were shaken, and each time they came close to falling off. Stretching herself across Harvey's back and holding him in her arms, Kieli clutched Mane's hair as hard as she could. They almost plunged straight into the agitated group of soldiers until Mane veered away at the last moment—and she saw a wall of rubble looming in front of them—

We're going to hit it!, she thought—

But then they swerved to the side with so little room to spare that Mane's wings scraped most of the way along the side of the wall before they shot through a gap in the piping over the deck and soared into the air.

"Wah…"

All at once the sky spread out before her. The sea of clouds covering the whole tiny gorge sky was closer than she'd ever seen it before. It looked as if they'd shoot out of the valley and straight into the clouds, and Kieli felt dizzy.

Mane rotated high in the air, and the radio tower below them entered her vision again. Rust swept up the steel tower from its base toward the summit. The whole thing changed from gray to red even as she watched. Like the spreading roots of a great tree, the pipes on the deck swiftly went red-brown with rust too, starting at the steel tower and spreading outward in every direction—and though the spreading phenomenon was definitely, unmistakably decay, what it *looked* like was a bed of red flowers putting down roots in a gray, barren land and blossoming, and Kieli watched it play out below her, wide-eyed and wordless.

The red steel tower cloaked in rust all the way to its tip seemed just like a colossal petrified tree.

And at the great tree's roots stood a solitary smaller tree. Such a tiny tree compared to its companion, and yet it had been plenty big enough to protect them. A red-brown tree in the shape of a large-bodied man in misshapen armor. One lone branch stretched up in the sky as if to wave to them; in that position the assistant had turned into an unmoving hunk of steel and rust.

"Mane, go back…!"

Mane did move to go back once, but in the end all he did was circle once in the air above the radio tower, and then he turned his back on it and began flying away, apparently giving up.

The great tree that was the remains of the radio tower and the tree of armor that stood nestled up against its base grew steadily smaller in the distance until they were swallowed up by the valley and disappeared from sight. Whether it could truly see them or not, Kieli didn't know, but the tree of armor seemed to watch them go the whole time with one hand held overhead.

Owooo…nn…

Was that the sound of the sharp wind against her cheeks, or was she hearing Mane howl for the first time? The sorrowful sound made her heart squeeze. Low, and long, and lingering before it vanished into the sky above the gorge.

"What the hell just happened…?"

The officer looked dazedly around him at the results of the bizarre phenomenon that had just happened before his eyes, wanting to doubt his own senses and his mind itself. A landscape of decay, everything blanketed with seasoned rust as though decades, maybe even centuries, had passed in the space of just a few minutes—but when he thought about how long ago this place had been built, he seemed to feel at the same time as though this moldering wreck was its true form, and it didn't strike him as strange—a fact which itself struck him as strange.

He assumed what had started it all was a power surge in the reactor, but oddly enough, there wasn't much fire damage. The violent quakes had died down, too. Time might as well have frozen, it was so quiet.

"How many casualties?" he asked his adjutant, recalling his job even if he hadn't quite recovered from his shock. "Report immediately." The other man had been standing stock-still, looking as stunned as he felt, but at his order, he anxiously set about confirming their status.

"Eleven men with minor injuries and two with major injuries. No deaths."

"I see…"

Whatever that might have been, for the moment he could feel relief that they hadn't lost anyone, at least. It'd be tough to clean up the mess caused by a big problem happening while he was using the unit for a private errand, so there was that— but more importantly than anything else, he didn't like to let any of his men die. That should go without saying, but unfortunately, lots of people tended to forget it once they were given a large command.

He looked into the distance of the night-dark gorge ahead, in the direction where a funny-winged beast the likes of which he'd never seen before had fled after saving the man who'd fallen from the steel tower. That one-armed redhead had struck a chord in his memory, though he hadn't been able to figure out exactly why right away. Now he remembered: the description of a certain fugitive the Undying Hunters had a bounty out on fit him like a glove. Anybody the Undying Hunters were paying a reward for wasn't just some ordinary human, obviously. He must be one of *those*.

And, although just for a brief moment, he'd clearly seen a girl clinging to the beast's back.

He was fairly certain he wasn't mistaken about who it was. Although he found himself somehow wanting to doubt his own eyes…

"Get Lord Sigri's envoy on the line."

After they'd zigzagged wildly through the gorge for a stretch, they eventually crashed into a protruding rock, and it was just too much to hold on through; this time Kieli was thrown off. "Gyah!" Fortunately she was saved by a ledge sticking out just far enough from the rock wall, so while she slammed her back hard, she escaped more or less unscathed.

Just as she began to sit up, coughing, Mane's black body thumped down next to her in an artless heap. One wing was bent unnaturally underneath him when he landed, broken from its base. It hurt Kieli just to look at it. "Mane!"

"Don't worry about it. It's not like these originally belonged to me," Mane declared bluntly. He pinned the broken wing down with a hind leg and ripped it off. "Is he alive?"

Harvey was lying over by the edge of the rock ledge. Kieli

crawled over to him on all fours and peered into his face. "Harvey?!" Harvey shifted his head slightly with a little groan, but put it right back down again and pressed his cheek into the rock. He had a horrible sore on his left cheek that went all the way up to his temple; it looked just as if the iron rust had infested his skin.

"Got caught in the fallout from *it*, eh? Can you see?"

A beast's snout thrust itself forward beside Kieli to peer down at him. At Mane's question Harvey cracked open his left eye, only to shake his head slightly, just once, and cover it with his hand. The hand itself looked as if it might break at the slightest touch: sunken flesh, bones standing out with grotesque sharpness. Half-crying, Kieli threw her arms around him.

"Harvey, no, not this…!"

His lips parted just a fraction, and she heard a scratchy voice say something she couldn't quite catch.

"……li……ine…"

"What? Harvey, what is it?" She crouched down low and brought her face close to his, straining to hear him.

"I'm fine……so, the Corporal…?"

He repeated the same thing several times in a painfully raw voice. He almost sounded like someone in a nightmare. Jolted, Kieli looked around her. She spotted the radio on the ground on Harvey's opposite side, and went to fetch it. All the parts had been put back together again, but no matter how much she fiddled with it or shook it, she didn't hear the usual white noise, or the Corporal's voice, either. "I dunno; I can't hear anything. I don't think he's working…!" she reported tearfully.

"We're walking a little farther. We can get out of the gorge."

Mane grabbed Harvey by the scruff of his neck and dragged him. Kieli helped by leaning Harvey's tall form onto Mane's back, and they started walking, more or less dragging him with them.

The path of narrow ledges along the rock wall stretched on, twisting and turning uncertainly until it disappeared into the darkness far ahead.

"Whoa…"

The small patch of night sky visible from the gorge was beginning to lighten faintly into the sandy color of morning. Captivated by the view that spread out beneath her eyes, a little exclamation escaped her along with her sigh of relief.

In the dimness ahead of them, at the end of the path of rock ledges, a single thin thread of weak light had seeped in through a gap in the rock walls as they walked. Now they'd passed through that gap to the other side, at a point about halfway up the towering rocks of the fault. Blue-gray predawn wilderness spread out far down below, shrouded in a light mist.

She could see the outlines of a ghost town in the foothills at the base of the fault, and a single railroad track that curved in a gentle arc out of sight.

In the pantry of a kitchen blanketed with dust she found a sealed bottle of alcohol. When she stumblingly read the type and proof on the label out loud to Harvey, he said, "Eh, that'll do it. Give it here," and carelessly accepted the bottle. He was slumped heavily against the wall. He felt around for the cork without looking at it, and used his mouth to pull it out when he had to. No sooner had he brought the bottle to his lips and tossed back a gulp of it than he suddenly choked.

"A-are you okay?"

Harvey coughed. "I'm fine," he said, shoving her off with an elbow when she tried to rub his back. Rather than drink the rest of it, he tilted his head back to face the ceiling and up-ended it over his face. Clear liquid dripped from the inflamed skin around his left eye all the way down his neck, soaking his clothes.

They were in a humble shack that consisted of just one room with an attached kitchen, plus a little loft underneath the roof. It showed no signs of use; Kieli guessed it had been abandoned decades ago now. Mane, who'd gone up to the loft to look around, descended smoothly back down to sit beside her.

"Want me to do it?" he offered, displaying the sharp talons of a great bird that crowned one leg.

Harvey shook his head without uncovering his eyes. "I'll do it myself." Kieli alone didn't quite grasp what Harvey planned to do next. When she directed a questioning glance at Mane, who looked sort of disappointed that his offer had been refused, he told her calmly, "He's going to gouge his eye out."

Kieli forgot to exhale. Struck speechless, she couldn't immediately formulate a reply, and Mane's detached explanation continued. "Hopefully it's only the eyeball itself that's done in, but probably the decay's eaten at some of his optic nerve, too. If he leaves the eye in, there's a possibility it'll travel farther and farther inside him. Right now there's no other way, and there's no time to hesitate. If we're unlucky, it'll get all the way to his brai—"

"Kieli. You go wait outside," Harvey interrupted in a slightly offhand voice, cutting off Mane's easy flow of words. He looked as if he wanted to tell him *Don't explain it in that much detail.*

"I'll be done fast, so wait outside...please."

After this repeated plea, she heard him add in a barely audible voice, "I don't want you to see this." He was covering his face with his hand. Between his slim fingers, though, she caught a glimpse of the left eye beneath them, pointed down and to the side at nothing in particular. His copper eye had darkened to a cloudy blackish color. Kieli'd wanted to stay with him, but after seeing that, she couldn't insist anymore. She could only nod.

"Hey, Kieli..."

When she moved to leave the room, entrusting the rest to Mane, Harvey suddenly called out to stop her as if he realized he'd forgotten something. She stopped moving halfway through the process of standing up, propped on one hand. Harvey's hand scrabbled anxiously along the floor, found hers, and gripped it lightly.

"Mm. What?"

"About the Corporal...I think things maybe turned out for the best this way."

At that, Kieli pressed her lips together and looked down at

the radio hanging around her neck. It dangled from her neck just like it always did; it looked ready to speak up any moment just like it always did. And yet the radio didn't say anything to her anymore. Apparently they hadn't gotten the repairs done in time.

When she stayed stonily silent and didn't answer him, Harvey rested for a breath and then went on. His normally gravelly voice sounded even scratchier than usual.

"Kieli, it's just, I want you to understand...Let's bring him with us to Easterbury. I want to take one last journey together, just the three of us, and go back to Easterbury...and let the Corporal relax and rest in peace. I'll be with you, Kieli, I'll still be with you...Won't that do...?"

She could tell that he was thinking hard, carefully choosing words that felt strange on his tongue. He was being good to her, trying with all he had to convince her after she'd stubbornly refused to listen to him. Even though really, the Harvey she knew hated to talk for so long...If he wanted to, he could've done what he always did: decide on his own and just do it, whether Kieli agreed or not. But instead he was trying to consider her feelings.

There was an uneasy silence while he waited for her answer. After a little bit, Kieli blinked back the tears threatening to spill down her cheeks and nodded. Harvey kept waiting, though, the unease not gone from his face yet. She belatedly realized he couldn't see her very well with only his right eye, so she opened her mouth and answered again out loud.

"...Okay."

She turned the hand he gripped palm-up and squeezed it back, and Harvey's expression relaxed a little, relieved at last.

The northwestern mining district. This was the district where countless mine shafts were dug along the enormous ore-containing fault, and Kieli and the others had come out of the gorge into its outskirts.

It was an old mineral vein that had been mined even before the War; here were the remains of an old mine where people even found relics of the high-level civilization before the War. There was a market for those relics, too, and this area had been prosperous once (apparently the mobile radio station Mane had lived in had stayed in the western part of this region for a long time). But fossil resources were running dry even here, and according to Mane the number of mine shafts left was less than half of what it had been in its heyday.

Kieli sat on the stone steps in front of the shack, looking down at the view before her. A desolate mining town clung to the foothills of the fault down below, where the land was hazy with white morning air. That town had almost certainly been a lot livelier once, but there didn't seem to be a single operating shaft in the vicinity, and all the tunnel entrances that dotted the middle stratum of the rock face were boarded over. She thought the shack they'd found while walking along the rock wall must have been a rest area for miners once, but it wasn't in use now. There were several other ramshackle buildings here that looked to have been storehouses and processing stations. Steep stairs and paths jutted out of the rock face and stretched down to the town in the foothills. Shovels, carts, and various other tools of the trade lay forlornly here and there, abandoned like children's toys scattered at the park and forgotten.

"Corporal…" Kieli called experimentally, pressing her forehead against the radio she hugged between her knees and chest. Her only answer was the cold feeling of the metal. The angular parts of the speaker hurt where they ground into her forehead, but she pressed against it even harder anyway, and started whispering to him. She didn't even care if he didn't answer back.

"Corporal, get angry with me…I'm—a really bad person…"

She was just like that woman from the mansion. No, that woman had just been simpleminded; Kieli knew her own heart must be even uglier inside. She hurt people without a second thought when she thought they'd take something precious from her.

I don't mind killing a person or two if it's for you. In that moment the words had just flown out of her mouth without passing through her brain, but when she considered it now, she didn't think she'd lied. In the end, what she'd said without thinking was what she really felt. No matter what Harvey said, even if Mane had killed that man, Kieli might as well have been the one to kill him. Because in her mind, she'd been bringing the ax down on his head.

If something like that happened again, and she happened to have an ax in her hand, she'd bring it down on the attacker's head without hesitation. She was sure of it. She hated that part of herself, and it scared her, and she wanted to run away from it, and yet she was sure that's what she would do. But that would also pierce Harvey's heart at the same time. The bad things Kieli did always came back to bite Harvey and hurt him when she'd meant to protect him.

She didn't want to hurt people anymore. She didn't want to make any more missteps. Suddenly it struck her that in that case, maybe it would be best to just leave everyone's lives. *Maybe I should just go away somewhere where I won't cause anybody any trouble. Where would I go...?* She couldn't think of anywhere to go but to Becca or her grandmother or her mom. But she was sure not one of them would welcome her the way she was now.

... What am I thinking?

Kieli shook her head back and forth. The hard body of the radio chafed her forehead until it stung, which thankfully cut off her line of thought that was getting so mixed up. She pulled her head back from the radio a little and gazed into the speaker. She got the feeling it was silently telling her *Nobody's going to give you advice about something like this.*

Could she really become someone who could protect the people she loved on her own, without relying on anyone else, without hurting anyone else? Somehow she thought that might be way, way beyond her.

By chance, her downcast eyes found something that looked very much like an exposed water pipe. A good ways down the slope sat what looked like a tap for drinking water. A pail was lying on the ground nearby, even.

Water...

Kieli looked over her shoulder at the door of the shack. *Harvey might want some water to drink.* She'd left her flask back at the radio tower along with her bag, and he'd been gulping alcohol when he hardly ever drank any-thing... Although she was disappointed in herself that a tiny little thing like this was the best help she could think of to give him, it was something, and she couldn't stand to sit there much longer anyway. So she put the radio around her neck again and stood up.

Kieli walked somewhat unsteadily down the steep, rocky incline, as if magnetically pulled toward the place where she'd seen the water. There was a big hole in the bottom of the tin pail, but luckily the spout was working at least, and rust-red water trickled out when she turned on the faucet. It must be drawing from a layer deep underground, because as she let it run it started coming up relatively clear. Kieli felt a little moved. It still smelled thickly of rust when she brought her face to the faucet, but she put her mouth under it and drank a little, and then let both hands fill up with it so she could wash her face.

"Fwahh!"

Letting the cold water contact the skin of her face seemed to perk up her feelings a bit, too. She ended the ritual by slapping both cheeks a few times, and then told the radio, "Okay, Corporal, I'm awake now."

She spoke to him just like always, even though she knew he wouldn't answer. She did it to convince herself to behave just like always. "I'm sorry I whined at you, Corporal. It's okay; I'll try to do my best on my own... I'm fine without you now, so don't worry." She had to admit her voice as she said so sounded too feeble to be very convincing.

Plop…a sphere sticky with blood and slime and wisps of nerve fiber fell on the floor in front of his face. Lukewarm fluid spilled out of his empty eye socket onto the cheek resting on the floor. He'd cut off his sense of pain, but more than the pain it was the unbearable unpleasantness of it all that made him feel like throwing up. Harvey pressed his palm over his hollow left eye, then closed his right eye too to shut off all visual input from the outside.

"Huh," said a boyish voice at his side, sounding impressed. "First time I've ever seen a human do that in his right mind."

"I'm not in my right mind," Harvey spat tiredly without getting up.

"…I'm guessing you know this, but that'll probably only be a temporary fix no matter what. I think the decay will still eat its way into your nerves. That'll only slow down the progression."

"Better than dying now," he answered half-automatically, without actually thinking about it, and received a somewhat surprised silence in reply. Harvey himself was surprised at his words too. He couldn't help the thin, self-deprecating smile that came to his lips beneath the hand over his face. "Is that funny? Heh, it is funny, isn't it? *Me*, struggling to survive like this. Right now…I'm clinging to life no matter what I have to do. I mean, what choice do I have, Corporal? It's…it's your fault for ending up like that. Now if something happens to me, Kieli'll be all alone and…" *Ugh*, he thought, *I've been talking up a storm today; I hate that*, but somehow he kept going, and the more he talked the less he knew what he was say-ing. With his eyes closed he felt as though he were drifting in deep, dark water, and it sucked his consciousness down into the darkness with it.

A guy with no will to live isn't worth killing.

The Corporal had told him that. Harvey could still remem-ber it vividly.

Does that mean right now I'm worth killing, at least? I won-der if you finally acknowledged me in the end. I hope so... He mumbled to himself for some time with no real awareness of whether or not he was doing it out loud. At some point he re-alized, *Huh, I think I might be talking crazy right now,* but he couldn't think about it very clearly. Apparently he really actu-ally *wasn't* in his right mind; his thoughts spun dizzily. *Wait, who was I just talking to...?*

Splish.

With a warm, wet sound, a thick drop of water fell on the floor in front of him.

About a tenth of his brain was wondering skeptically what the sound meant when a damp muzzle loomed toward him and prodded his cheek. Foul animal breath and the smell of old blood and new blood. The beast's snout pushed aside the hand he'd been holding over his left eye—

—and with no warning, something was shoved into the empty socket.

"Augghhh!"

The anguish attacked him out of nowhere, no time to pre-pare, and ripped the scream right out of his lungs. Unable to take it, he rolled around on the floor, hitting a wall after about three rolls and not even caring because he was just trying to claw the foreign object out of his eye—but someone seized his shoulders and pinned him down. It took every ounce of his strength to crack open his right eye and look up. Mane was straddling him, and his left eyehole was empty and dripping cloudy, viscous fluid.

"What—?!"

"Just bear it for a little while. Don't take it out; I don't just hand that out to people every day."

All Harvey's concentration was scattered by the agony and the feeling of wrongness, as though someone had stuck a chunk of rock in his head, and he couldn't quite manage to shut out the pain. The creature's face was right in front of him, but the voice seemed warped and far away. "This is my owner's eye. I got it when I ate him. It ought to stick right to you too, so I'll let you have it. You should be able to use it for a while, anyway."

In just that eye his senses were bizarrely amplified into hypersensitivity, and he could clearly feel the severed ends of nerve fibers stretching from the intrusion, crawling like tentacles deeper behind the socket. He tried to grind his teeth together and accidentally bit the inside of his mouth instead. The taste of blood spread on his tongue. When it came, the sensation of those tentacles pulsating as they encroached into his brain was too much. He vomited pure gastric juice.

While Kieli was walking around by the watering place looking for something to serve as a canteen, she heard a sort of muffled shout. She looked toward the shack and heard what sounded like a violent struggle in the distance coming from that direction. After a little while, it went quiet.

Harvey…?

When she wondered what was happening, she felt afraid. She started climbing up the path, thinking she'd go back and check on him, but on second thought, maybe she shouldn't go back inside yet; she changed her mind, and stopped. She went back and forth on it for a while. Just when she'd decided to go back down to the water after all, she caught sight of a group dressed in white approaching from the foothills. They were still a long way off, but the wind carried the sound of metal chinking against metal up to her.

Church Soldiers—! After freezing on the spot for a moment, she started and hid herself behind a rock, holding a hand over her racing heart as she peeked out at them. It was a safe bet that they were coming after her and Harvey and Mane, but evidently they hadn't actually pinpointed their location yet, because it looked as if they were methodically searching everywhere. *A "platoon," is that what that's called?* It was a group of about a dozen men in white clerical robes reinforced with armor plating over their vital points, carrying rifles at their shoulders.

What do I do? We might not be able to move Harvey yet. But I have to go let them know; that's the first thing.

Kieli avoided the path the platoon was climbing, circling around to a narrow staircase between two rock walls, and ran smack into another platoon coming down from the other side.

"Oh!" She'd stopped still and let out the gasp before she

could think. But apparently the soldiers hadn't expected the encounter any more than she had; their reaction was simple surprise. So Kieli took advantage of that opening to turn around and take off like lightning.

"Stop!" someone ordered behind her. Ignoring it, she fled down the staircase, taking the steps two at a time. *I can't let them go toward the shack; I have to go in a different direction and confuse them.*

Her own momentum ran away with her and two steps turned into two and a half, making her miss her footing on the next one and fall. She heard the smack of the radio hitting rock and cradled it to her stomach the best she could, curling herself up into a ball as she tumbled down the stone stairs. There was a flat rock ledge immediately below it, so she stopped there, but she'd hit her elbows and knees badly enough that she couldn't get up for several seconds. In that time the metallic footsteps of several soldiers overtook her.

A square, gloved hand grabbed her upper arm and dragged her up. Squirming and flailing all her limbs, Kieli shouted random noises at the top of her lungs. Best-case scenario, she'd make her captor flinch, and hopefully even if she didn't manage that, Harvey or Mane would hear her and realize that something was wrong.

"H-hey, pipe down! Just come quietly!"

"Waahhh! Waa—"

Along with the nonplussed soldier's shout came a blow to the back of her head, and for a moment the sound of her own voice faded from her ears.

"Hey, she dropped her letter. Pick it up for her," the radio ordered him in an *Obviously that's your job* sort of way. Resignedly, Harvey stooped forward and collected the stationery that had slid to the floor and landed by his feet. He slipped it as softly as he could underneath the girl's hands where they lay on her lap, sighing.

"Where is she gonna send that letter?"

"She's got nowhere to send it."

"Why did she write such a pointless letter?"

"Everybody has someone they want to write a letter to, even if they're not gonna send it."

"I don't."

"That's nothing to be proud of."

The put-down that came as quickly as Harvey's own response ought to have been just another of their exchanges, sickeningly routine, and yet Harvey felt strangely as though it had been a long time. He was oddly relieved, somehow.

He leaned his head against the cold window glass and let his gaze roam the scenery outside the train. The vast red-brown wilderness and sand-colored sky were sickeningly routine, too, and they flowed sluggishly by without inspiring any particular emotion. *Chug, chug, chug…* The constant thumping vibration against the bottom of his seat reinforced the unchanging ordinariness of it all even more.

When Harvey took his eyes away from the boringly familiar scenery in the window, the portable radio who seemed to live for nagging him was sitting by the sill just as always.

The soft sounds of sleep came from the seat kitty-corner from him. He glanced at the girl's face, and his shoulders twitched a little when he thought about how unguarded her face looked in sleep.

"Herbie."

"Harvey."

"Are you enjoying this?"

"What is this all of a sudden…? I don't enjoy talking to you."

Harvey was lighting a cigarette, giving vague answers without paying overmuch attention to the conversation. "I'm serious," said the radio in a lower tone, like Harvey'd hurt his feelings. "Do you wish you'd stayed dead at the abandoned mine, or—"…Huh? Wait a second. Isn't this something he already said to me, way back in the day? No, more like this whole conversation is from back then.

"—are you glad that you're alive right now?"

When he belatedly registered his déjà vu, the scene inside the train car warped like melting taffy, and then immediately it began to be pulled away, stretching farther into the distance before his eyes. Kieli and the radio were taken away along with the rapidly stretching train, and he was left behind alone.

"Wait…"

The instant he stood up, the floor at his feet vanished. No tracks sprinting by, no train car; just a void that swallowed him up when he fell into it headlong.

Where am I…?

Now he was walking all alone along the floor of a dark valley. He didn't know when he'd started walking or where he was going or why, but here he was, walking.

Through a long, long winding ravine wrapped in dimly staticky darkness. The air felt disgusting. Cold and coarse. *Owooo...nn...* The sorrowfully moaning wind had a grainy texture that filed away at his skin rather than caressing it. He had the sense of pain to feel that, and yet, strangely, he couldn't see any evidence of his presence. He tried holding up his hand to get it into his field of vision, but nothing happened. Did he really have a body in the first place? He started to lose confidence that he'd existed as a discrete individual at all. There was a lump of nausea and pain somewhere at the core of his consciousness, and he clung fast to it as the only fragile thread that let him perceive his own existence.

Somehow he tripped over something, even though he didn't have any legs as far as he could see. When he looked down, there was a corpse there. The corpse of a redheaded man lying in a patch of wilderness where some battle had taken place, with the right half of its body burned to cinders—*Who is that, again?* he wondered. After giving it some thought, he realized it was him. *Oh yeah, that's what my face looks like.* Remembering that made his existence feel just that little bit more real. Seeing himself dead just as he was finally starting to feel real seemed like kind of a shame.

When was this self from, again? I guess it must be from a long time ago, when I was still fighting the War. Looking around, he saw other selves lying here and there too, ones who probably would've died there if they'd been a little un-luckier. Most of them were from the War era, but there were also a lot from pretty recently.

The one buried in the sand with all those white-boned corpses at the bottom of the sand ship,

and the one lying like a rag doll in front of a white town wall early one morning,

and the one lying faceup at the bottom of the mine lift with his heart gouged out…

Oh, this one's from Easterbury…

He looked up along the dangling wires of the lift overhead to see the shaft's exit. But the top of the deep shaft was painted over in black so that it looked as if *it* were the bottom instead, and he felt as though he might start falling upward.

If the timing of anything at all had been even a tiny bit dif-ferent, it wouldn't have been surprising for any of these selves to have died for real. And the fact was that he remembered once thinking that he was fine with dying anywhere at any time…but now, gazing at each corpse in turn, he thought with all his heart, *I'm glad I didn't die there.*

I have to go home. I've still got things to do.

As he started walking in search of the way back home, something grabbed him from below. He looked down. The corpse of the self buried in sand was hanging on to his ankle. Not that he could actually see his ankle; still, the leg that as far as he knew wasn't there was nevertheless being dragged deep down into a whirlpool of sand. He tried to fight back, but there was no way to fight when he couldn't perceive his own limbs, and so he was buried up to his face in no time.

Coarse grains of sand scraped off bits of his skin and even invaded his mouth, until at last he couldn't breathe.

No, not yet...! He tried to shout, but the sand filled his throat and no sound came out. His whole field of vision was buried in sand. *No, I need a little longer; I can't die yet! Someone—*

His eyes abruptly surfaced out of the sand. Someone's hand was there, grasping his arm and pulling him up. Through the touch of that someone's hand the existence of his own arm felt clearly real, and in the same moment he experienced it as real, his invisible arm became visible as something physically real.

The hand that hoisted him out of the sand was the rugged hand of a man in a shabby dark green military uniform. With the hand still tugging him along, he climbed up the mine shaft toward the top. A thin ray of light shone down from the exit that had been colored solid, opaque black. The slightly clouded sand-colored light that shone on all the land on the planet.

The hand let go of him when they came into the light, and he was flung all alone into a white space where he lost all sense of which way was up. He heard a final sharp whisper of warning in his ear, and then the man's hand dissolved into static.

Wait, Corporal—! he shouted for all he was worth, and tried to grab on to the disappearing hand. Even to his own ears he sounded like an abandoned kid now. *No, Corporal. Wait, I don't want this after all. I don't want you to go yet—*

* * *

The sound of his own voice pulled him back to himself. "Ugh!" Instantly, a sharp agony behind his left eye. Harvey doubled over and writhed until he hit the wall, fell back the other way with a thud, and planted his face into the floor. Gathering his scattered thoughts, he managed to bring the sharp throbbing under control, but the dull pain weighing heavily on the center of his head remained.

"You okay?"

He cracked his eyes open at the sound of a boy's voice. A vague gray floor floated in front of him. Then his eyes started to adjust a little better, and he could see the forelegs of the black beast standing beside him.

"You passed out for a second there."

"A second…?" His throat was bone-dry.

"Not even a minute's gone by. Are you starting to see out of it a little?"

"……." Without lifting his cheek from the floor, Harvey let his muddled brain take in what he could see. His left eye's field of vision covered his right eye's with a hazy film. He was in the same boat he'd been in not long ago, just with left and right reversed. The daylight filtering through the tiny window from outside cut a single, slanting beam of sandy light through the dimness of the room, making a pool of sunlight on the floor. Just like the light that had filtered down into the mine shaft: light the color of their planet.

Harvey spaced out for several seconds before abruptly coming back to his senses and lifting his head. It felt heavy, as if his brain had turned into a dense mass, and he felt dizzy. His left eye's focus was still fuzzy. Relying on his good right eye, he stood up, letting his hand follow him up the wall for balance. Mane's voice followed him. "You should wait a little longer. It'll take some time for the nerves to finish hooking up."

"Kieli's…" The Corporal had warned him. *Kieli's in trouble…!*

The back of her head throbbed. She was being pressed against the ground where she'd fallen forward when she was hit, and her hands were restrained behind her back. The radio cut into her stomach where it was trapped underneath her, and her face twisted as she glared hard up at the soldiers in front of her. Blood seeped out of her cheek where it'd scraped against the rocky ground.

If only Harvey—no, if only Mane would come…But they were a long way from the shack here, so maybe even Mane hadn't heard her. Kieli stuck to her brave attitude, but on the inside she felt ready to cry any second. *Harvey…!*

Help came from a totally unexpected direction. "Hey, hold on! Stop that! What are you doing?!" a voice broke in. But she'd never heard that intonation before in her life: something without the hard tones particular to Church Soldiers, something relatively soft. "She's not some kind of rebel. There's no call for violence! Let her go right now!"

At his order, the soldier holding her down relaxed his grip somewhat. When Kieli raised her head from the ground, the person climbing up the mountain into view wasn't a Church Soldier in a white robe; he was a man in a long, jet-black

greatcoat—a priest. Her arms were still held captive, but the grip around them had relaxed, so she sat up on the ground, coughing, and looked suspiciously up at the priest running toward her. He was a comparatively young, wimpy-looking man; Kieli doubted he was the soldiers' superior. Priests and Church Soldiers weren't even in the same organization to begin with.

Waving the platoon back, this particular priest came to stand in front of Kieli. "I'm very sorry. That violence was my responsibility; I didn't make my instructions explicit enough. I promise you, we mean you no harm," he apologized frankly. Kieli was a little startled at that, but she quickly refocused and cordoned herself off from them again, glaring daggers up at the priest through her lashes. "Truly, um…I'm not going to do anything to you, so please don't glare at me like that." He looked discomfited by Kieli's blatantly hostile attitude before straightening himself with a little cough and executing a neat bow. It was the polished gesture of a capital priest.

"I'm here…I have come here on orders from Father Sigri, the Eleventh Elder on the Council of Elders, as an envoy with full authority in this matter. At Father Sigri's request, I'm extending an invitation for you to come to the capital."

"……?"

Blindsided by this totally incomprehensible announcement, Kieli gaped. "…What kind of joke is this, sir?"

"No, I haven't said anything to laugh at…"

The priest trailed off hesitantly, bewildered at her entirely incredulous answer, but after another cough, he persevered. In slightly uncertain tones, as if he himself were only reciting a speech someone else had given him to memorize: "Well, now…sixteen years ago, Father Sigri's wife, Setsuri, took their baby, who was about to turn one year old, and disappeared from the capital. You are that lady's gift to this world, and…well, that makes you Eleventh Elder Father Sigri's daughter."

The priest stopped talking, looking relieved to have finished with this summary explanation, and watched for Kieli's next response. Several seconds of blank silence passed.

And then the priest cried a loud "Ack!" as Kieli took him off guard with another escape attempt. Paying him no mind, Kieli ran as fast as she could. "C-catch her!" The Church Soldiers chased after her at the anxious priest's instruction; while she did manage to get a good distance down the path, in the end it didn't take them long to subdue her. The priest caught up a while later, panting hard and kicking up the hem of his long coat as he ran.

"Why are you running away?!"

"Let me go! Let! Me! Go!"

With her arms locked in a full nelson by a Church Soldier behind her, Kieli thrashed her legs as hard as she could, aiming to kick over the priest standing in front of her. As he dodged hastily, looking nonplussed, he tried a different tack. "Oh, dear…Ahem, well, I didn't want to play this card, but…" And, his tone becoming a bit pompous, the priest broached a new subject.

Specifically, that of a person Kieli wouldn't have expected in a million years to hear about from him.

"We have an acquaintance of yours in our custody…Does

the phrase "Witch of Toulouse" ring any bells? She's safe for the moment, but her treatment in the future will depend on you. So I'm asking you, please, listen to—"

"Beatrix!" Kieli cried, almost screamed, in fact, cutting off whatever the priest had been about to say.

After the reflexive shout, she was too astonished to speak. The blond woman's face the last time they'd talked at that bar on the parish border sprang up in the back of her mind. Kieli'd told her off for keeping Harvey's letter a secret, and she'd gotten this expression that was sort of sulky yet ashamed at the same time, and then started smoking there at the counter as if she didn't know what else to do with herself, and then a customer had come into the bar and the moment to start up the conversation again had never come.

Kieli'd worried. She'd worried for so long. There were things she had to apologize for when they saw each other again, but she was sure Beatrix would tell her she was an idiot for worrying about them and forgive her right away, and once they made up they could talk so much more than they used to, and go clothes shopping together, and all kinds of things. That's what she'd thought.

And she's been in the capital this whole time...?

A seething rage boiled up within her and erupted.

"Did you do something to Beatrix?! If you did, I'll never forgive you!"

"I-I told you, we haven't done anything!" The priest, who'd shied back when Kieli interrupted him and had stood stiff ever since, hastened to explain further. "She's just fine, I promise. So listen to what I—"

"Why should I believe *you*?! You say all this stuff that makes no sense, and you bring *my mother's name* into your lies! Just who does this 'Sigri' jerk think he is, anyway?! I've had enough!" Kieli screamed hysterically, fighting back with everything she had. When the soldier behind her flinched back, she took advantage of the opportunity to shake free and try to make a break for it, but they caught her and overpowered her again in no time.

"Augghh!"

A husky scream, and then the soldier gripping Kieli's arm bent backward, holding his face in his hand. She whirled around, stumbling with how suddenly she'd been released, to see a jet-black beast with one bird's leg and one grotesquely twisted protruding wing landing between her and the soldiers, protecting her.

"Mane!"

The beast glanced back to her when she called his name and nodded pointedly to reassure her everything was fine. When she got a good look at him, her momentary relief was gone in a flash: his left eyehole, the one where a dark brown eye should have been, was pitifully crushed in.

"What happened to you…?!"

"Don't worry about it," Mane answered easily, giving a glance at the enemy with his remaining amber eye. The platoon was daunted by the strange beast's appearance, but they resumed their formation and readied their rifles. Mane didn't give them a chance to fire. He closed the distance between them with one powerful leap, getting right into the heart of their camp and beginning to bite one soldier after another.

For several moments Kieli was too stunned to do anything but watch the uproar begin, but then she jerked back to her senses with a start. "No killing, Mane!"

He paused for only an instant at her voice, and in that instant there was the *bang* of a bullet slamming through the air—the bizarrely shaped wing seemed to leap into the air, broken right at the base, and his black body staggered, equally black bodily fluids pouring from it. However, he planted his feet and kept himself upright, immediately hurling himself at the soldier who'd fired, mauling him with his forelegs and knocking him to the ground.

"Mane...!"

"Get uphill!" he snapped. So Kieli wrenched herself away, turning on her heel to find a single soldier standing in her path up the slope.

She somehow managed to duck underneath the gloved hand reaching out for her, but she couldn't hold enough of her balance to stand back up again, and she ended up landing on her butt on the ground. Just as she thought she wouldn't be able to evade the soldier again, he suddenly stopped moving.

Holding her body stiff, Kieli looked up with her eyes to see a tall, thin redhead standing behind the soldier. He was holding the soldier by the throat with one hand and squeezing. Long, bony fingers bit deep into the struggling soldier's throat as he gasped tiny, thready noises, and she heard an uncanny creaking—from the bones in the soldier's neck, and, she suspected, from the ones in his throttler's arm, too.

"Harvey, wait..."

As Kieli called out for him to stop, right before her eyes,

a bullet grazed Harvey's arm with the sharp sound of a gun-shot—his lower arm—and tore off a chunk of his skin. Kieli gave a raspy shriek, frozen to the spot.

Harvey casually dropped the soldier, who was beginning to foam at the mouth, and rolled his eyes slowly toward the man who'd fired the shot. After first glancing down at the blood dribbling freely from his arm and tilting his head al-most questioningly—

"—!"

With a battle cry that Kieli could hardly even hear, he suddenly leapt at the shooter with no warning movement whatsoever, closing the distance between them and seizing the barrel of the soldier's gun faster than her eyes could fol-low. Never mind Kieli; it all happened so quickly that the now weaponless soldier himself was equally dumbfounded, and before he could recover, Harvey had shifted to an underhand grip and felled him with a blow to the jaw from below.

The black-robed priest who'd been standing behind him collapsed nervelessly to the ground, blabbering. Harvey just thrust the mouth of the rifle against the priest's head, support-ing its whole weight with just his left arm, and put his finger on the trigger. There wasn't any conspicuous hesitation in his coppery right eye—or in his inky brown left eye, either. "Har-vey, wait, stop...!" Something was wrong; there was too little uncertainty in his actions. *I think he's kind of snapped a little.*

And then Harvey abruptly swung the barrel straight out to the side. There was a dull metallic impact—the man who'd been on the verge of stepping in managed to raise the hilt of his saber just in time block the attack. Upon which they both immediately jumped a step backward and faced off from that distance.

The soldier who'd inserted himself between Harvey and the priest as a shield wasn't like the ordinary Church Soldiers; he was a man in the prime of life wearing a highly decorated white greatcoat. Kieli realized right away that he was the officer who'd come to the radio tower.

"Oho…" Squaring off against an opponent with some skill, Harvey let out a surprised noise that also sounded fairly amused. The officer, on the other hand, looked tenser. He licked his lips lightly, and then resolutely, though with a surprisingly mild attitude, set about the task of talking Harvey down.

"We apologize for our bad form. We don't want to fight you. We'd like you to listen to what—"

Without waiting for the man to finish, Harvey gripped the rifle like a saber and lunged at him. Kieli wouldn't be able to stop him in time—

"Will you just cut that out, you damn fool?!"

As the bellow rang out, the air in front of Kieli's chest swelled up, and a shock wave gushed forth that hit the rifle Harvey was about to mow down his rival with dead center and smashed it in half. Harvey was blasted backward along with the broken rifle, rolling downhill in a backward somersault. Knocked off her feet herself by the recoil, Kieli looked down at her chest with her mouth hanging dumbly open.

"C-Corporal…?"

Dark green bits of static spewed noisily from the speaker of the radio around her neck, and an image started to form in midair. The face floating within it diffused and laboriously re-formed several times as it opened its mouth and spoke. The low voice coming from the speaker in time with its movements was distorted, filled with awful static, but it still had an intimidating air.

"Very well, then ... let's hear what you have to say."

Thus addressed by a strange, unknown body of noise, the officer widened his eyes. He was still holding up his saber to parry the blow. Behind him, the priest was sitting on his rear, white as a sheet. The other soldiers that Mane had been attacking stopped moving too, stunned, and all the uproar abruptly died down into silence. A few men here and there did panic and run, but their cries sounded feeble and far away.

"Herbie," the body of noise whispered to the youth behind him, all the while keeping the men around them in check with the force of his glower.

That pet name Kieli hadn't heard in so long, the one that as far as she knew only one person in this world used; that mispronounced pet name, and that rough but warm tone.

"Calm down, Herbie. What the hell do you think you're doing, for God's sake?"

"But—" Harvey was just sitting there where he'd landed with a poleaxed expression on his face, but now he opened his mouth and started to make some kind of excuse for a moment before closing it again, seeming to forget how to speak. Then something in his face shifted, and he looked as though he were about to cry. To Kieli, it looked like the face of a little boy who'd just been scolded by his father.

She thought he reminded her of someone. He was a really high-ranking officer in the Capital Security Forces, and yet he didn't come off as so high and mighty. He seemed trustworthy. *Could he be...?* Maybe she should've asked him if he had a son, but she missed the right moment to do it, and then he was boarding his truck and leaving.

They stood on a rock ledge about halfway up the slope of the fault, watching the men at the armored trucks on standby down in the foothills collect the injured. Mane was lying on a rock a little ways down from them, keeping a sharp eye on the scene below him, at once watchful and menacing. Before long, the line of trucks began to withdraw, leaving behind only a circle of smaller trucks hanging back at a distance for observation. Leaving a surveillance team to watch them had been the one condition they wouldn't budge on, and Harvey had accepted it without argument.

They'd heard the priest who called himself the "envoy of the Eleventh Elder on the Council of Elders" state his business again from the beginning, and after a considering expression, Harvey had answered fairly readily. "We'll accept your invitation." Kieli felt lost. She couldn't figure out what he was really thinking.

Harvey fixed his eyes not on the priest envoy, but on the Capital Security Forces officer who claimed to have brought his men to serve as their escort at the Father's personal request, as he continued. His attitude was unruffled.

"But we're not interested in being hauled in like criminals. We'll get there on our own steam. Kieli's being invited there as an honored guest, you said. Is that how you people treat your guests? You take them prisoner and force them to come with you?"

It was a valid point, and moreover, thanks to Mane's mauling spree, half of the escort platoon was currently nonfunctional; even if what he'd said had been pretty absurd, their side was in control here anyway. Not to mention the sheer nature of the group who'd placed themselves around Kieli as a barricade. To start with, the one-eyed black beast curled up on the ground at her feet glaring intimidatingly—who periodically terrorized the soldiers by opening his mouth wide from ear to ear to display his bright red tongue and sawlike teeth. And particles of noise gathered around the radio in her arms to form the face of a soldier's ghost opening its mouth to growl at them before dissolving and then starting the whole process over again. And last but not least, there was the half-copper-eyed, half-dark-brown-eyed, one-armed Undying…He was standing at Kieli's side looking unconcerned, but every now and then he'd glance over at the circle of lower-level soldiers as though some thought had struck him, and whichever one his eyes happened to meet would gasp in terror and back away.

As for Kieli, the key figure in their conversation, her legs were trembling so hard she thought they might crumple beneath her any moment, but she drew reassurance and courage from everyone protecting her and managed to hold her ground.

"I'm afraid that, er, won't do. We'll need her to come with us…" the priest had persisted through his own obvious fear. But then the officer leading their escort force had taken over the negotiations and accepted Harvey's terms on the condition that a small unit stay behind with them to keep watch ("escort" though he might be, he was clearly higher-ranking than the young priest).

We'll get there on our own steam—hearing Harvey say that so casually made Kieli happy, but more than that it made her scared. There was no way Harvey could possibly think that an Undying going to the capital would get by there without incident. And yet nonetheless, he intended to go there with her, as if it was just a given that he come.

The Council's Eleventh Elder's… daughter?

As if she could believe something like that all of a sudden. Since the priest had specifically brought up her mother's name, it seemed as though they weren't just completely mistaking her for someone else, but that only made it harder to figure out what they were after. Doubt and unease and confusion just swirled around and around inside her.

Keeping watch over the procession of trucks receding into the distance out of her peripheral vision, Kieli darted a glance behind her and to the side. Harvey was sitting on a ledge a level above her (it was plain that he was sitting because standing was too painful), inspecting the radio. It was lecturing him about something or other as he fiddled with its tuning knob and grumbled back with a sullen pout. At one point she heard him saying, "Shut up; you let me do all the work and then just stole the limelight."

The armored station assistant's repairs had been almost finished. Evidently when Kieli'd fallen on top of him, the last connection had been knocked into place, and the radio had started working again.

The Corporal coming back to them was the one thing, the one real, true saving grace of all of this.

Noticing her gaze, Harvey turned his face toward her. The moment their eyes met, he grinned and said, "Hey, you. What's with that face?" Embarrassed, Kieli turned away. Was she really making such a weird face? Lately seeing Harvey's smile made her chest hurt for some reason, and it was hard to look at it. She'd always liked it when he smiled at her before…

"I was always planning to go to the capital sooner or later anyway, so if they're not going to get in my way, that suits me fine. And if they really are holding Beatrix there, I *have* to go."

"I…think it's some kind of trap."

"What kind of trap?"

"Well, I'm not sure, but…"

Kieli looked down, faltering. She didn't have any grounds for thinking it; she just did. After a short pause, she heard a rustle of fabric coming from the rock ledge above, and then she felt a faint warmth of body heat over her shoulder. When she looked back just briefly, Harvey was crouching close over her shoulder, peering at her.

"But you know, if what they said was true, it would mean you've still got relatives."

"I don't want any," she answered curtly, turning her head away again with a huff.

"...Hey, Kieli," a quiet voice reasoned in her ear. "You don't have to overthink this. You might have a father there. Just meet him and see what he's like."

"I don't *want* to meet him."

A father in the capital? Even if that was actually true, it didn't make her one bit happy. Just the idea that she might be related to someone in the Church actually gave her chills. To think that she was on the side of the people who'd made Harvey, and Beatrix, and all the other Undyings suffer for so long...

She hadn't wanted to learn *that*, not now. It would've been enough for her just not to lose what she already had. There wasn't anything else she'd wanted beyond what she already had—she'd never wanted to know something like *that*, something that was only good for upsetting her.

"Kieli."

When she stared at the ground and stayed quiet, he tugged lightly at her hair. Reluctantly, she tilted her face up to look at him, not bothering to hide the scowl. When they were squatting on the rock ledge like this, Harvey's eye level was actually a bit lower than Kieli's even without her completely raising her head, and he looked up into her face at an angle. His inky dark brown left eye looked strangely at home against the inflamed skin of his cheek; if anything, the fact that it didn't seem out of place to her made it more distressing to look at, making her feel conflicted.

"I hope it's true. 'Cause I've always wanted to help you meet a living, breathing parent. So let's go find out. The Corporal and I will both come with you. Okay?"

"……"

Kieli couldn't find any response to make, and she hung her head again, unable to meet his eyes any longer. When her eyes turned downward, Harvey's hand tugging at the hair hanging off her shoulder entered her line of sight. Joints even more prominent than before made it look all the more slender, and it was such a wreck, and yet this hand kept on trying to protect Kieli as it always had…Why did God treat him so unkindly, and rip away a little more of his life like this every time something happened? Kieli was the one who deserved to be punished, so why couldn't Kieli take his place?

Harvey'd always been planning to go to the capital sooner or later, even if this hadn't happened. And if that were the case—if Harvey would take her with him, and not abandon her yet, mess though she was, to Kieli that all by itself was enough reason to accept the invitation from the capital. More than enough, if it would let them stay together a little longer. Because Kieli wanted to protect Harvey just as he always tried to protect her.

Because she might not know what to do just yet…but in the end, rather than running away from the thought of hurting what was in front of her, she wanted to become strong enough to protect it.

Softly, she laid her own hand over the long fingers threading through her hair. After a short hesitation at the feeling of those bony knuckles, she wrapped her hand around his pointer finger, and nodded. It gripped back lightly, as if to nod back. For as much as she felt heartened, she also thought she could see the end of the fragile thread binding them together, the one that had almost slipped off, that could snap any moment, but she squeezed Harvey's finger tightly as if to hold on to it.

All along she'd been thinking, *Will we still be journeying together when we leave this gorge? What if we all end up going our separate ways there? What if our final destinations are different?*

But for now, at least, their journeys still all led in the same direction.

I don't want to cut this thread yet. I want to protect him.

So let's go to the capital—.

THE STORY OF A CERTAIN UNDYING,
GIRL, RADIO, AND WINGED BEAST UNDER
THE TWILIT SKY

Take care, she whispered, hugging him tightly around the neck and burying her face in his black mane. The hair standing out around his neck was stiff at the tip, but it was soft farther down, and when she breathed in it smelled like animal and blood.

"Kieli. Let him go."

At Harvey's rather hesitant words, she forced herself to unwind her arms and lift her face, though not without hanging on a while longer first. Bringing her nose in almost close enough to bump against his slightly moist black muzzle, she gazed into his eyes, one amber, one crushed in. In giving Harvey an eye, Mane had lost one.

"I'm sorry…" she murmured with a heavy heart.

"Why are you apologizing?"

Mane looked offended, and Kieli blinked.

"…Thanks," she amended.

"There you go, that's better," Mane sniffed, and smiled a little. To Kieli, the smile looked embarrassed. She smiled back at him just a little, and took a step back as she stood up, returning to Harvey's side. Looking up at her with his lone amber eye, Mane ducked his head a bit apologetically. Both bizarre wings were wrenched off by now. All that remained of them were the scars on his shoulder blades where they'd cracked open, and the faint remnants of the protrusions.

Even though Kieli knew with her rational mind that she mustn't say anything selfish to him, her heart still couldn't accept this. She let her eyes fall to the ground, crestfallen. She'd just assumed that Mane would come with them, too…

"Sorry, but I don't feel like going all the way to the capital with you. I'm not counting myself a member of your group, and anyway, we mountain lions have to live footloose and fancy-free. It's our nature, see?"—When he'd begun his good-byes in his usual easy tone, Kieli had tried to stop him, shocked, but Harvey seemed to have some tacit understanding with him, and didn't really say anything. He just nodded lightly, lowering the dark brown eye that had been a gift from Mane, and said, "Okay. Thanks for everything." Once Harvey'd agreed, Kieli couldn't very well insist any further.

That said…apparently he had no intention of acknowledging he was a dog to the very end.

"Okay then, I'm off. You hang in there."

And with those simple parting words, Mane turned around with a swish of his tail and began walking rhythmically away into the valley. The long tail like a mountain lion's had lost its fur; bare like that, it looked like a thin, pathetic string.

Evening-tinged sunshine filtered down from the narrow scrap of sky enclosed between the rock walls, faintly illuminating the outlines of the rock ledges that jutted out like shelves. Kieli couldn't see all the way to the end of the valley, but she closed her eyes and pictured the sight of the single great, withered tree the radio station had become that must still be out there, deep in the gorge far, far along that path of ledges. The rust-red grave where the armored guardian, now done with his mission after protecting the tower for so long, slept, and Mane's owner, too.

Burnt tail swaying back and forth, the jet-black beast with remnant wings on his back ambled easily along the rock ledge, far less like a mountain lion than like an old cat setting off for its spot to die. As they stood seeing him off from the valley entrance, though, he did turn back to them one last time.

"Listen, you! Smoked meat and chickpeas—"

"Huh?!" Kieli answered, bewildered at the sudden angry-sounding shout.

"That was my favorite meal back when I was alive!"

And with that, he loped nimbly off. His gait was just the littlest bit lopsided as he alternated between three padded animal legs and one bird's leg, but he vaulted lightly from one foothold to the next without seeming to mind at all. The hair around his neck caught a ray of sunset and gave off sparkles of golden light just like a real mountain lion's mane.

"Ah…!"

Kieli's eyes widened. For just a moment, it looked as if his ripped-off wings had grown back again. She blinked, and then bit her lip and swallowed back her tears.

The sparkles faded into afterimages as Mane ran too fast for the light to catch up, trailing down his back and then his long tail before scattering with twinkles into the air. He looked just as majestic as if he'd been given new golden wings of light in place of the black ones and gone soaring into the sky.

The wind from the gorge whipped Kieli and Harvey's hair in all directions. She'd like to believe that when its howl sounded for an instant like the music from the radio tower that they'd never hear again, it wasn't just a coincidence. Even now, that mobile radio station was parked in a quiet spot somewhere in this valley, and a large man in armor...no, a gentle elderly station assistant was wryly murmuring as a young station chief next to him happily picked out records, while a black dog with a strange ring of hair around its neck munched away at his meal of milky bread, smoked meat, and chickpeas. And surely the radio tower's speakers were crooning soft, staticky rock music as it watched over them.

The single tear that tracked down Kieli's cheek was scattered by the wind into tiny droplets that mingled into the sparkles of twilight filling the valley.

Kieli woke up at the sound of faint static from the radio. She slowly poked her head around the edge of the blanket she'd pulled up over her and blinked sleepily, looking around the room. The patch of blue-gray night sky in the shack's tiny window was just starting to lighten.

She could hear muffled noise and voices coming from the doorway. Harvey and the Corporal...apparently they were right outside. Kieli wriggled out from underneath the blanket and crawled over to the door.

"Take me to my grave?! Don't go off brooding on your own and deciding crap like that! I don't intend to retire for a good while yet, you hear? I can't leave you alone for two seconds. You always go and pull stupid stuff like that..."

"Shut up, you piece of junk. You're the one that told me to before you broke down. God, there you go, just happily laying into me the minute you start working again."

"If I don't say anything, who's going to fix that tiresome personality of yours, you moron?!"

"Don't call me a moron. Call me 'Master.'"

She thought about going out to join the conversation, then suddenly changed her mind and squatted in front of the doorway instead, hugging her knees. Propping her chin on them, she closed her eyes softly and let the sounds of their usual belligerent but strangely comfortable exchanges wash over her.

The Corporal had asked to listen to some rock before bed, so they'd fiddled with the radio's tuner and antenna for a long time, but no matter what they did, they never picked up the frequency of a guerrilla radio station. All they heard was static. When she realized the only guerrilla station playing music in this area had been that radio tower, Kieli's heart ached. The radio tower's music would never ride the waves to them again.

After a little while of brooding, she realized the bickering outside had stopped. She waited for them to start up again, but the silence continued for a while. Maybe they'd run out of things to talk about. Just when Kieli thought she'd take advantage of the good timing to go outside too, she heard a soft voice murmur, "Sorry, Corporal..."

She stopped the hand she'd been reaching toward the door.

"Mm? For what?" the radio's voice asked suspiciously.

The next reply didn't come right away; after another silence, a scratchy, slightly uncertain voice went on. "...I... haven't kept my promise yet. I'm the one who convinced Kieli, but in the end I still...I still thought, 'Don't go. I don't want you to go yet.'"

"*There you go talking like a damn kid again... For God's sake, I keep telling you, I'm not going anywhere. I'm guardian to you both, aren't I?*" The radio's voice was far more static-filled and scratchy than it had ever been before, getting awfully distorted each time it rose and fell.

Kieli's heart thumped hard. She realized that while she'd only been casually eavesdropping on them, she'd been listening to a conversation she never should have heard.

"*Don't look at me like that. It's fine; I'll stick with you to the end, okay? Don't just take everyone on yourself. So... don't you go up and dying either. You got that?*"

"Yeah... I can still keep going."

Something made a noise on the other side of the door at his back. The moment he looked over his shoulder, he heard softly pattering footsteps retreating. When Harvey gently pulled on the knob and peeked inside, in the still-dim dawn a small body was lying in one corner of the shack, facing the wall with her blanket pulled all the way up over her head.

So she heard that...

He wavered about whether to call out to her, but he couldn't really think of anything he could say, so he ultimately decided against it. He walked over on silent feet and bent over a little to put the radio by her pillow. Kieli kept facing the wall and pretending to sleep, but after he drew away, he could hear her feel out blindly for the radio with one hand and yank it under the covers with her.

Harvey went back outside by himself. Early morning

midway up the rocky tract. The chill, cloudy air felt just right against his skin. When he lowered his gaze to the foothills below, he could vaguely make out a quiet mining town and a single railroad track, hazy in the morning mist. The thin sea of clouds that blanketed the slate sky as far as his eyes could see were gradually taking on a sandy color.

He intended to set out today.

Kieli's parents, and the lab where Jude was, and Beatrix—if all the issues he had to take care of were gathered together in the capital now, that suited him well enough. Now he didn't need any more hesitation or any more waiting. He could just go.

…Not that he knew whether he'd be able to come back.

He felt a dull throb behind his left eye. Before his right eye had quite recovered it had been like a thin, milky-white film hung over the right half of his vision, but now it was the opposite: the left half of his vision looked a tiny bit darker.

—*You should be able to use it for a while, anyway.*

He turned over Mane's words in his mind.

But the nerves will probably be infested little by little no matter what, so I think you'll end up blind eventually. You're getting off easy if you only lose the eye, though…But since you've chosen to fight it as long as you can anyway for that girl's sake, here's a parting gift from me.

Harvey took a walk down the train track. There were weirdly flurried movements in the surveillance truck on standby. Apparently they were on alert, wondering what he'd come down here for so early in the morning. He'd come on a whim, but their random fear was too comical; he couldn't help laughing a little.

The he felt his shoulders relax at the unprompted laugh.

Yeah, that's right…

He stood on the ballast of the tracks and squinted along the tracks into the misty distance ahead. He couldn't see all the way to their final destination, naturally. But when he dropped his gaze from there to the ground, the twin rails stretched forward from the tips of his shoes through the whole range of vision, their crossties planted into the ground at regularly spaced intervals. He couldn't see where he was going, but he could still more or less see where he was standing.

Yeah, let's be a little more carefree about this. He had the feeling he'd been in an uncharacteristic hurry for some reason lately. Maybe it was because he was starting to understand that there was an end to his journey? But thinking about it now, he guessed that finding out it had an end was probably exactly the reason he didn't want to let it end.

Looking at it that way, it might be a little fun to do his best for once.

I'll take a shot at doing everything I can. And then after I've taken care of everything, yeah, that's when I'll go back to Easterbury to see off the Corporal. I'd like to be able to make that my last trip. Until then…I really don't want to let it end, if I can help it.

Harvey sighed out loud. His white breath melted into the morning mist and was gone right away. He stuck his hand in his pocket and walked for a while, hopping along the regularly spaced railroad ties. *Come to think of it, train tracks are*

made on the same standard all over this planet, aren't they? He'd never really registered that fact before. For some reason the thought came as kind of a relief.

I'll try just putting one foot in front of the other, and walk a step at a time without rushing. So I can burn the path into my memory while I can still see it. So that when all this is over, I can find my way back.

Because I intend to come back. Hopefully with all of us together.

AFTERWORD

....

Sneak, sneak, sneak…

It's been, um, eleven months since the last volume. I'd like to apologize to all of you who've been waiting for the next chapter of the story. Because I got to do a volume of something that I've been pestering my editor to please, please, *please* let me write for a long time now in between Volumes 6 and 7 of *Kieli* (I think you'll see it listed in the back of this book, but, anyway, they let me write my first non-*Kieli* new work, *Custom Child*), a bit of extra time ended up going by.

At any rate, here we are at the seventh volume of the *Kieli* series.

A journey takes center stage here for the first time in a long while—before I plunged into the series climax, I wanted to do one more "traveling story" like I'd started off with in the beginning. What's more, it's a story about falling in love with a giant structure that puffs billows of smoke from a bunch of smokestacks (…is it really?). It's a story about a man with a tiresome personality distressed by the plunge-in-headlong tendencies of girl with a complicated personality, and about a man who's tired of living finding meaning in life again. Somehow this stock line is starting to get less and less comprehensible with each volume…

Um, I'm not sure if it's okay for me to write about my plans here…but I plan to finish the *Kieli* story in one more episode. I'm not sure yet if that final episode will be one thick book or if it'll be split into two books, but right now I'm constructing the story with the idea of doing it in two volumes if possible, for a total of nine volumes. Long stories take a huge toll on me mentally and physically, so I'm already intimidated, but I intend to give this all I've got and write the whole thing through to the last scene so that I'll have no regrets. Okay, let's do this thing.

Oh, and also, before the next volume comes out, I believe I'll be releasing a *Kieli* "visual novel." It will be a stand-alone volume structured like a picture book. And since it's a picture book, naturally it will be brimming with Taue-san's illustrations. Tee hee. It's still in the works, but I hope to make it a book worth treasuring, so please check it out when it's released.

Still, how is it that I've already put out eight books at this point, yet I still haven't been able to write a single one of them smoothly, without causing any trouble for Taue-san? In fact, it feels as though our meetings are actually getting longer... This is the fourth (maybe? I think?) year I've been working with the editing department, and yet it's also the first time I've literally sobbed through a meeting. A-and I'm a grown woman, too!

The next day I was completely down in the dumps and I couldn't get any work done, so I decided to make curry. (I have a habit of making a giant potful of curry right before crunch time, because that way I don't have to think about what I'm going to eat for several days.) And so I went out and bought the ingredients, came home, and got more or less to the final stage, to the point where all I had left to do was add the roux, when suddenly—it hit me.

I'd forgotten to buy roux.

After a while spent being dumbfounded by myself ("What did you think you were going to cook, exactly?!"), I mechanically dragged my coat on, called up Hiro Arikawa in Hyogo, and one-sidedly blabbered out all my woe at him as I walked through the night to the supermarket in front of the train station. I-I'm really sorry about that. I swear I'll return your kindness someday.

As you can see, I pretty much fail at adulthood, but I like writing about people who fail at adulthood, so I tell myself maybe it's all good. So all told, I'm taking a laid-back attitude about it and getting along pretty happily in life.

Anyway, to my managing editor who buckled down and suffered with me through endlessly long meetings, to Taue-san, who made me pleased as punch savoring the return of his wonderful illustrations, to Reiko-san and Fujiwara-san who always help me polish my writing, and to all the rest of you whom I owe so much to, I thank you once again for this volume.

And above all, I give my very finest thanks to you who are holding this book in your hands and have come so far with me.

I hope…well, I hope you'll follow this story just a little longer.

Yukako Kabei

Kieli sees ghosts.
Harvey cannot die.
He will throw
her world into
chaos...
...and become her
one true friend.

STORY BY **Yukako Kabei**
ART BY **Shiori Teshirogi**

KIELI